THE EXCOMS

ALSO BY BRETT BATTLES

THE JONATHAN QUINN THRILLERS
THE CLEANER
THE DECEIVED
SHADOW OF BETRAYAL (U.S.)/THE UNWANTED (U.K.)
THE SILENCED
BECOMING QUINN
THE DESTROYED
THE COLLECTED
THE ENRAGED
THE DISCARDED
THE BURIED
THE UNLEASHED

THE EXCOMS
THE EXCOMS (No.1)

THE REWINDER THRILLERS
REWINDER
DESTROYER

THE LOGAN HARPER THRILLERS
LITTLE GIRL GONE
EVERY PRECIOUS THING

THE PROJECT EDEN THRILLERS
SICK
EXIT NINE
PALE HORSE
ASHES
EDEN RISING
DREAM SKY
DOWN

THE ALEXANDRA POE THRILLERS
(with Robert Gregory Browne)
POE
TAKEDOWN

STANDALONES
THE PULL OF GRAVITY
NO RETURN
MINE

For Younger Readers

THE TROUBLE FAMILY CHRONICLES
HERE COMES MR. TROUBLE

THE EXCOMS

The Excoms Thrillers No. 1

BRETT BATTLES

To Jill Fulkerson Marnell,
not only a dear friend,
but also a much appreciated set of eyes
in my writing process

ONE

February 5
Croatia

IN THE FUTURE, all meetings of the Committee would take place virtually. On this, the day of their inaugural conclave, however, the members would be convening in person.

Though there were many differences between the seven voting Committee members, they had at least one very important thing in common. Each had experienced a personal loss in which forces that could have prevented the tragedies had not lifted a finger. These scars ideologically aligned them and made them well suited for the work the Committee had been created to undertake.

Like the members themselves, the gathering's location had been meticulously chosen. A place grand enough to honor what was about to take place, but one that would make it nearly impossible for anyone to eavesdrop on the Committee's proceedings.

Though built under a different name, the ancient fortress overlooking the Mediterranean Sea had been known as the Angel's Keep for most of its existence. The oldest parts of the castle had protected the Balkan coast since the time of the Romans.

The armory room, buried deep beneath what was known as the old saints' tower, had only one way in and out.

A circular table filled the middle of the room, eight chairs spaced evenly around it. Behind the chairs were eight flat-screen monitors, positioned so that no matter where someone was sitting, a screen would be visible.

Placards sat at seven of the places, but instead of displaying members' names, on each tag was written a different day of the week. At each of the seven spots were also a glass of water, a pen, and an envelope containing a single sheet of paper.

Nothing sat at the eighth place.

The Committee members arrived with their personal security details via prearranged SUVs that dropped off each party in a scheduled order that saw no two members arriving at the same time. Though bodyguards were welcomed on the castle grounds, they were not allowed in the meeting room. A waiting area with comfortable seating, food, drinks, and entertainment was provided for them in the caretakers' lodge along the castle's north wall.

Upon entering the armory, each member silently took one of the placard places and waited, some more patiently than others. This was the first time any of them learned who else would be serving on the Committee, so each new arrival was scrutinized by those already in attendance. Given the lofty world the members traveled in, it was inevitable several knew each other from elsewhere. In these cases, a nod was exchanged but no words were spoken.

Two minutes after the seventh member arrived and took her seat, the acting Administrator entered the room, locked the door, and sat in the eighth chair. Unlike the others, who had all come empty handed, he carried a leather portfolio that he laid on the table, unzipped, and opened like a book. Inside was a short stack of papers, topped by the meeting agenda. He studied the rundown for several seconds before looking at the others.

"Good evening," he said.

The members returned the greeting.

"It is my honor to call to order the first meeting of the Committee."

In the weeks prior to the meeting, the acting Administrator had made personal visits to each member so there was no need to introduce himself. He glanced at the agenda again. He knew every word on it, but the pause would provide a sense of order he knew the others were expecting.

When the appropriate amount of time had passed, he said, "Your transfers have all been received, so I am therefore able to certify that the Committee is fully funded and ready to begin its work. The first item of business is member designations. With the exception of critical votes, these names are what will be used in meetings and communications. Are there questions?"

This was one of the things he'd discussed in detail during his personal visits. No one spoke up.

"Written on the placards in front of you is the name you will be known as from this day forward."

The members looked at the cards with little expression, and then returned their attention to the acting Administrator, who worked through a handful of other housekeeping tasks before reaching the more important matters.

"The bylaws dictate that day-to-day operations of Committee-sanctioned activities will be overseen by the Administrator. It is the Committee's responsibility to choose the person who will fill that role. Nominees may be presented now."

"Isn't that your job?" Saturday asked. As a child, she had witnessed her twelve-year-old cousin married off to a man four times the girl's age, and had attended the same cousin's funeral a year later when the girl had been beaten to death for burning her husband's dinner. The man had moved on and married someone else, never paying for his crime. Saturday had used her rage at this injustice to rise far above her station, amassing a communications empire that spread into fifteen countries and was worth several billion dollars. And yet, even with all that power, she hadn't been able to stop atrocities like what befell her cousin.

"I am the *acting* Administrator. My job has been to shepherd the organization to this point. When this meeting adjourns my term is over. It is the responsibility of the Committee to decide who will hold the position going forward."

"Do you not want the job?"

He bowed his head slightly. "It would be my great pleasure to serve if the Committee so desires."

"Then I see no reason to make a change at this point." Saturday looked around at the others. "Does anyone have an objection?"

A few members shook their heads.

Saturday turned back. "Acting Administrator, please take the vote."

The tally was 7-0.

"Thank you," the Administrator said. "I am honored by your trust in me."

Though pleased by the ease of his permanent appointment, he was not the least surprised. The real power behind the Committee—a man sitting in one of the chairs around the table—would not have had it any other way.

"Next on the agenda is the field team," he said.

From a pocket of his portfolio, he removed a thin remote control. When he pushed the power button, all eight television screens came to life. In quick succession, he relayed to the Committee the particulars of the five primary field-team targets, and the ten alternates. As he described each candidate's attributes and how he or she would function on the team, pictures of the individual appeared on the screens.

When he was through, he said, "The floor is open for debate."

Wednesday, one of the growing class of Chinese billionaires and sole surviving family member of the Cultural Revolution, leaned forward and said, "In regards to your suggestion for team leader, would it not be best if the position were filled by someone with more…operational experience?"

"An excellent question," the Administrator said. "Naturally, given her profession, one would think she would be more suited for solo work. That is definitely true of others who do what she does, but our candidate has considerable operational experience and possesses both the temperament and the leadership qualities we require." He cited a dozen examples that illustrated the candidate's qualification.

Tuesday, a nouveau riche Silicon Valley tycoon whose first wife fell victim to a suicide bomber in Tel Aviv when she was on vacation with her sister, said, "If you're convinced, Administrator, I'd say we give it a go. After all, isn't the idea that we can change pieces of the team as necessary? If she doesn't live up to our expectations, we move on."

The back and forth continued for nearly a quarter hour before a vote was taken and the full team as presented was approved.

"Our final matter today is the choice of our initial mission. If you will open your envelopes, please."

The members did so.

The piece of paper they pulled out was a ballot containing two numbered boxes. The Administrator described both potential missions, once more utilizing the video screens to help illustrate the specific problem that needed righting. Since this would be the Committee's first operation, the options involved issues that were not overly time dependent. "As a critical vote, please mark the ballot with your choice and sign your legal name at the bottom."

There was no missing the apprehension in the room. Making decisions on trivial matters by verbal vote was one thing, but putting their signatures on a vote for a job that could easily go awry was something else altogether. But this had also been part of the agreement they had to accept before being allowed into the Committee.

"This is how we succeed or fail," the Administrator's true boss had told him when they had been drawing up the plans for the Committee. "Everyone involved needs to feel responsible. The field team. The Committee. You."

The Administrator waited until he'd collected all the votes before he tabulated the results. The decision was a close one, 4 to 3. Both missions were worthy, but the winner had the added benefit of being in a remote location. If things went wrong, there would be no undue attention.

He set the ballots down and said, "The Lambert matter in Alaska."

"How long until we begin?" Saturday asked.

"The candidates will have to be put into positions where they will be primed to accept our job offers first. That will take a bit of time. These efforts will also need to be coordinated so that all five are ready at the same time."

"How long?" she repeated.

"Two months should be enough."

The meeting was adjourned.

Two

Three Hours Later
Elsewhere

THE KNOCK ON the door echoed through the cavernous office.

"Come in," Avanti growled from behind his desk.

Warren, his chief spook, entered and walked across the room, the hardwood floor creaking. He stopped in front of the desk but did not take one of the guest seats.

"Good afternoon, Mr. Avanti."

"Well?" Avanti asked.

"Cassidy just reported in. He's flying home now."

"The meeting. I want to know about the meeting."

"As expected."

"So they've officially begun."

"Yes, sir."

Avanti folded his arms across his chest and grinned. "I knew it. I knew that son of a bitch couldn't resist. After all these years, he's finally got his Committee." He looked back at his spook. "And their first mission? Did Cassidy say anything about that?"

Warren relayed the information their mole on the Committee had given him.

When he finished, Avanti said, "You're keeping an eye on these field-team targets?"

"Of course."

"And the disruption?"

"Ready to go. As soon as the Committee has collected its team and is on the brink of activating the mission, the disruption will commence. As soon as the first phase is complete, Cassidy will anonymously feed our Committee member target the information that will trigger a change."

The disruption was designed to test both the abilities of the field team and the resilience of the Committee. In the worst case, Avanti and Warren would learn where the organization's flaws were, and in the best, the whole Committee would come crashing down while still in its infancy.

"What if they don't make the change?"

"Then there will be one very bitter Committee member who Cassidy can manipulate even more in the future."

"The first option would be preferable," Avanti said, and then returned his attention to the file on his desk, signaling the meeting was over.

THREE

April 3
Manila, Republic of the Philippines

ANANKE CARRIED A tray through the ballroom, a ghost among the event attendees.

Like the rest of the serving staff, she wore a white shirt, black bow tie, and black pants. Her shoes, also black, were killing her. Whosever idea it was for the female servers to wear heels should have been shot. Something she might do herself once the job was over.

The shoes wouldn't have been as much of an issue if she'd been allowed to show up right before the target arrived at the event, do her business, and split. But the client had been terrified of something going awry, and had insisted the utmost care be taken.

Noah Perkins, the op leader, translated this to mean Ananke needed to be serving the guests from the moment the party started in order to sell her cover. She'd already been handing out champagne to members of the Philippine elite for over an hour and a half, helping them get sufficiently lubricated before the guest of honor arrived.

According to the brief, Fernando Alonzo, candidate for the Philippine presidency, had two other stops to make before his arrival in the ballroom for his final campaign speech of the night.

Alonzo, the current governor of one of the northern provinces, was running on an antiestablishment platform and billing himself as the People's Candidate. Given the enthusiasm of the crowd, Ananke seemed to be the only one present who found it hilarious he was in Manila courting that very same establishment.

Funny or not, his attempt to gain more votes wasn't going to matter. She was there to put a stop to his campaign.

A ripple of excitement rushed through the crowd.

"He's on his way."

"He's almost here."

"He's coming."

"He's coming."

This wasn't the first rumor of Alonzo's arrival that night, but this time it was true. A moment before the nervous chatter began, Ananke had heard two beeps through her undetectable earpiece, alerting her that the target's car had entered the hotel driveway. She eased through a gap in the mob and headed back toward the kitchen.

Perkins had arranged for her to win the lottery that Mr. Reyes, the catering coordinator, had held that afternoon to choose who would present Alonzo and his wife with their drinks.

The moment Ananke entered the kitchen, Reyes shouted, "Jessica, over here." Jessica Santos was her cover name.

As she weaved her way toward him, he set an ornate tray on the prep table and placed two beautiful crystal flutes on it. "They're here," he said, barely glancing at her as he filled each glass with champagne.

"Why do you think I'm here, asshole," is what she wanted to say, but she just smiled and nodded and picked up the tray.

Reyes put a hand on each of her arms and looked her over. She'd seen the same unhappy expression on his face when she'd won the honor of serving the Alonzos. She was giant for a Filipina, over six feet in her heels. Clearly she didn't fit his image of what a woman from his country should look like.

Again, she couldn't help but see the humor.

She wasn't Filipino. According to the DNA test she'd taken a few years earlier, she had no Asian heritage whatsoever.

What she did have, however, were excellent facial prosthetics and highly effective makeup. If Reyes or anyone

20

else at the party had seen her without her disguise, they wouldn't have looked at her twice. Well, they might have *looked* twice, but they wouldn't have connected her to Jessica Santos in a million years.

"You remember what to do," he asked.

"Of course."

"Are you to say anything to them?"

"No."

"And if they say something to you?"

"I smile and act like I can't hear them above the crowd noise."

He straightened her bow tie and took another look at her. "All right. Just…whatever you do, do not spill anything on them."

"I promise," she said, then turned and walked toward the exit.

In a well practiced move, she used her back to pass through the swinging door into the ballroom, steadied the glasses with her free hand, and rubbed the bottom pad of her index finger across the flute destined for Alonzo. From a pouch designed to look like her skin, several dozen microscopic R-ToFF pellets dropped into the glass. As soon as they plunged into the champagne, the pellets dissolved.

The false skin was off her finger before she finished her first step into the ballroom. With a subtle flick, she dropped it onto the floor and stepped on it, her specially treated sole starting a chemical reaction that dissolved the drug pouch into a small spot of harmless liquid.

In the time she'd been in the kitchen, the crowd had surged toward the dais where Alonzo would soon be speaking. Sticking near the wall, Ananke worked her way around until she reached the security guards blocking access to the area behind the stage.

She flashed the special card she'd been given for the occasion.

After a quick pat down, the guards let her enter, and the older one said, "Follow me."

The crowd was nearly as thick behind the platform as out

front. Ananke had to shield her cargo with her free arm as she made her way to the stairs. Twice, revelers tried to take one of the glasses, but her escort was there each time with a glare and a "Not for you" that was more than enough to scare everyone off.

The guard led her onto the dais where about two dozen people were waiting for the man of the hour. Ananke was taken to a spot along the back edge where she could wait out of the way.

A few minutes later, the rumble of the crowd grew louder, starting on the left side and spreading through the ballroom like wildfire.

Alonzo had arrived.

Too many people were on the stage for Ananke to visually track the man's progress, but the yells and whoops and shouts gave her a pretty good idea of where he was at any moment. Finally, he and his entourage climbed the steps and walked onto the stage.

Alonzo was wearing a traditional Filipino barong—shirt made from white thin fabric with intricate designs embroidered down the front—over a white undershirt. His wife, a woman at least fifteen years younger than he was, wore a golden floor-length dress and a double strand of pearls. While the president looked genuinely pleased to be there, the woman looked ready to call it a night.

There was much hand shaking and hugging as the candidate made his way to the podium at the center. When he finally reached it, he shouted something into the mic that made the crowd go wild. From Ananke's position, it was near impossible to hear what he'd said, but it wasn't important. The only thing that mattered was her cue. That came seven and a half minutes later, after Alonzo had made additional remarks and one of his aides waved Ananke forward.

As she approached the podium, she received a raised eyebrow from her target. It wasn't a look of suspicion, only surprise. Her height again, she guessed.

She handed the untainted flute to the man's wife, and the other to the man himself, and then took a step back.

The couple raised their glasses, and Alonzo said in Tagalog, "Your support and belief in me will carry us to victory. And our country will be great once more."

It didn't matter where she was, Ananke thought, politicians—regardless of ideology or language—always said the same damn things.

The Alonzos lifted their glasses and drank.

And there it was. R-ToFF delivered. Ananke's job done.

In approximately twenty-four hours, Alonzo would start feeling a slight headache. He'd likely play it off as a side effect of being so busy. The next day, his throat would be sore, and soon after he'd start coughing. On day three, he would be in a hospital's intensive care unit, struck down by a severe case of the flu that would prevent him from campaigning during the critical final month of the election.

Ananke started toward the stairs to finish her shift. This was the part of the night she had been dreading most. Perkins had been insistent. "We can't do anything that might cause someone to wonder if the target's illness was anything but natural. You'll stay until the event is over and make everyone believe you're nothing but a server."

As she reached the end of the stage, she heard someone shout behind her. Not in excitement or congratulations, but in terror.

She glanced over her shoulder.

Those who'd been on the dais had coalesced at the podium, most trying to peek around the person in front of them at something on the ground. Missing from the group was Alonzo.

Ananke lowered her gaze so she could see through a gap that had appeared in the crowd. She spotted the candidate's face for only a moment, but it was long enough for her to see his eyes had rolled back, his skin was turning blue, and white foam was dripping from the corner of his mouth.

As an assassin, there was always the potential for an "oh, shit" moment. Ananke did everything she could to mitigate that possibility, but some things, like the true identity of a drug she had been given by her handler, were out of her control.

Oh, shit.

Acting like the commotion wasn't her business, she moved down the stairs at her former pace and headed toward the checkpoint. While a few of those behind the stage were looking curiously at the backdrop that separated them from the platform, most seemed unaware anything had happened.

Before she reached the guards, though, shouts rang out from the stage, informing all those in earshot that Alonzo was down.

The guards at the checkpoint ran toward the stairs. The first sped past Ananke without even looking at her. The second, however, did a double take, and then seemed to connect the dots that the server who had brought the champagne might have had something to do with the chaos on stage.

Skidding to a stop, the guard yelled, "Don't move."

She looked at him, her eyes wide and innocent as she stepped toward him. "What? Why?"

Another shout caused the guard to glance toward the stage. Before he could look back at her, Ananke kneed him in the groin, then leaned next to him as he doubled over, like she was checking to see if he was okay, and deftly removed the pistol from its holster.

She shoved the barrel into his belly and scanned the room to see if anyone was watching her. A few moments earlier, the assault would have been witnessed by dozens of people. Now, everyone's attention was on the dais.

"You want to stay alive, you keep your mouth shut and stay bent over," she whispered. "Nod if you understand."

His face still twisted in pain, he nodded.

She guided him through the abandoned checkpoint toward the back side of the room. Plenty of people rushed past them, but none paid them any attention.

In preparation for the mission, Ananke had memorized the hotel's layout. She headed for a door along the back wall near the corner. As expected, it opened onto a hallway that led to several storage rooms and, via a locked door at the far end, the loading docks.

She hustled the guard into the first storage room.

"Do you have handcuffs?" she asked.

"No," he grunted.

"In that case, sorry about this."

She meant it. The guy had only been doing his job—in fact, by suspecting her, had done it exceedingly well—and didn't deserve the knee to his groin, or the one she now sent into his stomach.

As he groaned, she wrapped an arm around his neck and cut off circulation to his brain. Within seconds he passed out.

After dragging him behind a shelving unit, she returned to the door. All was quiet on the other side, so she slipped out and sprinted to the end of the hall.

There, she removed both of her shoes, broke off the heel of the left one, and pulled out a key made entirely of plastic. If Perkins had given it to her, she would have suspected it wouldn't work. But she had done her own recon and obtained temporary possession of a master key from which the plastic one was created. The door opened without a problem.

Several cameras were mounted over the loading dock. Perkins had told her it was live-view only, no recording, but given what had just happened in the ballroom, she had to assume he was lying. Either way, they could aid in her escape. As she ran into the loading area, she made sure to face one of the cameras like she didn't know it was there. If it was recording, soon the image of a tall Filipino female murder suspect would be everywhere.

Fortunately, Manila did not have a citywide CCTV system like London did, so beyond the hotel, there was no organized surveillance network. Four blocks away, she found a quiet spot down a dark alley where she removed the applications from her face that had drastically changed the way she looked. She wiped away what she could of the makeup that altered the color of her skin, but because she couldn't risk the time to do a thorough job, she knew she didn't get it all. If she steered clear of any bright lights, though, she should be okay. Off, too, came the white shirt and bow tie, leaving her in a white spaghetti-strap top and the black pants. She disassembled the guard's gun and dropped several of the pieces on the ground.

One street over, she tossed more of the gun and the heel of her broken left shoe into the bed of a passing truck. The rest of that shoe and all of her right one were dumped next to a pile of garbage from where they would likely be stolen within the hour. The last pieces of the gun went into a drain.

Now she was just an unarmed foreigner walking through the city, albeit barefoot.

As a professional assassin, Ananke had developed a survival guide over the years.

Rule number one: the client was not her friend.

Her employers were a mix of agencies and other individuals operating in the murky world of intelligence, and they all had their own agendas. Most of the time they played fair, but even then their goals would always take precedence over those of any temporary employees.

Rule number two: safeguards, safeguards, safeguards.

An example of this was the recon she'd done at the hotel and the master key she had duplicated. In addition, and also unbeknownst to op leader Perkins, she had arranged for a safe house if things went sideways. Located three miles from the hotel, the gardener's quarters sat at the back of a sprawling property owned by a family with old Filipino money, and was secured using Ananke's new favorite tool, Airbnb.

She arrived nineteen minutes after handing Alonzo his champagne. She had no intention of staying for long. First thing she did was wash away the remaining makeup, restoring her skin to its natural caramel tone. She then released her hair from the bun it had been in and pulled it into a ponytail.

A black plain T-shirt, a pair of jeans, sneakers, and a Tokyo Giants baseball cap completed her transition from Filipino server to African-American tourist. From a slit she'd cut into the bottom of the mattress, she extracted a messenger bag containing three sets of false IDs, two sets of hard plastic lock picks, a stack of Philippine pesos, and three thousand US dollars. She left the equivalent of a thousand dollars in pesos on the dresser with a note explaining a family emergency had taken her away in the middle of the night.

Her last stop was back in the bathroom, where she

removed the fan vent and retrieved a Glock 39, a matching suppressor, and full box of .45-caliber ammo. These went into a special section of the bag. Though they wouldn't go undetected during a physical search, they would be invisible to visual checks and most scanners. She reached back into the vent and grabbed a plastic bag containing four disposable phones and two dozen SIM cards.

She stuck a SIM card into one of the phones and called Shinji.

He picked up before the fourth ring and said in Japanese, "Nakamura Restaurant. Sorry we're about to close, so—"

"It's me," she said in English.

"Oh, hey. Didn't expect to hear from you for another day or two." Shinji's English was flawless, which made sense given that he'd been born and raised in the San Gabriel Valley east of Los Angeles, and had yet to set foot in his ancestral home of Japan.

"I need a way out," she told him.

"Can do." A click and the line went silent. Thirty seconds, another click. "The earliest flight leaves in ninety minutes. Can you get to the airport in time?"

"No planes."

"Oh, well, you should have told me that."

"No passport checks."

A pause. "Is there something I should know about?"

"Correct me if I'm wrong, but aren't you supposed to be monitoring the news?"

"Of course I am, but if you've seen one Filipino soap opera, you've seen them…oh, wait."

Over the line, the sound of a television increased, and Ananke could now hear a correspondent reporting that presidential candidate Alonzo had collapsed.

"That wasn't supposed to happen, was it?" Shinji said.

"No."

"So probably not good."

"Your deduction skills never cease to amaze me."

"How about a ship?"

"Given that I'm on an island, that seems the logical

27

choice."

Shinji found a Panamanian registered ship called *Loretta's Star* that was due to leave Manila an hour before sunrise. An agreed-to sum was transferred into a Cayman Island account, and arrangements were made for a skiff to ferry the "girlfriend" of the captain to the ship after it was underway.

Until then, Ananke had a few hours to kill.

F(OUR

ANANKE CAUGHT A cab two blocks from the safe house and gave the driver the address of the building where she'd last met with Perkins. The driver had his radio on so loud she couldn't help but hear the latest news about Alonzo's condition.

Most of it was no more than rumors. The reporter even said several people in the ballroom claimed to have heard gunshots right before Alonzo collapsed. The reporter had already turned the story into a possible assassination attempt. Though he was overdramatizing it—as his lot was wont to do, he was actually right. Which annoyed her because it would only legitimize sensationalism in the future.

Ananke did learn one piece of news. Alonzo had been taken from the ballroom to a nearby hospital. No updates on his condition, though. Of course, she didn't need them. If he wasn't dead already, he would be soon enough.

That son of a bitch Perkins had done a masterful job of setting her up.

"Since we're only putting him out of action temporarily, I'm thinking a nice case of R-ToFF Flu would work great. How's that sound to you?" That's how he'd presented her with his plan for dealing with Alonzo.

That sounded good to her. Many kinds of synthetic flu had been developed for just such purposes. R-ToFF's appeal was that it would gestate in a target's system for twenty-four hours before laying him up for weeks and likely leaving him frail for a long time after that.

Though her job was usually to kill, there were a few times when she'd been hired to deliver a less permanent type of hit.

As she cursed Perkins under her breath again, a report

came over the radio saying police were looking for a tall Filipina last seen at the hotel.

If the cabbie only knew who he has riding in his backseat.

At least Perkins hadn't leaked details of what she really looked like.

Yet.

The taxi turned onto the street where Perkins had been staying.

When they were still half a block away from his building, Ananke said, "This is fine."

As soon as the cabbie pulled over, she paid and hopped out.

A few scattered businesses were still open, restaurants mostly, the rest having locked their metal shutters for the night. Unusually, no one seemed to be eating at any of the outside tables, though at a few of the restaurants several customers stood in the doorways, looking inside. When Ananke walked by one of these places, she discovered why. Everyone's attention was on a television broadcasting a chaotic scene outside what appeared to be a hospital. Even the restaurant's staff had stopped to watch.

She wondered how long it would be before word got out that Alonzo was dead.

Dear God, let me be on the ship by then, she thought as she moved down the street.

Perkins had been using a set of rooms above a dress shop. She approached the building from the other side of the street and stopped before she got too close.

At least one light was still on in his flat. She pulled out the disposable phone. The crappy device came with a crappy camera that had a crappy zoom, but it was better than nothing. She pointed it at the second-story window and zoomed in. Though the curtains were closed, she hoped to see movement, but either Perkins was staying away from the lamp or he was already gone.

From her previous visits, she knew he'd rigged the main building door so that a buzzer sounded in his room every time it was opened. He'd also put a camera on the street somewhere.

She'd seen the live feed playing on a dedicated monitor next to his computer. Unfortunately, she'd never taken the time to figure out where the camera was. All she knew was that she couldn't go much farther without entering the frame.

She backtracked to a gap between buildings that led to the next street over. The narrow passage stank so strongly of garbage and God knew what else, she was forced to pinch her nose to keep from retching, and it wasn't until she reached the uneven sidewalk of the other street that she could really breathe again.

There were no restaurants on this street, only rundown apartment buildings and a few empty lots.

Perkins wasn't a stupid man. Not completely, anyway. So Ananke knew he'd likely extended his surveillance to the building behind his. She allowed herself a minute to search for where he might have placed a camera, but spotted none. To play it safe, she broke into the building next to the one behind Perkins's place and took the stairs to the roof, then crept onto the place directly behind his.

At the back, she looked down on the roof to Perkins's building.

Quiet and empty. Just how she liked it.

His building was a floor shorter than the one she was on, so she lowered herself over the side and dropped the remaining few feet. The stairwell door was locked, but the mechanism was cheap and she picked it in no time.

She moved inside and sneaked down the stairs, searching ahead for cameras. As far as she could tell, she reached the landing of Perkins's floor undetected. She eased the door open and peered into the hallway.

Camera, mounted on the wall opposite Perkins's door.

She didn't recall it being there before.

She might be able to disable it by tossing something at it, but a) she didn't have anything to toss, and b), the resulting noise would alert Perkins if he was inside.

Screw it. She'd have to hope he wasn't watching.

Lock pick in hand, she rushed out of the stairwell and inserted the pick and tension wrench into the lock on Perkins's door. Seven seconds later, she shoved the door open and rolled into the room, coming to her feet—ready to fight—halfway to the desk Perkins had set up as his control center.

The computer and monitors were gone. She looked toward the mattress Perkins had slept on. His bag was also missing.

"Dammit," she muttered.

She knew finding him there had been a long shot at best, but God, how she had hoped she would.

Having no time to waste on disappointment, she sloughed it off and searched the room, hoping he'd left something behind that would tell her where he went. But there wasn't even a scrap of trash in the bin.

Probably headed to the airport the minute I reported for work at the hotel. In all likelihood, he'd been safely in the air when Alonzo sipped his deadly champagne.

Sirens. Distant, and not unusual for a place like Manila, but given her current circumstances, she gave them a bit more attention than she would have normally, and realized they were moving closer.

She hurried back to the doorway and examined it.

"Ah, come on," she whined as soon as she spotted the disk near the bottom of the jamb.

She checked the door. Sure enough, there was a matching one on it. Both had been dirtied up to not appear obvious, but now that she'd seen them, she knew them for what they were—contact points.

When she'd opened the door and moved them out of alignment, she'd likely triggered an automated phone call to the police.

She looked back into the room. She was willing to bet that somewhere in the flat—maybe hidden under a floorboard or in the walls—was evidence of the plot to assassinate Alonzo. If the police found her, they'd find that, too.

Perkins covering all his bases like a champ.

I'm going to find you, you son of a bitch. And when I do…

She wiped down the few surfaces she had touched and headed back up the stairs. On the roof, she moved to the front of the building and looked down just as the first police vehicle arrived. A moment later, two more joined it. That was more than enough for her.

Using a discarded box and the imperfections of the wall, she climbed back the way she'd come, ran over to the stairwell entrance, and had just reached the door when—

BOOM!

She flew several feet before smacking down on the roof.

Dazed, she blinked a few times before glancing over her shoulder. A roiling column of smoke and fire was rising from the space where Perkins's building had been.

There was only one logical explanation. Perkins had wired the place to blow up, most likely assuming she would be caught in the explosion.

Her former op leader had reached a whole new level of asshole.

FIVE

THE VOYAGE FROM Manila to Singapore took two and a half long, quiet, maddening days. When the harbor finally came into view, Ananke gladly paid the captain extra to have a skiff take her ashore instead of waiting until they docked.

Though she still had the four disposable phones and handful of SIM cards, the SIMs were all for Philippine networks and wouldn't work in Singapore. So the first thing she did upon reaching land was find a cab driver who would take US dollars, and had him drive her to a convenience store where she could buy several local SIMs.

At a nearby park, she checked her voice mail. There was only one message.

"This is Marcus Denton. You will return my call immediately." Short and sweet and delivered with barely contained fury.

Denton was the client contact on the Alonzo job, a job for which he'd stressed numerous times that no one was to die. Especially not Alonzo.

He undoubtedly wanted an explanation.

Or, she supposed, he could be calling to inform her that if she ever set foot in the States again, she would immediately be arrested and hauled off someplace like Gitmo to spend every day of the rest of her life as a guinea pig for experimental torture techniques.

The message had been left only a few hours after she'd been taken to the *Loretta's Star* so it was two days old already. Had that forty-eight hours of not responding destroyed her chance to convince him she wasn't to blame for the assassination? Likely.

Still, she'd have to try.

Her first call, though, was to Shinji.

"Huh?" he answered, more asleep than awake. "I mean, Nakamura Restau—"

"Just tell me everything's all right."

"Ananke? Are you in Singapore already?" She heard something falling to the floor, and then an annoyed mumble. A moment later, Shinji said, "Oh, wow. I guess you are, huh? Totally thought I'd set my alarm. Um, what was the question?"

"Tell me that everything's okay."

"Could you, uh, define 'okay'?"

"Shinji!"

"Sorry, sorry. Yeah, so, um, I wouldn't exactly say everything's...well, okay. Mr. Denton called."

"Yeah, I heard his message."

"I mean he called me."

"You?"

"I know, right? How did he get *my* number?"

The 'getting' of Shinji's number wouldn't be that hard for someone with high-level NSA clearance like Denton. The real question was how her client knew Shinji worked for Ananke in the first place. The partnership was not one she advertised.

"What did he want?"

"To talk to you. I explained to him that you were incommunicado and that—"

"Please tell me you didn't use that word."

"Why not? It's accurate."

She closed her eyes and rubbed her forehead. "So you told him I was out of touch. And?"

"And that I'd make sure you give him a call as soon as you surfaced."

"What did he say to that?"

"Something different every time."

"What do you mean, every time? How many times has he called?"

"Seven. No, wait. Eight times."

Ananke sighed. "He didn't ask about the job?"

"Once or twice, but I said I only handled getting you in

and out, and didn't know anything about what happened in between."

"Anyone besides Denton call?"

While Shinji's number was not known to any of her clients—except for Denton, apparently—Shinji did monitor the automated line that job requests came in on.

"No new jobs, but, um, we've had some cancellations."

"How many?"

"Five."

"Did you say five?"

"I did."

"How many do we have lined up?"

"Before cancellations, seven. So now two."

"Thanks. I can do the math."

A pause. "You're not going to like this."

"As opposed to all the things I've liked so far?"

"You're *really* not going to like this."

"Just tell me."

He took a deep breath and blurted out, "All five want full refunds."

Up until that point, Ananke had been pacing a path at a quiet end of the park, but Shinji's words stopped her in her tracks. To book Ananke required a deposit of half her fee. If the job went away, the money stayed. That was industry standard.

"Did you remind them what nonrefundable means?"

"They claim it doesn't apply in this situation."

"In what situation?"

"Right, um, soooo…I did a little checking around, and apparently, well, uh, you've been excommunicated."

Ananke had not been rendered speechless for years, but that counter had just reset to zero.

Shinji said, "Are you still there?"

"Yes," she managed.

"What do you want me to do?"

She blinked. "About what?"

"The money. Should I refund them?"

"Not yet. I'll…um…I'll get back to you." She hung up.

Denton.

He must have been the one behind the blackballing. Perkins wouldn't have had that kind of pull.

She needed to talk to her client.

She needed to talk to him *right now*.

It was a little after 3:30 p.m. in Singapore, which meant it was twelve hours earlier in New York, where Denton worked. But he did say return his call immediately.

"Yes?" The crisp, no-nonsense male voice that answered did not belong to Denton.

"I'm returning a call."

"Name?"

"Ananke."

A pause that could have meant nothing, but she knew better.

"Hold," the man said.

The wait lasted ninety seconds before Denton came on. "I assumed you weren't going to call at all."

"As my colleague told you, I was indisposed."

"That's unfortunate." The words were stated matter-of-factly, the angry tone of his voice mail nowhere to be found.

"Not sure I agree. It was better than ending up in a Philippine jail."

"Well, you *did* commit murder."

"I definitely disagree with you on that."

"So you're saying that you were not the one who delivered the drug that killed Alonzo?"

"What I'm saying is that the drug I was told I was delivering was R-ToFF. I performed my job exactly as presented."

"And yet a man is dead."

"Ultimately not by my hand."

Denton said nothing for several seconds. "I take it you're accusing Mr. Perkins."

"It's not an accusation. Perkins supplied the drug. He had to know what it was. If he won't tell you the truth, put him in a room and I'll get it out of him."

"If only that were possible."

"What do you mean?"

"I'm not playing this game with you. Please do not—"

"Wait," she said, sensing he was about to hang up. "I had no knowledge of Perkins's plan whatsoever. I'm being set up. You have to see that. If necessary, I'll find him and make him tell you the truth."

"Here's what I suggest you do. Go someplace quiet. Don't do anything to draw attention to yourself, and maybe, just maybe, you'll live through the week. Good-bye, Ananke. Don't call this number again."

"Hold on! What are you—"

But the line was dead.

She almost hit redial, but what more could she say that she hadn't already? She needed to give Denton more than assurances. She needed to give him Perkins, tied up and talking. And to do so, she needed help.

She called Shinji back.

GIVEN ANANKE'S—TEMPORARY, she hoped—banishment from the intelligence world, she thought it best to keep as low a profile as possible while she hunted for Perkins. To this end, she took a cheap room in a hotel far from the city center, using a brand-spanking-new, never-before-seen ID. Once ensconced in her new hideaway, she dropped her things on the bed and turned on the TV to BBC International.

Not surprisingly, news of Alonzo's collapse and death dominated the broadcast.

Fan-freakin'-tastic, Ananke thought as she popped another aspirin.

A photo from his final campaign event appeared on the screen. In it, Alonzo and his wife had just taken glasses of champagne from a server who was turning away. The picture zoomed in until the server's face—Ananke's altered face—was in profile. The screen was then split between a close-up of this photo and a clearer one of her looking toward the loading-dock camera.

"Philippine authorities are looking for a woman named Jessica Santos," the reporter said. "She worked that night as a server, and was the one who presented Mr. Alonzo with the champagne he drank seconds before he collapsed."

The only bright spot Ananke learned from the broadcast was that Perkins still hadn't fed the authorities information about who she really was.

The next story was about Alonzo's funeral, scheduled for the following day. Crowds were expected to fill the streets in his hometown around the church where services were to be held, and for those who couldn't attend, it was to be shown live on all the major networks.

She muted the volume and jumped into the shower. Unfortunately, all the hot water in the world wasn't going to wash away the layers of anger and guilt that clung to her. Unwittingly or not, she had allowed herself to be used as Perkins's puppet. And that was a stain she would have a hard time removing.

Hearing her phone ringing forced her to finally get out. After a quick wipe down, she grabbed the cell off the counter and checked the caller ID: SHINJI.

"Tell me you found him," she said.

"Kinda."

"Kinda?"

"You're not going to like it."

"I wish you'd stop saying that."

"Sorry. What should I say?"

"You should just tell me what you found."

"Perkins is dead."

For a second it was as if all the noises of the world had stopped. "What?"

"Perkins is dead."

"I heard you the first time."

"Then why did you say 'what'?"

"How did it happen?"

"There was an explosion in Manila the same night as the mission. According to the police report, it took out a whole building. They found his body in the rubble."

The skin on Ananke's arms began to tingle. "Where was this explosion?"

"You want the exact address?"

"If it doesn't inconvenience you."

The sound of a keyboard clacking. "Here we go. Paz Street. Crap, no number listed. According to the news report, the body was found in a dress shop on the ground floor. The place is just south of—"

"I know where it is."

"You do?"

"Was Perkins mentioned by name in the news report?"

"Nah, just 'body found.' His ID came from one of my contacts."

"How good is this contact?"

"Never had a problem before."

Even ignoring the evidence she'd seen that Perkins had already fled the building, the explosion had been large enough to rip apart anyone inside. Meaning identification would have needed to be made by DNA, a process that took time. The results would then need to be cross-referenced to find a match, in this case with someone not even from the same country. It had been less than seventy-two hours since the blast. Even a week wouldn't have been enough time.

"Forget about the body. It's not him."

"It isn't?"

"He's still out there. Find him."

Six

ANANKE ARRIVED IN Shanghai skeptical of the tip from the anonymous source Shinji had dug up. The informant claimed Perkins's employer had secured a thirty-fourth-floor apartment in a building along the Huangpu River. Though the employer's identity was not given, the implication was that it was a large Chinese firm that did a lot of business in the Philippines and was not pleased with the possibility of Alonzo becoming the next leader.

While the explanation felt far too detailed and ready-made, Ananke had no other tangible leads so had little choice but to check it out. She would do so very carefully, however.

Under the cover of darkness, she flew a whisper-tech miniature drone with mounted camera—arranged by Shinji—around skyscrapers along the river toward the target building. Within the first two minutes after the device arrived at its destination, Ananke picked out half a dozen suspicious men loitering outside the building, and three others she positively identified as hunters she had worked with in the past. She flew the drone up to the thirty-fourth floor and spied inside the supposed safe house.

Two men lounged on a couch in front of the TV, neither one Perkins. On the coffee table in front of them was a pair of pistols. A check through the other windows of the apartment revealed no one else.

The safe house was not so safe.

After that disappointment, Shinji found a promising lead in Seoul, so off Ananke went.

Though Perkins was not there, either, she found evidence he had been less than a day earlier. Using Korea as the starting point, Shinji traced Perkins's trail, sending Ananke to New Delhi, then Abu Dhabi, then Cyprus, and finally to Rome.

In the Italian capital, the clues took Ananke to an unused storefront on the east end of the city. A check inside revealed it was empty, but someone had been present very recently, probably even spent the night.

Ananke discreetly showed a picture of Perkins to people working at the shops along the street. She received only shaking heads until she entered a small market half a block away.

Like elsewhere, the clerk was already in the process of saying no before Ananke had even finished setting the picture down, but once the woman actually saw the image, her head stopped moving.

"*Si*," she said, her lip curling in disdain. "I have seen him before."

It turned out Perkins had purchased some cigarettes, but it was the way he looked at her teenage daughter that had made the impression on the woman.

"When was this?" Ananke asked, her Italian flawless.

"Two hours ago. Maybe a little more."

The moment Ananke exited the shop, she contacted Shinji.

"Motorway footage, street cams, whatever you can get your hands on," she said. "Look back no more than three hours. You'll find him somewhere."

She was right.

Exactly forty-three minutes before she'd arrived at the store, Perkins appeared on a security camera feed four blocks away. He was on foot and in the company of three men— bodyguard types and armed, if the bulges under their jackets were any indication.

Shinji bounced from camera to camera, tracing Perkins's route.

Ananke hurried back to the motorcycle she'd obtained upon arriving in Rome, and then, with Shinji's voice in her ear guiding her, followed Perkins through the city, past the Vatican, and toward the airport.

"He must be leaving the country," she said as she sped southwest. "Check flights. Whatever he's booked on, get me a ticket."

By the time she reached Fiumicino airport, Shinji had determined Perkins was scheduled to fly out on a Delta Airlines nonstop flight to Atlanta, Georgia. He was using the name Carl Pinter and had a ticket for business class, row 3, seat A. Shinji had purchased Ananke a seat in the same section, only at the back on the other side, row 9 seat J.

She reached the gate just as boarding began. From the cover of the economy-class crowd, she watched the business-class passengers file past the gate agents into the tunnel to the plane.

The sixth person to have his boarding pass scanned was the very not dead Noah Perkins.

Ananke grinned.

She waited until the bulk of the passengers were boarding before she checked in, and then used the economy entrance onto the aircraft instead of the one for business class. When she reached her seat, she peeked over the center aisle toward the front of the plane.

She had a moment of panic when she saw his seat was empty, but then she spotted him emerging from the front galley area where he must have been using the toilet. She ducked until enough time had passed for him to settle in before she checked again, and found him exactly where he was supposed to be—belted into seat 3A.

Just in case he planned a last-minute exit, she continued checking on him until the doors were shut and the aircraft was taxiing toward the runway. At that point she allowed herself to relax.

She had him now.

Lunch was served not long after they were in the air. Ananke watched *Ex Machina* while she ate. It was the kind of film she loved. Men who thought they were smart, and women who were smarter. Okay, technically an android, but a *female* android.

Before the movie ended, the cabin lights were dimmed so

passengers could get some sleep. She paused the film and glanced at Perkins. He had turned his chair into a flat bed and was lying back, wearing an eye mask.

As she watched the rest of the film, she extracted a small kit from the bag she had obtained, with Shinji's help, in Abu Dhabi. It looked like a simple bathroom pouch. Inside was a comb, a small cake of soap, a half dozen cotton swabs, and two small pill containers—one labeled IBUPROFEN and one SLEEP.

The comb broke down into several predesigned pieces, which, when combined with parts from two of the specially made swabs, created a ring that, if worn correctly, looked unremarkable, but if the wearer were to turn her hand palm up, four thin needles would be visible sticking out of the band.

She set the device down and poured a cap full of bottled water into her unused coffee cup. She dumped in two of the pills from the SLEEP bottle and three from IBUPROFEN. The water boiled for a moment as it chemically reacted to the combined ingredients. Once the bubbling stopped, the drug was ready.

Next, she pulled on a pair of puncture-resistant, skin-colored gloves and dipped the ring's needles into the solution. She then slipped the ring over her finger. All that was left to do now was touch the metal tips to Perkins's exposed skin, and he would remain asleep for the duration of the flight.

And several hours afterward.

If Shinji had done his job, a "medical" team would be waiting in Atlanta for the inevitable request for medical assistance.

She peeked across the cabin to make sure Perkins hadn't woken, and then eased into the aisle and headed toward the front galley. As she neared the front, she heard someone behind her lumber out of their seat. A glance over her shoulder revealed the passenger was a tired-looking, middle-aged woman clutching the toiletry bag all business-class passengers received. No one for Ananke to concern herself with.

When she entered the galley, a flight attendant sitting near the door started to stand.

Ananke smiled and said, "Just stretching my legs. Don't

need anything."

The flight attendant resettled into her seat.

The curtain was drawn across the entrance to Perkins's aisle. Ananke pulled it to the side and stepped through.

The first thing she noted was that all the passengers along the aisle appeared to be either asleep or watching their TV screens—just how she wanted it.

The second thing she noticed was the prick of a needle against her arm.

Before she could turn to see the source, the world disappeared.

SEVEN

Dublin, Ireland

DYLAN BRODY SAT on his favorite barstool, convinced he was in a fix.

No one had told him there was a problem. In fact, just the opposite. The meet was on. The goods would be ready to move. And the deal would be done.

So said Harmon, the logistics guy, who'd just called with the update.

But Harmon was the problem. In Dylan's experience, even the most mundane packages he was hired to transport came with a layer of paranoia affecting everyone involved. A little nervousness would have been expected, but Harmon sounded as cool as Tom Hiddleston ordering room service.

Hence Dylan's suspicion.

He thought about calling Harmon's boss, Mr. Lyne, and expressing his concern, but then there was the whole Dylan-really-needing-this-job thing. Yes, the money for sure would be helpful, but what he really needed was the successful completion of the job.

He'd had a bit of a bad run as of late, culminating in several months of intense rehab for fractures to his right leg and arm. Once he felt well enough to work again, he quickly learned no one wanted to hire him anymore. Potential employers were more interested in someone with—as he had heard several times—"a better track record." He'd been seriously considering a career change when Mr. Lyne called.

Having never worked with the man before, Dylan had, of course, done his due diligence and made sure Lyne was on the up and up. But in reality, even if Lyne's reputation had been sketchy, Dylan would have taken the job. He was that desperate.

Which was why he grudgingly knew it would be a mistake to call Lyne now. Dylan needed to finish this job so he could show the world he could be trusted again. Even if something fishy was going on, he couldn't allow himself to worry about that. He needed to keep his head down, do what he'd been hired to do, and not ask any questions.

That's what couriers did.

He downed the last of the pint he'd been brooding over and hopped off the stool.

"That it for you, Dylan?" John, the bartender, asked.

"Things to do, I'm afraid."

"See ya tomorrow, then."

"See ya tomorrow."

Dylan headed out, his limp barely noticeable anymore.

THE PICKUP WAS to take place on the fourth floor of the car park at the bend in St. Andrew's Lane, a few blocks east of Trinity College.

Dylan wanted nothing more than to get inside the building for a little pre-event scouting, but knew the people he was receiving the package from might be doing the same. If they found him wandering around, it could foul things up well and good.

A courier's job was to show up where he was told to show up, take possession of what he was given to transport, and take it to where he was instructed to go. There would be no recon, no surveillance, nothing outside the assigned tasks. Those details were the responsibilities of others. Even though that meant no walk-through of the garage, checking the place out from down the street was something he thought he could get away with.

He found a drainpipe running up the side of a building near the corner of St. Andrew's Lane and Exchequer Street. He waited until there was a gap in the foot traffic, and then scaled the pipe to the top of the wall. It took a few moments to maneuver over the top, but soon enough he was on the roof. From the back end, he used a pair of cheap binoculars to scan the garage.

Each floor had five arched large openings filled with angled blue slats that made it difficult to see anything inside. He turned his attention to the roof. All but one of the parking spots were empty. The lone car there had someone sitting in the driver's seat.

Dylan frowned. The meeting was still an hour and a half away. Did the guy have something to do with it?

Hold on there, he told himself. *You're just on edge. Maybe he's part of the advance team. You know, making sure the place is safe for when you arrive.*

Not convinced, Dylan switched his view back to the slatted windows and checked each one individually.

His gaze paused on the window right above the ground-level garage entrance he'd been instructed to use. A black rod that looked far too much like a rifle barrel was sticking out between two of the slats.

More protection? Or someone waiting to pick off the meeting's participants as they arrived?

Or was Dylan the only one who was supposed to use that entrance?

Just relax! You're making something out of nothing.

Was he?

Again he considered calling Mr. Lyne, and again he talked himself out of it.

It's going to be fine. In a few hours, you'll be finished and home again.

He thought if he repeated it a few hundred more times, he might start to believe it.

DYLAN SPENT THE remaining pre-arrival time at a pub called the Banker's Lounge on Trinity Street, a block away from the garage. As much as he wanted another pint, though, he stuck with tea.

Five minutes before the appointed hour, he headed out again.

By entering St. Andrew's Lane via Trinity, he came at the garage from the east. Along this side were more of the arched openings, only these weren't filled with slats. An idea poked at him from the back of his mind. It was probably ridiculous and unnecessary, but he couldn't shake himself of the notion, so seconds later he was rolling a nearby trash bin under one of the windows.

Getting on top of the bin was relatively simple. Pulling himself up through the arched opening took a bit more work.

After catching his breath, he used the cover of the parked cars to sneak up to the next floor. This was the floor with the slatted window where he'd seen the rifle barrel sticking out. Several vehicles were parked between him and the window, so he dipped his head toward the floor and looked under the vehicles. Sure enough, someone was crouching right where the rifle should be.

Dylan took extra care moving to the next ramp, his journey aided by the fact the rifleman was more focused on the world outside than the one within. When Dylan reached the next level—where the meet was to take place—he scanned the space from the safety of a concrete barrier at the top.

He immediately spotted the gray panel van parked near the stairs, with a logo on the side that read FLOWERS BY MAUREEN. It was exactly as Harmon had described. As were the two men standing impatiently in front of it.

See, everything's fine.

He double-checked to make sure no one else was around, took a calming breath, and walked out.

The two men didn't notice him until he'd covered almost half the distance to the van. When they did, the larger one drew a weapon from a holster under his jacket.

"Not another step," he ordered.

Dylan halted. "I'm here about the flowers. Katie sent me," he said, reciting his portion of the recognition signal.

For a few moments, no one moved.

Finally, the guy who wasn't holding a gun said, "Where did you come from?"

"I'm here about the flowers," Dylan repeated. "Katie sent

me."

The men exchanged a look, and then the armed one said, "You're the courier?"

Dylan stayed silent, allowing them to finish the greeting. When they didn't, he said, "Perhaps I'm in the wrong place. Have a good evening, gentlemen."

"Your, um, flowers are ready," the smaller man said. "I just need you to…sign the receipt."

It wasn't the best delivery of a counter-sign in the history of espionage, but it was good enough.

Dylan smiled. "Then let's get down to business, shall we?"

"No," the big man replied, his gun still aimed at Dylan. "First you tell us where you came from. You were instructed to come in through the front entrance, but my man woulda seen you if you did."

"My job was to meet you here, and here I am. There's no reason you need more than that." He was playing tougher than he felt, but it was the Irish way.

"It's okay, Tom," the smaller one said. "We don't need to lose any more time."

After another beat, the man's partner lowered his weapon.

"All right, then," the unarmed one said to Dylan. "Get yourself over here."

Four minutes later, Dylan drove the van through the garage and out the main entrance. He couldn't help but fidget as he emerged onto St. Andrew's Lane, knowing if the guy with the rifle was going to take a shot at him, now would be the time, but he made it all the way onto Exchequer without anything hitting the van.

You're an overthinking ass, Dylan Brody. That's what you are.

As he headed toward the drop-off point north of the city, he started thinking about his future again. He'd be able to use his success on this job to leverage another. It might take him a while to build his business back to what it had once been, but bit by bit he'd get there.

Traffic was light, adding to his increasingly buoyant

mood. After a while, he was feeling so good that he even smiled at a red-headed beauty crossing the street in front of him while he was stopped at a light a few kilometers shy of the countryside. It didn't hurt that even though she was talking on her phone, she seemed to be checking him out, too.

Yes, things would definitely be better now.

When the light turned green and he was on his way again, he began to hum that old Black Eyed Peas song he loved, "I Gotta Feeling." Soon he was bouncing his head to the rhythm. This private concert was the reason it took him a moment to notice the flashing lights behind him.

When he saw the garda car in his side-view mirror, he muttered, "Not now," and then quickly checked his speedometer to make sure he wasn't going too fast.

Nope. He was well within the speed limit.

Take it down a notch. The car is probably on its way elsewhere.

Dylan kept shooting glances at the mirror, expecting the car to go around him, but it stayed right on his tail.

"This cannot be happening."

Maybe it was a faulty taillight, or something stupid like that. It wasn't his driving, that was for sure. He'd driven with even more care than usual, following the law to a fault. Not counting his potentially illegal cargo, of course. But if he was being stopped about what he was transporting, then he would have expected more than one car with a single officer inside.

At his first opportunity, he guided the van to the side of the road, hoping he wouldn't be there long. The garda pulled in behind him and stopped.

For the next few minutes, Dylan nervously tapped the steering wheel and stared at the side mirror, waiting for the officer to get out of his car.

When the door finally opened and the garda climbed out, Dylan said, "Whoa."

The guy was big. Like rugby full-back big, over a hundred and eighty-five centimeters tall and as broad as an elephant across the shoulders.

As the garda drew near, Dylan rolled down his window

and put on his most cooperative smile. "Good evening, Officer."

The man nodded and said, "Driver's license, please."

"Sure, sure. Of course." Dylan pulled out his wallet, fumbled his license loose, and handed it through the window. The name was fake but the license was real.

The cop looked at it for a second and then said, "What's in the back?"

Dylan motioned back toward the logo on the side of the van. "Flowers."

"What kind of flowers?"

"I'm not sure about the type. I do the deliveries, not the packing."

"Is that so? Show me."

"Don't you need a search warrant to do that?" The moment the question was out of Dylan's mouth, he regretted it.

"Is there a reason why I should need one?"

"Not at all, not at all. Just curious, that's all."

"Then you don't mind showing me."

Some employers were great at prepping a vehicle so that nothing questionable would be visible if a door was opened. Dylan had no idea if Mr. Lyne's people fell into that category. He sent up a prayer that they were as he said, "It would be my pleasure."

When he turned away from the officer to unlock his seat belt, he felt the prick of a bee sting on the back of his neck. His instinct was to slap down and squash the insect, but before he could, he slumped over, unconscious.

E|GHT

Mexico City, Mexico

ONE OF THESE days it would be fun to attempt something a little more challenging, Rosario thought, and then immediately snorted.

Who was she kidding? Nothing was challenging enough for her anymore.

Just look at where she was now compared to where she'd started life. Clawing up that cliff was probably the most challenging thing she would ever do.

Of course, her birth parents were partly responsible. Sure, they'd left her at the back door of that godforsaken storefront church in Tuxtla Gutiérrez when she'd been only a few weeks old, but the mixing of their DNA had given her genius-level smarts.

Her surrogate parents? Well, they had contributed, too, in their own way.

The church had been one of those radical evangelical offshoot-type places, filled with uneducated zealots who didn't know the difference between the square root of four and the round root of a *chaca* tree. Science was the enemy. And the church's champion was the self-righteous bastard of a preacher named Morales.

The preacher and his wife had taken Rosario in, telling everyone she was their daughter. What she really was to "Papa" Morales was his servant. Some of Rosario's earliest memories were of cleaning toilets and scrubbing dishes and being whipped with a switch for not dusting the living room properly.

And the sermons—she couldn't forget those, either.

Everything was an opportunity to preach for Morales. His favorite refrain was telling Rosario she'd been abandoned because she was not worthy of God's love, and that it was only through her obedience to Morales and her strict adherence to his teachings that she could even hope for a slim chance of entering heaven.

If Rosario had been an ordinary girl, she would have probably been crushed by his mental torture and become a meek follower of his every word. But even at a young age she was more than smart enough to know he was full of shit, though not quite smart enough to avoid the beatings.

Soon enough, however, she realized her best course of action was to pretend his methods were working. She carried out every task she was given, kowtowed when contrition was called for, and always acted the repentant daughter who was thankful for any scrap of attention she received. She was merely biding her time, learning as much as she could, and planning for the moment when she could make her break.

She was twelve when that day finally came. In the years leading up to that moment, she had obtained a robust self-education that far exceeded the institutional ones kids her age were getting. She'd learned a decent amount of English, mostly from movies and TV, and could write in her native Spanish at a near college level.

The day prior to escape day, she and the two people everyone called her parents had traveled west to a church in Oaxaca where Morales had been asked to speak. On the afternoon of Rosario's independence day, Morales had left her and his wife at the home of the preacher who had brought them to town, while Morales went to check out the church in advance of his big sermon that evening.

Rosario had not known when she'd make her move, only that the trip to Oaxaca would provide the best opportunity she might ever get, so she had come prepared.

Buried in the bag of clothes Morales had selected for her was a small backpack she had taken from a store two years earlier. In it was the money she had been secretly skimming from the church's offerings for as long as she could remember—nearly fourteen hundred pesos now, more than enough to get her on a bus out of town. There was also a set of clothes *she* liked, and a pair of never used sneakers she had stolen the day after she was told about the trip.

With Morales not planning on returning until after the evening service, she had decided that afternoon would be go time.

The only obstacle was Rosario's "mother." Though the woman was not the tyrant her husband was, Rosario didn't think she'd just let Rosario walk out the front door. Fortunately, that wasn't the only exit.

Most of the time when the two were alone together, they never talked. When they did, it was usually about a task Rosario needed to perform. Rosario decided to use that to her advantage.

"Father told me I should take some private reflection time before tonight," Rosario told the woman after they'd been sitting quietly for a few minutes. "I thought I could use the bedroom."

With a nod, the preacher's wife said, "Bless you, child."

Rosario wanted to run to the back of the house, but she kept her pace unhurried, like it was just another afternoon in the life of the Morales family. Once she had the door closed, however, she began to shake in excitement. Unless the preacher's wife became suspicious—and she wouldn't—Rosario would have at least two hours before anyone knew she was gone. By then, she would already be on a bus heading north.

She retrieved the book bag, pulled out her never worn jeans and T-shirt, and changed. After she donned the sneakers and tied them up, she allowed herself a moment to enjoy her forbidden wardrobe.

She briefly considered shoving the clothes she'd taken off into her backpack so she'd have something else to wear, but she wanted no reminders of Morales, so she stuffed them in the big bag she was leaving behind.

Quietly she opened the window, climbed out, and snuck down the side of the house toward the street. An old sedan that probably hadn't run for years was parked at the front corner of the house. She figured if she slipped around it, she could get away without anyone in the living room seeing her.

She began creeping along the car.

"Rosario," the preacher's wife said, right before she rounded the other end of the car.

Rosario was caught. When Morales found out, the beating would be magnitudes greater than any he'd ever given her. And she might as well kiss the idea of freedom good-bye, because he would never leave her unsupervised again.

Unless she made a run for it.

The preacher's wife was far from athletic, and if Rosario could get past her, the woman would never be able to catch her. What the woman *would* do was alert her husband, who would then enlist the help of others to track down Rosario.

The bus station would be the first place they went, which meant it was no longer an option.

She could either try to hitch a ride out of town, or hide in Oaxaca until Morales and his wife finally went home. Neither was the scenario she'd been planning for, but they were both better than returning to Tuxtla Gutiérrez.

She rocked forward, about to run.

"I'm not going to tell him," the woman said.

Rosario paused, her brow furrowing.

"I just…I wanted to give you this."

The woman held out an envelope.

It had to be a trick, Rosario thought. She'd reach for the envelope and the woman would grab her arm.

As if reading her mind, the preacher's wife set the envelope on the car and backed away several meters.

Rosario didn't move.

"Please, I'm not going to stop you."

Rosario didn't know what to think. This was the most personal conversation they'd ever had. She decided to risk checking the envelope. She crept forward, ready to spring away if the woman even twitched, and snatched the envelope.

As she untucked the flap, she kept one eye on the woman to make sure nothing funny happened. But when she saw what was inside, she simply stared at it.

"It's not a lot, but maybe it will help," the woman said.

Money. At least ten times more than what Rosario had saved up. She looked at the woman again. "Why?"

Wearing a pained smile, the preacher's wife said, "I'll tell him you were ill. He won't know you're gone until we come home tonight. Get as far away as you can. Get as far away and never come back."

With that, the only mother Rosario had ever known walked back into the house.

Rosario did exactly as the woman urged, and was three hours into a bus ride north to Mexico City by the time she figured Morales and his wife returned home.

She never found out if Morales looked for her. When she finally went back to Tuxtla Gutiérrez after she'd become an adult, she discovered his church had been turned into a hardware supply store, and that the apartment above it where they had lived was occupied by a young couple who'd never heard of the Morales family.

Rosario found only one person who remembered the "crazy" preacher. The man couldn't recall the specifics of what had happened to him, something about a falling out with his flock but the man wasn't sure.

The discovery was disappointing. Rosario had really hoped to tear Morales's church apart herself. In the end, though, the only thing that mattered was the new life she'd created in Mexico City.

When she first arrived in the capital, she shed the Morales name and began calling herself Rosario Blanca. To survive, she began executing petty crimes for people older and bigger than she was, and found she had a special talent for it. She obtained whatever her "clients" asked for, and they gave her the protection she needed as she matured. By the time she was sixteen, she had taught herself how to use computers, and had moved on to doing regular work for investigators, both private and governmental. Her clients never knew how old she was, of course. All contact was conducted via the Internet, where the only qualification that mattered was her reputation for finding things.

Her ability to obtain items was not confined to the Web.

Since she'd basically been putting on an act since the first time she felt the sting of Morales's switch, she could now easily transform herself into anyone she wanted at the spur of the moment. One of her favorite personas was a cute and naïve young woman. It was amazing what she could get others to say in front of her, and she had a dozen other personalities she could call on, depending on the situation.

And when neither computer expertise nor acting was called for, she was damn good at getting inside places where she shouldn't be, and finding papers and flash drives and photographs and whatever else a client might be looking for. It didn't matter if the items were in secure desks, padlocked cabinets, or even safes. With a little preparation, she could get into almost anything and be gone without anyone knowing she'd been there.

When she was nineteen, she took on a job for a new client. The company tried to hide its true identity from her, but it had no idea who it was dealing with. Turned out it was an organization known as TPG, an intelligence-gathering service based in the Czech Republic. Her successful completion of the assigned task opened a whole new market for her, and within a year all her clients were intelligence based.

They paid better.

And on time. She appreciated that.

Her current gig involved obtaining three software dongles from a safe in the Mexico City branch of a well-known chemical company. For this operation, she had transformed herself into a research assistant named Ivonne Perez, visiting from the company's facility in Monterrey. She'd created a working ID badge and planted the appropriate information in the corporate database. Unsurprisingly, it worked like a charm when she passed through security upon entering the building.

The research and development lab she wanted was on the fourth floor, in the southeast corner. Having memorized the floor plans, she navigated her way to her destination like she'd been there a million times, and tapped her badge against the reader outside the door.

A green light and a beep signaled the card had worked again.

The safe was in the lab director's office, along the back wall of the lab. Standing between her and it were more than two dozen occupied workstations, not to mention the director himself at his desk.

She garnered a few curious looks as she worked her way through the room, but no one tried to stop her or question her presence. Right before she reached the door to the director's office, she slipped her hand in her pocket and pushed the side button on her phone to start the countdown.

She knocked on the door and stepped inside. "Dr. Ruiz?"

He glanced up from his computer screen, clearly not pleased to be interrupted. "What is it?"

"I was sent by human resources. I understand you requested help with a documentation project."

"Documentation project? I don't know anything about a documentation project."

"That's all I was told."

"Obviously you've been sent to the wrong place. Now, if you don't mind, I am rather busy at the moment."

"Of course. I'm sorry to have—"

The main power cut off and the fire alarm started blaring. Panicked voices rose from the lab.

"What the hell?" Dr. Ruiz said, rising.

"That's the fire alarm," Rosario said. "We should probably…"

There was no reason for her to finish as Ruiz was already hurrying toward the door.

"Let's go," he said. "Out. Out."

He ushered her into the lab, where the others were filing into the hallway in the dim light of two battery-operated lamps. Rosario made her way to the back end of the crowd, with Ruiz right behind her. Then, in the confusion at the doorway, she allowed the director to scoot by her. The moment he crossed the threshold and the door swung shut, she hurried to one of the workstations and ducked beneath it, waiting in case the director sent someone back in to look for her.

When a minute had passed and no one returned, she scooted out and hurried over to the director's office.

The safe was embedded in the floor next to a metal cabinet. She turned on the flashlight function of her phone and mounted it on a stack of books so that it pointed at the safe. The first combination she tried was the one installed by the safe's maker. It didn't work.

She let out a soft *hmm* of appreciation. It was refreshing to see Ruiz had enough sense to assign a number of his own choosing.

She had an electric device in her pocket that could determine the new combination, but it took a few minutes to work. She decided to try the list of potential combinations she'd come up with based on an analysis of the director's life. The fourth set of numbers was the winner.

So, one credit to the director for not sticking with the factory-issued combo, and a demerit for using a mix of his daughter's birthday and the date he received his doctorate.

A good portion of the safe's interior was occupied by files. Shoved in among them were portable hard drives and a clear plastic box containing the three dongles. She removed the three items and put them in an empty pocket, then replaced them with fake dongles given to her by her client.

Forty-five seconds after the safe was closed again, she was heading down the stairs at the tail end of a group from one of the upper floors.

Walking away from the building was a snap. Many who had been driven outside by the alarm were heading toward one of the local shops, so she looked like just another employee taking advantage of the down time.

The moment she was out of sight of the building, she retrieved her phone and opened an app she'd named Chaos. From the OPERATIONS RUNNING list, she selected the entry that had killed the building's power and set off the alarm, and pressed COMPLETE. In ten minutes, power would "miraculously" cycle back on.

Next, she checked the app labeled MAKEUP and selected

the section called CONCEALER. Under this, she verified that the worm she had planted within the building's security system had destroyed video footage from all the cameras for the last thirty minutes.

See, not a challenge at all.

As she neared the car she'd parked four blocks from the job site, an older woman with a weather-worn face, dressed in clothes that had seen far better days, limped out of a doorway in front of Rosario.

Being raised by a mental abuser did not mean Rosario was without manners. She slowed, giving the woman the right of way, but the woman staggered to a stop as soon as she noticed Rosario.

"I'm sorry," the woman said. She waved a hand in front of her. "After you."

"It's all right. Go ahead."

But the woman waved her hand again and didn't move.

With a mental shrug, Rosario started walking again, curving her path around the woman. As she went by, the woman took a step but stumbled and grabbed Rosario.

"I'm so sorry," the woman said.

Before Rosario could respond, something stung her arm.

NINE

Avanti's Office

WARREN FOUND HIS boss standing at the floor-to-ceiling windows overlooking the city. He stopped a dozen feet behind the man and waited.

Three full minutes passed before Avanti turned around.

"Report," the man said.

"They've begun the recruitment."

"Good. Have we stuck our foot in their way yet?"

"We're about to."

"Even better."

TEN

Las Vegas, Nevada

LIESEL KESSLER STUDIED the crowd, wishing her boss had listened to her and skipped the fundraiser's red carpet entrance in favor of slipping in through the back door.

That, of course, was not the way Hans Wolf did things. His brand was built on grand displays of his toothy smile, chiseled jaw, and perfectly coiffed salt-and-pepper hair. The public had come to expect it, and more importantly, so had his investors. He often said his first hundred million had been made off his hard work, but the two billion after that was all due to his boyish charm.

Wolf held controlling interests in, among other things, two large-project construction firms, a high-volume cargo shipping company, several electronics manufacturing facilities, a dozen casinos located around the world—including the one Liesel and Wolf were about to enter—and was also the chairman of a professional football team in Germany.

All of which meant that though many people enjoyed his antics, even worshiped the man, not everyone held the same warm, fuzzy feelings for him. Hence the reason Liesel and the rest of the security team accompanied him everywhere he went.

Tonight he was attending a fundraiser hosted by perennial Las Vegas headliner and world renowned performer Kevin Larson. Liesel had heard of Larson, of course, but couldn't name one song he was famous for. His last big hit had been in the 1980s, so probably something her parents would have liked—if Larson's music had been allowed into East Germany back then.

Liesel kept five paces behind her boss as he made his way along the carpet, his model of the week draped on his arm. The crowd was a mix of professional photographers covering the event, attendees too common to walk the star route, and tourists who were drawn to the Wolf Hotel and Casino by the klieg lights and flashing cameras.

In other words, an unsecured situation.

Liesel didn't like unsecured situations.

So far, the crowd looked tame enough—tourists smiling and pointing at people they recognized, and photogs shouting for the famous to look their way. Here and there video camera crews were set up so celebrities could stop for a few quick words with wannabe Ryan Seacrests before continuing on.

A wrangler for one of the American networks approached Wolf, but Liesel stepped in the way before the man could get there.

Flustered, the man said, "I'm with Glitz. We'd love a moment with Mr. Wolf."

Liesel stared at him for a second, then looked over her shoulder at her boss and raised an eyebrow.

He gave her the slightest of nods before putting on a big smile and walking over to the man. "It would be my pleasure."

Liesel followed them to the cameras, stopping a few feet outside the bright lights so she could keep an eye on the crowd.

The interview was as inane as these interviews always were—a non-funny joke to start, a comment about Mr. Wolf's suit, an inquiry about his date's dress, and a softball question about the charity the event was supporting.

Liesel had heard all the answers, or ones like them, so many times, she could have done the interview herself. But she was glad she didn't have to. The fewer words she had to speak on any given day, the better.

Once they resumed walking down the carpet, she scanned the waist-high divider ahead that separated the crowd from the famous attendees. That's when a blond woman wearing sunglasses caught her eye. There was something familiar about her.

Not wanting to scare her off and risk losing track of where

the woman went, Liesel swept her gaze through the crowd while keeping the blond in her peripheral vision. Finally, recognition came to her. The lips. Liesel was used to seeing those lips smeared with bright pink lipstick, not unadorned as they were now. But they were the right shape, as was the woman's nose and the line of her jaw.

She couldn't be here. Even if the woman had been released from prison early, she shouldn't have been able to leave Germany.

No. It's someone who looks like her. That's all.

Liesel swung her gaze back to reassure herself.

Two A-list movie stars were close to the woman's position. Everyone but her was looking at them. The woman was staring right at Wolf.

Scheisse.

Liesel activated her comm. "Katarina Stolzer. Six meters from the door. Blond wig. Glasses. Go."

While the two other security team members on the carpet hurried ahead, Liesel stepped between her boss and his stalker.

Stolzer's obsession with Wolf had reached its high point when she'd snuck into one of his homes, armed and claiming they had agreed to a suicide pact. That event had landed the woman in prison.

"We need to go. Now," Liesel whispered as she motioned for one of the other backup men to approach her.

"What is it?" Wolf asked. Though his tone was hushed and serious, the lighthearted smile remained on his face for the photographers.

"Stolzer."

The smile faltered. "She's in jail."

"She's here."

He looked past her to where the other two men had gone.

Liesel put a hand on his shoulder. "We'll go back the way we came and get you to your room."

"Absolutely not. I'm expected inside. I'm not going to hide."

Like with the interview questions, she'd known this would be his response. "Fine. Then once it's safe, we'll get you there another way. Please, sir."

He looked annoyed, but let her turn him around. "Walk at a normal pace," he whispered. "I don't want to make a scene."

Liesel instructed the team members who'd joined them to quickly escort Wolf's date inside. She then guided Wolf back the way they'd come and clicked on her comm. "Did you get Stolzer?"

"We've looked all around," Miguel said. "She's not here. Are you sure you saw her?"

"Positive. Keep looking."

With Stolzer on the loose, Liesel wanted to grab Wolf by the arm and rush him inside to someplace safe, but she restrained herself and settled for staying as close to him as she could.

When they reached the start of the carpet, Liesel guided her boss toward a row of glass doors that had been closed to the public for the event. They were guarded but not locked.

"Open the door," she ordered as they neared one of the security men.

The guard, recognizing Wolf, yanked the door open.

An onslaught of dinging slot machines and human voices flooded over them as they stepped inside. A row of security guards stood five meters beyond the doors, facing the casino floor so they could point people to another exit.

Though Liesel visited the hotel only a few times a year when her boss had business there, she knew the layout well. Awareness of one's surroundings was critical to her job. She walked the buildings her boss visited frequently to see all the nooks and crannies with her own eyes.

Because of this, she knew there was an employee-only service corridor to the left, just past the guards, and inside that half a dozen rooms in which she could keep Wolf until the danger had passed.

No longer needing to maintain a calm demeanor for the press, Liesel hustled Wolf toward the security line. "Move, move, move," she ordered the guards.

Wolf was once again recognized and the guards stepped to the side.

A few of the patrons popping coins into slot machines looked over as Liesel hauled her boss along the walkway by the wall, but most continued donating their money to the casino without a glance.

The entrance to the employee service hall was inset about a meter into the wall and needed an authorized keycard to open. As a trusted member in Wolf's protection staff, Liesel possessed a card that would open any door in the building, including her boss's suite. She slapped it against the reader and shoved the door open the instant it buzzed.

They passed the toilets first—she refused to fall into the American habit of camouflaging what they were by calling them restrooms—then a couple of large storage closets that would have sufficed as safe rooms if the office of one of the assistant catering managers wasn't just ahead. The office had chairs, a phone, and, most importantly, a computer Liesel could use to access the security system and monitor the hallway.

She pulled the door open, ready to kick the assistant manager out, but no one was there. After locking the door, she propped one of the guest chairs under the handle. When she turned around, she saw Wolf about to sit in the manager's chair behind the desk.

"The other one. That's mine." She nodded at the computer to convey why.

With a wry smile, he circled back to the guest chair. "You'd better be right about this."

"No. Better if I'm wrong."

She took the desk chair and logged into the computer, using her security override. The camera feed from the outside hall showed two employees walking toward the far end, but that was it.

She turned on her mic again. "Update."

She waited several seconds, but there was no response.

"Miguel? Thomas?"

Nothing.

She clicked the button a couple of times to make sure the batteries hadn't died. She could hear the electronic snap so the mic was on.

"Miguel, report."

No response.

She reached for the phone to call casino security, but before she could lift the handset, she heard the door to the supply closet behind her swing open.

She swiveled around as she rose.

"I've been watching you," Katarina Stolzer said from the closet threshold. She held in her right hand a Smith & Wesson pistol. Liesel thought it was probably a 9mm but it was hard to tell, because taped to the end of the barrel was a large plastic cola bottle, stuffed with what looked like paper. A homemade suppressor that would likely catch fire when used. "I knew this is where you would come. Closest room to the red carpet that you could secure. They said you were predictable, and they were right, weren't they?"

Calmly, Liesel said, "Katarina, there's no reason for you—"

"Weren't they?" Stolzer demanded again, raising the gun. She didn't point it at Liesel, but at Wolf.

"Yes. You are right. I am predictable." As she spoke, Liesel began inching to the side to shield her boss.

"Stop or I'll shoot him right now!"

Liesel stopped. "No reason for anyone to get hurt. Why don't you put the gun down and we can talk."

"I'm not an idiot! If I put it down, you won't give me the chance to talk."

"Put it down, Katarina," Wolf said. "I know you don't want to hurt anyone."

Anger flared in the woman's eyes. "Shut up! And don't you call me Katarina. You have lost that privilege. You don't know anything about me, do you? I thought you did once, but you know *nothing*! You just wanted to put me away. You wanted everyone to think I was crazy. After all we meant to each other, how could you do that?"

"I never wanted—"

"Shut up!"

With zero hesitation, Liesel flung herself over the desk chair and reached for the suppressor.

At the same moment she heard the barely muted bang, Liesel felt the bullet pierce the soft tissue just below her collarbone and then burst from her back an inch from her neck. As she fell to the floor, Katarina shouted, "No!"

The woman rushed past the desk, out of Liesel's sightline.

Grunting in pain, Liesel rocked onto her knees and staggered to her feet, knowing she needed to stop Stolzer before the woman could hurt Wolf. But Liesel was already too late. Her boss lay back in the guest chair, a bullet hole two centimeters above his right eye.

Katarina dropped to her knees next to him and tried to pull him into her arms.

"Leave him alone," Liesel said.

Katarina turned to her, her face darkening as if just remembering Liesel was also in the room.

"You did this! You killed him! You took him from me!"

Stolzer rushed at Liesel and rammed into her chest, knocking her against the wall. Before Liesel could recover, Katarina snatched a pen off the desk and jammed it into Liesel's wound.

The whole world turned electric white. Liesel slid to the floor, her consciousness slipping away.

She could hear Katarina raging at her, but the words meant nothing.

Liesel's vision began going in and out.

Gray.

Stolzer sitting at the desk.

Gray.

Stolzer hunched over something, as if reading a book.

Gray.

Stolzer holding something in her hand.

Gray.

A bang. The desk, but Stolzer no longer there.

Gray, this time turning darker and darker and darker until there was nothing.

ELEVEN

THE ADMINISTRATOR HUNG up his phone, stunned.

There was, of course, a set of rules in place for dealing with what had just happened, but he had never expected to implement them.

But implement them he must.

He opened the video chat and clicked the button that would connect him to his boss.

Committee member Monday accepted the call after the fourth ring. "Good evening." He was dressed in a tux and had answered on his smartphone. From the scene behind him and the noise, it appeared he was at a party. "If you can wait a moment, I'll find someplace private. Unless that's not necessary."

"Unfortunately, sir, it is."

"I'll get right back to you."

Two minutes passed before the Administrator's computer buzzed with the return call.

"What's going on?" Monday asked. He appeared to be in a bedroom. All the noise from before was gone.

"Thursday has been murdered."

"What?"

As succinctly as possible, the Administrator related what he'd learned of the situation involving the now late Committee member Thursday, known to the world as Hans Wolf.

Monday cradled his forehead. Wolf had been one of the first he'd recruited, and someone whose judgment Monday had trusted implicitly. His would be a large hole to fill.

"Dear God. Do we know how this Stolzer woman even got to him?"

"I will be having people look into it, but I wanted to notify you first."

"I appreciate that." Monday grimaced. "Perhaps we should suspend operations. I need time to process this."

The Administrator had anticipated this response. "I understand, sir, but I would argue against doing so. The team is already in the process of being collected. If we suspend now, we will risk losing the opportunity of bringing them into the fold."

"Operating without the full board, especially now, is not ideal."

"It is a problem, sir, but we created protocols that will guide us if issues arise."

"I think what bothers me most is the timing. I don't like it."

"Nor do I."

"We need to know if this was coincidental or a shot at us."

"Absolutely."

Monday took another moment. "You're right. We continue. Please keep me posted of any changes."

"Sir, one last thing."

"Yes?"

"The woman."

"The woman?"

"The one Thursday was so high on. Perhaps we can bring her on in his memory."

Another pause, and then a nod. "Not a bad idea. What about the candidate we already selected for that position?"

"That operation has just begun, so it can be easily aborted."

"If you think that's feasible, let's do it."

"Should I call an emergency board meeting?"

"Everyone needs to know about Thursday, but I'd rather you call them individually. Let's wait on telling them about the woman until she's already in place. If anyone raises an objection, you can say that there was a problem with our primary candidate and you had to go with an alternate. Have an answer ready that will stand up to any scrutiny."

"Yes, sir."

TWELVE

Las Vegas, Nevada

LIESEL WASN'T SURE what she picked up on first—the odor of antiseptic or the rhythmic beeps of medical monitoring equipment. Either way, it meant only one thing.

Eyes still shut, she listened for signs of anyone nearby, but the beeps were her only company.

She parted her eyelids and confirmed she was alone in a hospital room. There was a window to her left, and through it she could see the twinkling lights of a neon city.

Las Vegas.

What was she doing in Las Vegas? In a hospital? What could have—

Her breath caught in her throat.

Mein Gott!

Memories flashed in her mind.

Katarina Stolzer, gun in hand.

Liesel's shoulder, lanced by a bullet.

Hans Wolf, a hole in his head.

It was my job to keep him alive.

She tensed. Had the police caught his killer? Or was Stolzer on the run? If the woman was still out there, Liesel had to go after her. The woman had to pay for what she'd done.

Liesel looked around until she spotted the mounted call button. Since her right arm was strapped to her chest, she reached with her left. Rather, she attempted to reach with her left, but was prevented from doing so by the handcuff securing it to the bed's railing.

Why would she be restrained? The only wrong thing she'd done was fail to keep her boss alive. While she would have to live with that horror for the rest of her life, it was not a crime.

She tried to shout, "Hello," in English to get someone's attention, but her dry throat caused her voice to crack. After a few swallows, she was able to shout loudly enough to get a response.

The young police officer who stuck his head in the room said, "Finally awake, huh?"

"Why am I…" Her mind still hazy, she couldn't remember the word she wanted, so she raised her left hand and rattled the cuff against the bar.

"The detectives will be back soon. You can ask them whatever you want." He shut the door.

She called again several times. When the door reopened, a stern-faced nurse came in. She took Liesel's vital signs, examined the wound, and redressed it. Though Liesel barraged her with questions, the nurse never responded.

Not long after she left, two men in suits entered and introduced themselves as Detectives Ferris and Montrose. She put them both in their forties, with Ferris the older of the two.

"Your lawyer not here yet?" Ferris asked.

"My lawyer?"

"He was here this morning. Mr…." He turned to his partner. "What the hell was his name?"

"I think he said Ramsey," Montrose said.

The older man smiled. "That's right. Ramsey." He looked back at Liesel. "So, has he come back yet?"

"I do not know a Mr. Ramsey," she said.

"Is that right? Huh. Would you be willing to answer a few questions while we wait for him?"

"No, she wouldn't, Detective." The words came from a third man who had just entered the room, his suit considerably more expensive than the cops', more like something Hans Wolf would wear.

"Well, there you are, counselor," Ferris said. "Seems your client here doesn't know who you are."

"That's because we've never met. Now, if you don't mind, I'd like a few minutes alone with Miss Kessler."

The detectives didn't look happy, but they vacated the room.

Once the door was shut, Ramsey pulled a chair over to her bed and sat down.

"I'm glad to see you're awake," he said in flawless German. "How are you feeling?"

"Who are you?"

"You heard Detective Ferris. I'm your lawyer."

"Who sent you? Someone from the company?"

"Oh, God, no. I'm pretty sure no one there wants anything to do with you."

"What do you mean? Why not?"

"Because you've been implicated in Mr. Wolf's murder."

"W-w-what? But I had nothing to do with it!"

"Were you there?"

"I was, but—"

"Then you had *something* to do with it."

"I had something to do with trying to stop it, yes."

He pointed at her shoulder. "Is that how you received the wound?"

She nodded. "I tried to grab Katarina Stolzer, but she pulled the trigger before I could reach her." Eyes hardening, she added, "*She's* the one who killed him."

"And?"

"And what?"

"What happened after she pulled the trigger?"

"The bullet went through me and hit Mr. Wolf."

"That is unfortunate."

Her brow furrowed. "Unfortunate? He's dead, Mr. Ramsey. Unfortunate doesn't even come close to describing it."

He smiled sympathetically. "I understand your feelings, and I'm sorry if I offended you." He paused. "But you have a bigger problem to worry about right now than being concerned about what words I use. When Mr. Wolf's and Miss Stolzer's bodies were found—"

"Stolzer? She's dead?"

"You didn't know that? She took her own life with the same gun that did that to you."

"I-I-I heard a second shot, but I blacked out."

"Miss Stolzer left a note in which she thanked you for arranging to get her inside the hotel and for bringing Mr. Wolf to her."

"I did no such thing! I was the one who saw her. I was trying to hide Mr. Wolf from her."

"Two men from your security detail have said you sent them to look for her."

"I *did* send them."

"In what turned out to be the exact opposite direction from where Stolzer was."

"I *saw* her standing near the doors in a blond wig and wearing sunglasses. That's where I sent them!"

"Miss Stolzer had no wig or sunglasses in her possession."

"She must have thrown them away."

"I'm sure you can see how it might look like you're

lying."

"You don't believe me?"

"I said how it might look, not that you are." He leaned toward the bed. "I actually know you're telling the truth." He waved toward the door. "The problem is, our friends out there are convinced you were in on it. There is a lot of evidence piled against you."

Liesel stared at the ceiling. She'd always been able to get herself out of trouble in the past, but she had no idea how to do that now. "Are you here to tell me I'm going to jail?"

"Not at all. It's my job to see that never happens."

As he stood up he pulled a ring out of his pocket and slipped it over his finger.

"How?" she asked.

"I'd tell you to just trust me, but you don't know me and, truthfully, trust isn't necessary."

"What's that supposed to mean?"

"It doesn't matter."

He clasped her cuffed hand, and something pricked her palm.

THIRTEEN

Karas Evonus

A QUICK, SHARP whistle ripped Ananke from sleep. She shot to her feet, ready to deal with any threat that might come at her.

It turned out she was alone in a small, metal walled room with a narrow bed that took up half the space, with a toilet and a sink at the other end. There was a single door and no windows.

A cell. She'd seen plenty in her life, even been in a few.

A shelf stuck out of the wall above the foot of the bed. On it was a stack of neatly folded clothes. She glanced down and realized she was wearing only a bra and panties.

Anger boiling, she grabbed the clothes and yanked them on. Though she'd never seen them before, the formfitting yet flexible slacks and the black, long-sleeve, light pullover sweater were items she would have picked out herself.

Someone was trying to prove they knew her, and that pissed her off more.

She tried the door but, no surprise, it didn't budge.

All right, assess.

Her last memory was of passing through an airplane galley kitchen on her way to deal with Perkins.

I remember feeling something. A...prick. She muttered a litany of swear words she saved for only the most special of occasions.

Someone had drugged her before she could do the same to Perkins.

Obviously, the asshole had not boarded alone, and Ananke had failed to identify his partner.

Hold on. Hadn't someone been following her?

She seemed to recall seeing a person behind her, but couldn't remember if it was a man or a woman, let alone what he or she looked like.

Ultimately, it wasn't important. Perkins had caught her and brought her to wherever the hell this place was. The only reason he hadn't killed her yet was so obvious, even an apprentice on her first day in the business could have figured it out. Ananke was the assassin of the people's candidate, and therefore a valuable commodity. Likely, this was some kind of high-security Philippine prison. Either that or she was in a holding cell waiting to be transported back to Manila. Given the whistle that had woken her, she figured she'd know the answer soon enough.

She stretched. Boy, was her back tight. As she raised her arms over her head, she felt a slight pull in the crook of her right elbow. She pulled back the sleeve of the sweater and found a small red circle of dry blood, like one made by a needle, surrounded by a small bruise.

An IV line?

Her eyes narrowed. Sore back. Needle mark on her arm. How long had she been out?

A metallic squeak rose from the bottom of the door. She whirled around, thinking it was opening, but instead of the whole door swinging out, it was only a hatch along the bottom. When the flap was out of the way, a covered tray slipped through the slot and then the hatch closed again.

"Hey!" she yelled. "Where am I?" She pounded her fist against the door. "Hey! Hey!"

But whoever had delivered the tray was either gone or had been instructed to say nothing.

Ananke's stomach rumbled.

She banged the door once more before giving in to her hunger, picking up the tray, and setting it on the bed. As she lifted the cover, the aroma that wafted out was both familiar and unexpected. Pork and sriracha sauce and fresh bread. She couldn't believe what she was seeing.

On a plate was what appeared to be a pork belly sandwich,

exactly like the ones made at one of her favorite restaurants in Los Angeles. Beside it was a bowl of fruit salad containing only the ones she loved, and a bottle of Pellegrino Sparkling Water—her drink of choice.

Again, she was being presented with a clear demonstration of how much her captors knew about her life. She knew she should be further enraged, but at the moment she was too hungry.

There would be plenty of time for anger when she finished eating.

DYLAN HAD THE headache of headaches, the kind where any move he made drove another hundred nails into his brain. So it didn't take long to figure out his best course of action was to lie perfectly still.

Though he had yet to open his eyes, he knew he was locked up in a garda cell. What he couldn't figure out was what the officer had done to him. Most garda only carried pepper spray and a baton. A few, detectives and the like, were allowed to carry guns, but if it had been a bullet that pierced the back of Dylan's neck, he'd be in a casket, not on a bed.

Taser?

Dylan knew for a fact some garda carried them. He'd been tased once, years ago. A night out with the boys, too many beers, and a little public drunkenness. Don't ask. What he remembered most was that after he finally sobered up, he could still feel an electric tingle under his skin. He didn't feel that tingle now.

Now that his mind was clearing a bit, he couldn't understand why the cop tased him in the first place. Even if the guy had suspected Dylan was up to no good, he would have tried to arrest him first, right? That would have been the civilized thing to do.

Before Dylan could take that thought any further, a howling whistle wailed down on him. He curled in on himself, his hands pressing on his ears but doing little to stanch the aural assault.

When the whistle finally—mercifully—stopped, Dylan

peeled his eyelids open a fraction of an inch and took his first look around. The room was a cell, but not like any he'd seen before. No bars, only solid walls and an equally impenetrable-looking—

—door, on which a small panel at the bottom had just groaned open. As he watched, a tray slid into his room and the panel dropped back into place.

Curious, Dylan started to push up, but a spike of pure torture reminded him why he'd been holding still. It was another hour before the crippling pain lifted enough that he could finally move, but the remnants hung in his skull like a cloud of anguish.

Instead of standing, he knelt on the floor—learning in the process he was clothed only in his underwear—and lifted the lid off the tray.

Garlic soup. And roasted chicken. And could it be?

He picked up a breaded ball and bit into it.

Yes. Fruit dumplings.

All of it exactly like how his Czechoslovakian-born grandmother used to make them. With his head still impaired, he didn't realize what feeding him such a personal meal said about his captors.

ROSARIO WENT FROM unconscious to full alert without any stops in between. It was a habit she'd learned growing up in the preacher's house.

There were times when he'd come into her room in the middle of the night and yank her out of bed, yelling at her about chores he said she hadn't done that she actually had. She'd discovered early on that if she displayed even the tiniest bit of sluggishness before doing what he demanded, he would bring out his switch and her backside would be red for days. So she quickly learned how to leave sleep behind in an instant.

Her second life benefited from this ability, too. She'd lost count of how many times waking in a flash had saved her from being robbed or beaten or raped, especially in her first year in Mexico City, before she'd found safer places to live.

Whatever room she was now in was pitch-black and dead

quiet. She clicked her tongue softly against the roof of her mouth. No echo, meaning the space was small.

With care, she lifted her arms straight up, and then moved them slowly to either side as if she were doing a yoga move. Her left arm touched the wall before it reached the forty-five-degree mark. Her right, however, went all the way down until her bicep was lying beside her on the mattress. She let it continue down until the tip of her index finger brushed the floor.

As she brought her right arm back up, she felt a tiny point of tightness in the crook of her elbow. She rubbed it and discovered a small bump. The area surrounding it was sore, too. It could have been a cut, but from its location and size, she was pretty sure it was a needle mark.

She assessed her body for other irregularities, but found nothing other than the fact she was almost nude. When she set her feet on the floor, it was cold and felt like metal.

Using the same careful approach she'd employed earlier, she determined the room was two meters wide by three long. She also found a shelf with clothes on it—a T-shirt, it felt like, and jeans that, when she pulled them on, were a perfect fit.

Not long after she dressed, the lights came on and a loud whistle screeched from a speaker in the ceiling. A few minutes later, a tray of what she assumed was food slid into the room. She didn't check. She'd already been drugged at least once, so until her stomach twisted with hunger pains, she wasn't going to consume anything.

Instead, she sat on the bed and stared at the door.

LIESEL SLEPT THROUGH the whistle and panel opening and the tray being pushed into her room.

She woke two hours later, rested, no headache, and momentarily believing she was in her hotel room at the Wolf casino. But reality quickly returned in an avalanche of crushing memories—the assistant catering manager's office, the gunshot, the head wound, the hospital, the police, and the man who'd said he was Liesel's lawyer.

Finally, the mental assault eased enough for her to notice

the silence.

Where were the beeps of the hospital equipment?

And the odor of medicine?

The bed felt different, too.

She opened her eyes and looked around.

"What the hell?"

FOURTEEN

Office of the Administrator

DESPITE THE DEATH of a Committee member and the last-minute field team substitution, everything was progressing within the expected parameters.

The four candidates had been woken from their induced sleep—Ananke's the longest at six days and Liesel's the shortest at thirteen hours—in preparation for the final stage of recruitment. Due to the special circumstances surrounding the fifth candidate, and the fact he would not be necessary on the Fairbanks mission, the Administrator had decided to let him stay where he was until a more appropriate job came along.

The Administrator checked the recruitment schedule, and was about to alert the monitoring team that they would begin shortly, when a *bong* from his computer signaled a request for a video chat from Committee member Tuesday.

The Administrator clicked ACCEPT. "Good afternoon, sir."

"Good afternoon. I know you're quite busy, but I wanted to confirm that the field team was in place." Though the man's tone was businesslike, the Administrator noticed an underlying concern, bordering on panic, in Tuesday's disposition.

"Our recruits are in place, yes, but we have not yet begun orientation."

"Why not? Shouldn't that happen right away?"

"Pardon me, Mr. Tuesday. You should have received a copy of the schedule. Did you not?"

"I have it. I just thought—" He paused, as if resetting himself. "I only wanted to confirm where things stood."

"Orientation will commence in the next few hours."

"And how long until they are operational?"

That, too, was in the schedule. But the Administrator replied, "Four days, as long as they accept our offers."

"The schedule needs to be sped up."

"I'm sorry?"

"And we need to change the mission."

Caught by surprise, the Administrator took a moment before saying, "I don't understand. Change to what?"

"Correct me if I'm wrong, but the Fairbanks job isn't time critical."

"That's not precisely true."

"What I mean is, the mission doesn't need to happen immediately, and can be put off for a week or two if necessary."

The Administrator worked hard to keep from frowning. "Technically, that's correct. But the same is true for all the proposed missions."

"I'm not talking about switching to one of the other choices. I'm talking about something entirely new that *is* time sensitive." Tuesday explained what he meant, finishing with, "I'm sure you can see that this is an even better test case for the field team than Fairbanks. And there's no question that it fits within the goals of the Committee."

The Administrator considered his response. "It's indeed a troubling situation," he said. "And, as you say, a suitable mission to undertake. But there are rules the Committee must operate under. If we ignore them, the program will quickly fall apart."

"Call the Committee into a special session. Let us vote on it. I'll stand by the decision."

"Very well. Mr. Tuesday, I am informing you that from this point forward, our conversation is being recorded." The truth, of course, was that the recording had been on since the start of the call. "Are you formally requesting an emergency meeting of the Committee?"

"Yes, dam—yes. That's exactly what I'm doing."

"Your request has been registered. Per Committee rules, I will convene the meeting at the earliest possible time."

"*Now* would be best."

"I'm sure you understand that is not in my control, but I will do everything I can to make it happen as soon as possible."

Looking frustrated but resigned, Tuesday said, "Of course. I understand. It's…never mind."

"Just so we're clear, Mr. Tuesday, I will also need to verify the events as you've presented them."

"I'll send you everything I have."

"One final question. As you know, Committee rules are very clear on a separation between ourselves and the missions we take on. I apologize for saying this, but your demeanor makes me wonder if you have a personal connection to this."

The lie flowed from Tuesday's eyes to his face as he donned a more detached expression. "Of course not. It's just…things like this…they affect me right here." He patted his chest above his heart. "Admittedly more than they probably should."

"I understand."

The Administrator called his boss and succinctly relayed the details of his conversation with Tuesday.

"I agree," Monday said after the Administrator finished. "Tuesday must have a connection to this. We need to find out what it is. But I'll tell you what troubles me most. It is far too convenient that this *alternate* mission just happens to come up not only right when the field team is being assembled, but when they are also nearby."

"I had the same thought," the Administrator said. "We might not be able to dig up Tuesday's connection soon enough to avoid an emergency meeting, but what I could do is recommend to the Committee that we don't make the change, for any number of practical reasons. At this point, I think they'll follow whatever I suggest."

Monday was silent for a moment. "They would, but I don't want you to do that. If this legitimately needs our attention, I want you to recommend it, and I want the Committee to vote for the switch. This is an opportunity for you and me, not a complication. If there *is* someone working against us through Tuesday, this could provide us with the means of finding out who they are."

"Whether he's aware of being used or not, if Tuesday has a tie to this, he will need to be replaced."

"Yes, he will."

Two empty Committee seats in a matter of weeks. The Administrator did not like that at all. "Should we pass on a warning to the other members to be more vigilant?"

"No. If they're not vigilant enough at this point, they don't deserve to be part of our work. Now, if there's nothing else, I have other—"

"Just one more thing, sir. Given the nature of the new mission, it would probably be a good idea to bring in the hunter."

"I concur. Bring him in."

Twenty-three minutes after the Administrator confirmed the details of Tuesday's proposal, the Committee convened via video conference.

The vote to switch missions was 6-0 in favor.

FIFTEEN

Elsewhere

WARREN WAS IN Avanti's office again.

"They've taken the bait," he said.

"As I knew they would." Avanti clasped his hands and set them on the desk. "And the babysitters? I'm assuming everything is under control."

"They've reached the encampment and have transferred the cargo to the shelter."

"Good. You've made it clear how they should proceed?"

"Yes, sir. McGowan has his orders on when to escalate."

"And the child?"

"I personally made it clear that she's not to be handed over under any circumstances. Once everything has run its course, she will be brought to us."

Avanti nodded and said, "Please tell Ms. Richmond I'll have my lunch on the patio."

Sixteen

ANOTHER TRAY SLID into Ananke's cell several hours after her first meal had been delivered.

Once more, the food was familiar. A raw kale salad with the blackened tofu she always requested at the vegan restaurant a few miles from her home in Boulder. If her captors were going to continue torturing her with food she loved, that was fine by her.

After she finished eating, she spent a half hour stretching, her body still sore and stiff, and then lay down on the bed. Somewhere in the middle of thinking about a job she'd done the previous fall, she dozed off for about twenty minutes, the normal length of one of her catnaps.

She yawned, sat up, and froze.

The door to her room was wide open.

She peered through the doorway. The subdued lighting on the other side kept her from being able to determine how big the room was. She could see only that the space right outside her room was empty.

Slowly, she approached the door, increasing her view of the room outside, but it remained unoccupied.

This is just plain weird.

Though logically she knew no one would be waiting to jump her since she was already a prisoner, she tensed as she stepped across the threshold. Of course, nothing happened. She was the only person in what turned out to be a wide, circular room.

Eleven other doors identical to hers were spread around the space in groups of three. Hers was the only one open. Between each group was an open entrance to what appeared to be a hallway. Three of them were dark, but the fourth was not only brightly lit, it also had a line of undulating LED lights embedded in the floor, rippling inward.

She stepped over to the closed door just left of hers. A chest-high, heavy metal bar lay across it, secured in place by an electronic lock.

She knocked. "Anyone in there?"

Not a peep from inside.

Maybe she was the only prisoner. For a second she considered checking the other doors, but *screw that*, she thought. She wouldn't learn anything from someone who'd also been locked up. What she needed was a jailer.

She checked the dark hallway entrance closest to her, and found it went only ten feet before being walled off by a temporary-looking metal wall.

She skipped the other two dark entrances, entered the lit hallway, half expecting a wall to open up into a Rube Goldberg killing machine that she'd have thirty seconds to defeat to keep from dying. Thankfully, the walls remained walls, and the only killing was going on in her head as she imagined what she was going to do to those who'd taken her prisoner.

She followed the moving LEDs down the hall. She passed several exits along the way, but all were blocked off by the same kind of metal wall she'd seen in the dark hallway. About fifty feet in, the hall took an elbow turn to the left, went on for another thirty feet or so before it and the rippling lights stopped at a set of double doors.

Feeling like a fish on a hook, she contemplated going back to her cell, but there were no answers there, so with extreme reluctance, she pulled one of the doors open and looked inside.

If she had created a list of the kind of spaces she expected to find, a conference room would not have even made the cut. But that's exactly what was on the other side of the doorway. Dominating the center of the space was a large rectangular table surrounded by five chairs—one directly in front of her, and two on each side. Like in her cell, there were no windows or additional exits.

She stepped onto the threshold and held the door wide

while she looked around, but she was the only one there. As she moved the rest of the way in, she reached around for the handle on the back of the door to keep it open, but there was no handle. The door slammed shut before she could grab it. Annoyed, she searched along the edges for enough surface to pull on, but everything fit together too well.

She looked back into the room.

"Crap."

DYLAN SHOT THROUGH the open cell doorway the moment he realized he was no longer locked in, and paused in the circular room just long enough for a quick look around. The second he spotted the lit corridor, he ran to it.

He didn't care if he was being led somewhere or not. In fact, he didn't even give it a thought. The only thing important to him was finding a way out.

When he reached the double doors at the end, he yanked them open and rushed in. Unfortunately, he had not anticipated finding furniture in the middle of his path. While he avoided the chair at the end of the table, he could not avoid the table itself, and slammed belly first into the edge.

Clutching his gut, he stumbled backward, groaning, and was completely unprepared when someone flew into him and knocked him to the ground.

He yelled out as he hit the floor. Hands on his shoulders rolled him onto his back, and before he could react, a woman who looked like a tall Thandie Newton straddled his aching stomach, pressed her hands against his shoulders, and tucked her legs back so her feet hooked around his thighs.

Lowering her face until it was only a few inches from his, she growled, "How do I get out of here?"

"I'm having a hard time…breathing. Can you let up a little?"

His request garnered him the exact opposite of what he wanted. "Answer the question."

"How…the hell…would…I…know?"

Her eyes narrowed. "Why are you holding me here?"

"You think I—"

91

"If you don't tell me what I want to know, I will kill you. Do you understand?"

"Yeah...but...but..."

"Answer me!"

"I   can't...I'm   not...holding   you...*I'm* the...one...who's...being held."

Uncertainty rippled through her eyes. She eased up on his torso enough for him to catch his breath. "Held where?"

"In a damn cell for I don't know how long," he said, his voice strained by the fact she was still on top of him. "I wake up and the door's open. So I decided to try to find a way out, and   then   you   body-slam   me   like   we're   starring   in WrestleMania. I'm not the one who needs to answer questions. You are."

"Maybe you're saying that just to trick me."

"Oh, for chrissake. Think what you want. But can you do it someplace that's not on top of me?"

ROSARIO SEARCHED EVERY inch of the round room before she ventured into the lit hallway.

Her most interesting finds were the two other open doors that led into cells identical to hers. From the crumpled bedding, it was clear both had been recently occupied.

She entered the hallway and inched along, alert for any sounds. Each time she came to one of the doorways covered by metal drop-down walls, she placed her ear against it. Not once did she hear anything on the other side.

When she did the same upon reaching the double doors, she heard a rhythmic squeak.

She eased the door toward her until the gap was wide enough to step through. Before she could—

"Don't let it shut!" The shout came from a tall woman standing beside a long table in the center of the room. Sitting on the opposite side was a man twirling in a chair that squeaked every few seconds.

When the woman started moving toward her, Rosario pulled back into the hallway and started to shut the door.

"No!" the woman yelled, halting. "Please, don't lock us in

here."

Rosario stopped, but stayed ready to shove the door closed if anyone made a wrong move. "Who are you?"

"If you're hoping to get a name out of her, good luck to you," the man said, his accent Irish. "She's not much for sharing. I'm Dylan. Dylan Brody."

"Did you just come out of one of the cells?" the woman asked.

Rosario kept her expression blank and said nothing.

"I was the first one out," the woman said. "About thirty minutes ago. This idiot stumbled in here fifteen minutes ago."

"Literally," the man tossed in.

"And now you." The woman motioned toward the table. "Five chairs. If the pattern holds, someone else will show up in another fifteen minutes, and someone else another fifteen after that."

"Why?" Rosario asked.

The man grunted a laugh. "Ain't that the question of the afternoon? Or evening. Hell, or morning. Do either of you know what time it is?"

Rosario looked back and forth between Dylan and the woman. "So it's just the two of you? You haven't seen anyone else?"

"Just you," the woman said.

Rosario eyed them for a moment, and then glanced at the inside of the door. No handle.

"Either of you have something we can jam this open with?" she asked.

Her question seemed to relax the woman.

"Use one of your shoes," Dylan said.

"I'd rather use one of yours," Rosario countered.

"Ha! I don't think so. I'll hold on to both of mine if you don't—"

"Give her a shoe," the woman said.

"Why me?"

"Did your mother not teach you any manners?"

Dylan groaned, pulled off one of his shoes, and tossed it toward the open door. "There you go. Everyone happy?"

Rosario opened the door all the way and jammed the toe of the shoe under it until the door wouldn't budge.

"Hey now," Dylan said, rising from his chair. "I still gotta wear that."

Rosario cautiously walked into the room, stopping several feet from the other woman. Petite to begin with, Rosario felt like a hobbit next to her. There had to be at least a twenty-centimeter difference between them and who knew how many kilos.

"I didn't get your name," Rosario said.

"And I didn't get yours."

They looked at each other, eyes locked, neither willing to go first.

"Oh, for the love of God," Dylan said. "You're worse than the boys back at school."

As if they'd been practicing it for hours, Rosario and the woman simultaneously said, "Shut up, Dylan."

The corner of the woman's mouth ticked up. "Ananke," she said, holding out a hand.

After a pause, Rosario took it. "Rosario."

LIESEL SAW THE open door as soon as she woke and knew it had not been left open by accident. Therefore, walking through it would be doing her captor's bidding.

She had no idea why she had been brought here or what her captors' intentions might be. But she did know she wasn't going to do anything to make their lives easy, so she sat cross-legged on the bed and proceeded to meditate.

At some point, the whistle blared from the speaker in the ceiling again, and then sounded off a third time a few minutes after that, but she was so deep in her nothingness that the intrusions were barely noted.

The footsteps, however? Those she did hear.

A RESONATING WHISTLE like the one that had initially woken Ananke screamed through the propped-open doorway into the conference room.

"Sounds like another guest just got up," Dylan said.

Ananke frowned. "A whistle didn't wake me this time."

"Me, neither," Rosario said.

"Come to think of it, I also didn't hear one," Dylan said.

Ananke walked over to the doorway and peered down the hall. A moment later, Rosario and Dylan joined her.

"Taking their time, aren't they?" Dylan said.

Rosario turned and studied him for a second. "You like to talk."

Though it obviously wasn't a compliment, Dylan beamed. "Well, I am Irish."

The whistle went off again.

Ananke exchanged a look with Rosario. "Perhaps someone should check it out." She turned to Dylan.

"Me?" he asked.

"I was thinking more that you could stay here in case someone else shows up."

"Alone? I don't think so. I think it's better if we all stick together for now, don't you?"

"He has a point," Rosario said.

They headed down the hall, Ananke first and then Rosario and finally, a few steps behind, Dylan.

"Not sure this is such a good idea," Dylan whispered.

Ananke turned to tell him to be quiet, but saw that a glare from Rosario had already taken care of the problem.

They paused at the entrance to the round room. Four doors were open now. Ananke pointed at her cell, and then at herself. Rosario indicated which was hers, and Dylan nodded toward his.

That left only the open door at their two o'clock unaccounted for.

Ananke mimed what she thought they should do. Rosario considered it, and then nodded. Ananke looked at Dylan, who gave her a sure-why-not-you're-not-going-to-listen-to-me-anyway shrug.

Instead of heading straight toward the open door, they went left to a spot directly across from it. Ananke's eyebrow rose when she spotted the woman sitting on the bed inside, legs crossed. One of her hands relaxed on a knee; the other appeared to be strapped across her chest. Rosario and Dylan looked as perplexed as Ananke felt.

There didn't appear to be any danger, so they approached the doorway.

The woman looked half Asian and half Caucasian. Ananke guessed she was a few inches shorter than herself, but it was hard to tell with the woman sitting as she was. Ananke could see the woman's arm was indeed restrained. No cast, though, which made her wonder if something had happened to the woman's shoulder and not the arm itself. Dislocated, perhaps?

Surprisingly, the woman still hadn't opened her eyes.

"I think the idea is that you're supposed to come out of there," Dylan said loudly into the room.

Ananke shot him an annoyed look.

"What? Someone had to say something sometime."

The sitting woman made no indication she'd heard him.

"Maybe she's sleeping?" Dylan whispered.

"You really do not know how to shut up, do you?" Rosario said.

"She's one of us. Why should I be quiet?"

The sitting woman suddenly breathed deeply and moved her free hand into her lap. Eyes still closed, she said in German-accented English, "What do you mean, one of us?"

With an I-told-you-so smile, Dylan said, "We're cell buddies."

The woman parted her eyelids.

"I'm Dylan," he said, stepping into the doorway. "And this is Rosario, and the tall one's Ananke. Who might you be?"

The woman untangled her legs and walked over to the toilet. As she started to unbutton her pants, she glanced back at them. "If you do not mind."

"Oh, right. Sure."

They moved away from the door so the woman would have some privacy.

The moment the toilet flushed, a male voice boomed from ceiling speakers scattered throughout the circular room. "Please make your way back to the conference room. We will begin in a few minutes."

Dylan looked up at the ceiling and yelled, "Begin what?"

There was no response.

SEVENTEEN

ANANKE SAT DOWN in the chair at the end of the conference table, while Rosario took one of those on the right and Dylan one on the left.

A few moments later the woman from the fourth cell warily entered the room.

"Glad you decided to join us," Dylan said. He tapped the seat next to him. "You can sit by me. I'm the friendly one."

She considered him for no more than a second, and then took the chair next to Rosario.

"Is it because I haven't showered?" He smelled under his arm. "Eww. Definitely. Good call on your part."

The lights dimmed, and the wall directly opposite Ananke split down the middle and slid out of sight, revealing a floor-to-ceiling, wall-to-wall screen. On it was the image of a man behind a desk, facing them. Short brown hair, graying on the sides.

Ananke put him somewhere between late forties and early fifties. And his stylish dark gray suit, black shirt, and black tie marked him as a man who likely didn't buy clothes off a rack. His hands sat on the desk, palms down, a stack of files between them.

"Good morning," he said.

"Who the hell are you?" Rosario asked. "And why are you holding us prisoner?"

"You are not prisoners. You are under our protection."

Dylan guffawed. "Protection? That's why you locked us away in those tiny closets?"

"The recovery rooms are no larger than they need to be. One does not need a penthouse suite when one is unconscious."

"How long were we out?" Ananke asked.

"Different for each of you. Mr. Brody has been out for four days."

"Four?" Dylan said. "Are you kidding me?"

"I am not."

"Four days gone," Dylan scoffed. "That explains my headache, then."

"No, your reaction to the medication explains your headache. We would have used something else but there was nothing in your records to indicate your particular intolerance."

"Oh, you want to talk about intolerance, do you? I can—"

"How long was I out?" Rosario asked.

"Just a little less than Mr. Brody. Fraulein Kessler has been with us for twenty-two hours."

"And me?" Ananke said.

"Seven days."

She'd been out for a whole week? That meant it had been eleven days since she fled Manila. "What the hell are we doing here?"

"You are here because each of your lives was in danger."

"In danger?" Dylan said. "What are you talking about? My life wasn't in danger."

"That van you were driving. Do you know what you were transporting?"

Dylan grinned. "Of course I do. Flowers."

"*Under* the flowers. Beneath the fake floor. And in the van's walls."

"Look, it's not my job to know what the cargo is."

"You're just the courier," the man said.

"Damn right."

The man pulled a file from his stack and opened it. "Your van was lined with C-4. Nearly four hundred pounds of it."

"I'm sure it's not the first time," Dylan said with an it's-no-big-deal shrug, but he couldn't keep the concern from creasing his brow.

"What would someone do with four hundred pounds of stolen plastic explosive?" the man asked. "You don't need to answer. I'll tell you. You were to deliver the van to an expediter who had been hired to obtain it for an organization I believe you are familiar with. ISIL, Daesh, whatever you want to call them."

"No, no. That can't be true. I would never involve myself with them."

"How would you know? You were just the courier. The explosives were supposed to be on their way to Berlin an hour after you delivered them. You, of course, would never have had the chance to know this because you'd have been dead not long after you arrived. They wouldn't have chanced you connecting them to the delivery." The man closed the file and put his hand on it. "The proof is right here. You will be given a copy, along with audio recordings and video footage that should alleviate any doubts."

Looking uncomfortable, Dylan said, "Well, even if you're right, they didn't receive the cargo."

"Also true. And they are none too happy about that. You are, as they say, on the run. But don't worry. We do have several solutions for you to choose from that should get you out of trouble." His line of sight switched to the other side of the table. "Señorita Blanca, your situation is somewhat similar to Mr. Brody's. The client you were working for before you joined us—who was it?"

"Does anyone actually fall for that trick?" she asked.

He smiled. "No. But it's all right. We already know." He picked out a different file, opened it, and scanned the top sheet. "The CIA, in the guise of their Mexico City station chief, Stephen Robinson."

Ananke glanced at Rosario. A slight tensing of her jaw confirmed the man was right.

"Politically the United States is at a very critical point right now. The population is largely polarized. A spark or two in the wrong place and there will be a wildfire that no one will be able to put out until the country has burned to the ground. Unbeknownst to his employer, Mr. Robinson is a believer in that fire. He thinks that everything needs to be destroyed so that something better can take its place. He also believes he's the one who will ignite that spark. The device you stole would have allowed him to move significantly closer to that goal."

"What do I care what happens in the States? They don't care what happens in my country."

"Nicely said, but I know you are not that naïve. The day after you would have delivered the device, you would have been killed in your own home, taken into the countryside, and buried in a hole no one would ever find."

"And how would you know that?" Rosario asked.

"Because the contract to end your life was arranged through associates of the people I represent. Instead, we made you disappear before you could complete the delivery."

"And now you're going to tell me that my client thinks I still have the dongles and is hunting me down to get them back."

"Technically, you *do* still have them. They're waiting with your other things. And, yes, Mr. Robinson is trying to find you. Rest assured, he will be taken care of soon enough, and the inquiries into your whereabouts will fade away. The larger problem is that there are others in his organization who know about the devices and will be looking for them and for you. We have a plan for that also." He closed the file and selected a third. "Fraulein Kessler, first let me say I'm sorry for your loss. Your employer's death is a tragedy for all those who knew him. But most especially for you."

The woman looked at the screen impassively.

"May I ask how your shoulder is feeling?" the man asked.

The woman said nothing.

The man acknowledged her silence with a sympathetic smile. "As you know, the police possess evidence implicating you in Mr. Wolf's death. We know your only involvement was that you were there when it happened. My regret is we did not anticipate this event and prevent that woman from getting anywhere near him."

"It was my job to anticipate," the woman said. "Not yours."

"That's not entirely true. You see, Mr. Wolf was a member of the group I represent. An instrumental member, as a matter of fact. You are here because of his faith in you."

The woman's eyes glistened, but she made no response.

"When we realized you had no chance of getting out of your situation without going to trial, we chose to intervene. Naturally, the police have not responded well. Notifications have been sent across the country and back to Germany asking that you be detained. We are dealing with that, plus working at clearing you of any involvement in Mr. Wolf's murder. It will take time, but it will get done. Until then, the safest place for you is with us."

He traded her file for the last in the stack. "Miss Ananke."

"It's just Ananke."

A bow of his head. "Ananke, then. In your case, the murder was your fault."

"I'm going to have to take exception to that."

"Understandable. We know your intention was not to kill, but you *did* deliver the fatal dose."

"I'm pretty sure you have the details in that little folder of yours, so I don't see the point of going over everything. Besides, you're not my client."

"Not at this point, no. The organization that did hire you is currently conducting a worldwide manhunt for you. You are, after all, the killer of the people's candidate."

Dylan spun in his seat, staring wide-eyed at Ananke.

"Holy crap. That guy in the Philippines? That was you?"

Rosario and the Kessler woman were both now looking at her, too, the former curiously, almost impressed, but the latter with more than a hint of disgust.

Ananke thought about telling them how it had all gone down, but really, why should she care what any of them thought?

To the man on the screen she said, "My client would have canceled the manhunt as soon as I walked off that airplane with my asshole backstabber of an op leader if you all hadn't stopped me."

"Ah, yes. Mr. Perkins. Do you think he was working on his own? That he alone decided to switch the drug you delivered to your target? Who do you think was pulling *his* strings?"

"Of course he was working for someone else. Which is even more reason for me to turn him over to my client."

"I didn't say anything about his working for a second employer."

She stared at him, and then narrowed her eyes. "Are you trying to tell me my client wanted me to kill Alonzo all along? He was as angry about what happened as I was when I talked to him."

"And everyone in your business speaks the truth all the time?"

That stopped her for a second, but then she shook her head. "I kill people. It's what I do. If they'd wanted me to kill Alonzo, they would have just said so."

"If they had, you would have planned the mission differently, made sure you were nowhere near your victim when he went down. Then your client would have been left without a scapegoat. This way they have pictures of the killer on the platform with Alonzo. My understanding is that you were to be caught before you could get out of the building. That you weren't is admirable."

"Gee, thanks. But if you want me to believe that the people who hired me were behind it, you're out of luck. I've worked with them for years. We have an excellent relationship."

"Even the best soldiers need to be sacrificed at times. But I understand your reluctance, which is why the evidence we've gathered will be made available to you, too."

The room fell quiet, Ananke and her fellow prisoners contemplating what the man on the screen had told them.

It was Ananke who finally broke the silence. "Let me get this straight. You 'saved' us, and brought us here to 'protect' us. Do I have that right?"

"In part, yes."

"So there is something more."

"Of course there's more."

"And this *more* has something to do with why we were kept unconscious until we were all here?"

"I promise, you will be told everything, but before we dive in, I think it would be best for each of you to familiarize yourself with your new quarters, and take some time to examine the evidence waiting for you there."

A distant *thump* echoed from somewhere behind Ananke. This was followed almost immediately by the low whine of an electric motor.

The man stacked his folders into a single pile again. "Follow the hall. You can't miss it. We'll meet again soon."

"Wait! You still haven't told us who the hell you are," Ananke said.

"An oversight. You can call me Administrator."

"Are you serious?" Dylan asked, snickering.

"I am," the man said.

"Well, Mr. Administrator, I have a question for you. Why are there five chairs here when there are only four of us?"

"Simple. The fifth member of your team has not joined you yet."

He started to reach offscreen for what Ananke assumed was a disconnect button.

"Hold on!" she yelled. "What do you mean by team?"

The man paused. "I thought that was obvious. We'd like you to do a job for us."

EIGHTEEN

Crestridge Federal Prison, Georgia

"THIS ONE GUY was a real problem," Ricky said.

His audience was bigger than usual. Five guys today. His two regulars—Tommy and Prance—plus three newbies who'd arrived the day before and hadn't had the chance to grow tired of his tales.

"I mean, I'd already found all his buddies, but this guy? He was proving elusive." Ricky paused when he saw the confused looks on two of the new guys' faces. "Elusive, it means, um, hard to find." That seemed to clear things up.

"I'd been tracking him for days, way longer than I expected, but finally I corner him at this campsite in upstate Michigan. You know what I'm talking about. A bunch of spots for people to park their trailers and feel like they're roughing it for the night? This was off-season, though, early November and already really cold, so the place had closed until spring. I knew he was there, though, and I knew he hadn't left because there was nowhere else he could go. But damn if I couldn't find that son of a bitch. I looked through the check-in cabin at the front of the camp. I looked *under* the cabin. I looked through the surrounding woods. You know where I finally found him?"

Tommy and Prance smiled but kept their mouths shut.

After a few moments, the youngest of the newbies, a kid not much more than eighteen, said, "Where?"

"Well, you remember this was a campground, right?"

Nods.

"Some people actually used tents instead of campers. If you were staying in one of them, and needed to take a piss in the middle of the night, you needed somewhere to go, right? So there was this row of outhouses off to the side."

"What's an outhouse?" another of the new guys asked.

"Where are you from?"

"New York."

"City?"

"You know it," he said with pride.

"Ever leave the city before? I mean, you know, other than coming here?"

"Why would I do that?"

Ricky grinned. "That explains it. An outhouse is a toilet."

"You mean a restroom."

"No. A toilet. That's all. The outhouses at this place were small wooden huts, with a wooden bench inside that had a hole cut in the top, and below the hole was a pit where the, you know, waste would go."

The new guy's face cringed. "You're making that up."

"If only I was. Now these particular pits had been emptied at the end of summer, but the truth is, you can never completely get everything out. My guy was at the bottom of the one in the center, and covered in crap. *Literally*. You know what literally means, right?"

"Oh, man," the kid said. "That's disgusting."

"You haven't heard it all yet," Ricky said. "Some must have gotten in his nose because as I was walking by, he started sneezing, must have gone on for a whole minute before he finally stopped and saw me smiling down at him. Let me tell you, getting him out was no fun. Thank God the pipes hadn't frozen and there was still running water in the community showers. Not hot, though. Made him strip down and wash off for twenty minutes, and then put him into the trunk of my car, sans clothes—that means without—and hauled him away. Job done." He flashed a smile. "Like I told you, Ricky Orbits always gets his man."

A born showman, Ricky had stretched his story out so that he finished just as the buzzer sounded, signaling the end of yard time.

With an "after you, boys," he followed the others into line

and began the long shuffle back to his cell.

As they neared the building entrance, a guard standing off to the side said, "Ricky Orbits," and motioned for Ricky to join him.

Tommy and Prance gave Ricky a quizzical look.

"Beats me," Ricky said. "You guys didn't nominate me for inmate of the month again, did you?"

They shared a laugh, and then he broke from the line and leisurely walked over to where the guard was waiting for him.

"Afternoon, Officer Cruz," he said. "What is it Ricky can do for you today?"

"That way." Cruz pointed down a path that ran along the edge of the yard.

Ricky went first, Cruz a step behind him.

They walked all the way to the administration building before Cruz again said, "That way," and pointed at a door Ricky had never used before.

Inside, they went down a short hallway that ended at a security door.

"Stand to the side," Cruz said.

Ricky stepped to his left. "What's this all about?"

"No idea." The guard looked at a camera above the door and said, "Officer Robert Cruz, transporting prisoner Orbits, Richard." He recited Ricky's prisoner number.

In the silence that followed, Ricky said, "Can you at least tell me who you're taking me to?"

"No idea means no idea."

"Officer Cruz, I'm disappointed in your lack of customer service."

The door buzzed. Cruz pushed it open and waved for Ricky to go through.

Aha, Ricky thought as he walked into the new space. The private visitation rooms. He'd heard about them, but no one had visited him after his incarceration so he'd had no reason to ever come here before.

The hall was wide enough for four people to walk abreast. Five doors were on each side, with windowed upper halves that would allow guards to keep an eye on what was going on inside. No watchers at the moment, though.

Cruz led him to the center door on the left. Unlike elsewhere, its window had been covered from the inside. The guard opened the door and stood to the side.

Ricky looked at him for a moment, then at the doorway, and then back at Cruz. "Seriously? Not even a hint?"

"Get in there."

"If I get one of those survey cards when this is all done, do not expect me to give you five stars." He stepped through the doorway.

The room was disappointingly bland. A table and a few chairs, that was it. There weren't even pictures on the walls. There were, however, two people present.

Sitting at the table was a woman in sharp business attire. Good-looking but in a serious way, like she'd forgotten how to have fun. Standing behind her was a man who was all height and muscle. No doubt he was a reminder for Ricky to behave.

"Mr. Orbits, thank you for coming," the woman said.

"Lucky for you I had a meeting canceled."

When he reached the empty chair across from her, she held out her hand. "You can call me Miss Marsh."

He cocked his head. "Miss March?"

"Marsh. As in swamp."

"I like my way better." He winked.

Apparently it was a joke she'd heard before, because her only reaction was to repeat her motion for him to sit.

"So, Miss Marsh," he said as he settled into the chair. "Do you visit random prisoners often?"

"Never."

"How lucky am I?" Another wink, and another nonreaction.

"Shall we get to business?" she said.

"You're calling the shots, so whatever you want to do. I would appreciate it, though, if we can stretch this out for as long as possible. It's a nice break from the usual routine, know what I mean?"

"Breaking from your usual routine is exactly why I'm here."

BRETT BATTLES

"Now you really have my attention."

"You are in the first year of a ten-year sentence on federal weapons charges. Is that correct?"

"I believe that's what it says on my paperwork." What he'd actually been imprisoned for was getting in the way of someone else's operation. There'd been no trial, only an agreement that it would be better for him to do some time than to die young.

"Your home is in Chicago?"

"That's where they forward my mail from."

"And you are thirty-eight years of age?"

"What is age, really, but a mental state?"

She tapped an impatient finger on the table. "Answer the question, please."

"There are…certain documents that claim I'm…" He tried to voice thirty-eight, but his lips refused to form the words. "…that number you mentioned."

Apparently, that was good enough for her because she moved on. "Your back, please. Show it to me."

"My back."

"Yes. Specifically, lower back, right side."

"Oh. The scar."

"Yes. The scar."

He stood, turned around, and pulled up the flap of his shirt. The scar was half an inch above his hip bone and looked like a sideways checkmark. It had been a gift from a wiry little punk who'd tried to rob Ricky in Nairobi.

Ricky nearly jumped when he felt the woman touch his back. She began pulling at the scar as if it were a sticker. When she let go, she said, "Thank you."

"You don't want to see my tattoo?" he asked as he tucked his shirt back in.

"Which one? The leopard on your thigh, or the name under your hair above your left ear?"

Good thing he wasn't looking at her, because he couldn't quite keep the surprise off his face. He didn't think anyone but the tattoo artist knew about the name on his head.

"Either one," he said as he turned back around, his

109

composure restored.

"Tattoos can be faked."

"So can scars."

"Yes, but yours isn't."

"Anything else you want to see while I'm up? I can stand on my hands and walk ten feet without falling."

"Thank you, but that won't be necessary."

Ricky retook his seat. "So did I pass the test? Am I to be a card-carrying member of the Illuminati now? Or does my scar mean I'm next in line for the British crown?"

"You're a funny man," Miss Marsh said, not laughing.

"Well, that's not news."

Miss Marsh stared at him with either mild amusement or borderline disdain. "I have a piece of paper in my possession that I think will please you."

"Do you? I like being pleased." Wink number three. Nonresponse number three. "What do you got?"

"An order for your immediate release."

He didn't even attempt to hide his surprise. "Excuse me?"

"If you agree to our terms, you will leave with me this afternoon."

"I agree," he said quickly.

"You have no idea what you're agreeing to."

"I don't care. Anything's better than staying here for the next nine and a half years."

"Under the agreement, you will have some independence, but you will not be entirely free."

"Sounds great."

"You will be working for us, likely to the end of your current sentence."

"Employment, too? Who are you? My guardian angel?"

"If you are ever perceived as more of a problem than as an asset, you'll be put back in a cell."

"I'll be on my best behavior." He crossed his heart and held up three fingers in a scout salute.

"You don't even know what we'll be asking you to do."

"All right, I'll bite. What do you want me to do?"

"Hunt, Mr. Orbits."

Ricky Orbits, the self-proclaimed best hunter in the world, said, "Where do I sign?"

NINETEEN

Karas Evonus

ANANKE AND THE others left the conference room in silence, each still processing their first meeting with the Administrator. When they rounded the hallway corner, they found a metal wall blocking the way to their cells. On the left side, however, another of the barriers had been lifted.

As they turned down the new hallway, Dylan sniffed the air.

"What are you doing?" Rosario asked.

"Trying to see if I can smell the cheese. There's always some at the end of the maze, isn't there?"

No one laughed, not even him.

After a few more turns, they emerged into a large, rectangular room. A long cafeteria-style table with attached benches sat in the center, while at least half a dozen wide-screen TVs hung from ceiling mounts throughout the space. Ananke had a feeling it would be difficult to find a spot in the room where she wouldn't be able to see at least one of the monitors.

Like the round room, this one was surrounded by doors, two instead of three on each of the four walls. A metal placard was affixed to the wall next to each door. The one closest to Ananke read: LIESEL KESSLER.

"Looks like we each have an assigned spot." She looked at the German woman. "Liesel, right? This one's yours."

Ananke went in search of her own door, finding it on the wall directly across from Liesel's. Before entering, she checked for any signs the door could be locked via remote control, but the only lock she found was a deadbolt that could only be engaged from the inside.

Before entering, she removed her shoes and placed one against the jamb, just in case the door did automatically shut.

This was no small cell, but rather an expansive suite. The living-room area was big enough to fit a dozen people comfortably, and beyond this was an equally large bedroom complete with king-size bed. There was even a spa tub in the en suite bathroom.

What drew her attention most was the thin black binder lying on the main-room coffee table. Beside it were a remote control and a piece of paper that contained instructions on how to access video and audio files through the wall-mounted television.

She started first with the binder, reading every word of the seventeen pages inside. As the Administrator had promised, they detailed how Noah Perkins, Marcus Denton, and Denton's organization had worked together to frame Ananke for Fernando Alonzo's murder. But as damning as the evidence was, it could have easily been a set of well-constructed forgeries filled with dreamed-up facts.

She picked up the remote and reviewed everything on the list, many several times. Though video and audio could also be fabricated, in her professional opinion everything she saw or heard was one hundred percent real.

She had no choice but to admit the Administrator had been right. Even if she'd captured Perkins and dropped him on Denton's doorstep, her fate would have been served on a platter to the world as Alonzo's assassin.

Returning to the common room, she found Rosario and Dylan sitting at the central table across from each other, lost in their own thoughts.

"Marked for death?" Dylan asked Ananke.

She nodded. "You?"

"Had to check my chest to make sure there wasn't already an X painted on it."

Ananke looked at Rosario, who nodded in confirmation that she was also a member of the should-be-dead gang.

"Any sign of Liesel?" Ananke asked.

"Not a peep," Dylan said.

Ananke walked over to the German woman's room. Liesel had also left a shoe against the jamb. Ananke tapped on the door. When she didn't get a response, she pushed it open and looked inside.

Liesel was sitting on the couch, staring at a paused image on her TV screen. It appeared to be a police crime scene photo of a man splayed across a chair, a bullet hole in his forehead.

"May I come in?" Ananke asked.

Liesel didn't move.

Ananke gave it a couple of seconds, then stepped into the room and joined Liesel on the couch. Tears glistened at the edges of the woman's eyes.

"Your boss?" Ananke asked, glancing at the screen.

"He was my responsibility."

"I'm sure you did everything you could."

Liesel turned to her, her expression blank. "If I had done everything I could, he would be alive and I would be the one dead."

"Your shoulder wound…you took a bullet for him, didn't you?"

Liesel self-consciously touched a spot along her collar. "It went through me before it hit him. If it hadn't, maybe it would have missed him."

"And maybe it wouldn't have. You tried to save him."

"It doesn't matter. He's dead. I didn't do my job."

"Blaming yourself isn't going to solve anything. He wouldn't want you doing that, would he?"

Liesel shot Ananke an angry look before turning back to the television without a word.

Ananke tried to get her talking again, but it was apparent Liesel was done. Ananke returned to the others.

"Still can't believe those bastards were going to kill me," Dylan said after she sat down. "Couriers are supposed to be protected. That's how the system works. No one's supposed to mess with us."

"Couriers die all the time," Ananke said.

"I've been doing this for a long time, and *I'm* still alive."

"You wouldn't have been if these people hadn't stepped in and saved you."

He had no response to that.

"So what do you do?" Ananke asked Rosario.

"What I do is none of your business."

"If we want to get out of here, we'll have to work together. Which means what each of us does is all of our business."

"What?" Dylan asked. "We're going to break out?"

"If that's what we need to do."

With a glance at the ceiling, Rosario said, "You do realize this place has to be bugged."

"I don't care. They may have helped us out of some difficult situations, but that makes me feel thankful, not beholden. I want them to know that I'm not staying here any longer than necessary." She turned her face toward the ceiling, and in a loud voice said, "In case you didn't hear me, I'm not staying!"

A grin brushed the edge of Rosario's mouth. "I am an obtainer."

The Administrator's voice suddenly boomed from an overhead speaker. "Ananke, would you please join me in the conference room?"

"Alone?" she asked, not sure he would answer.

"If you don't mind."

She shared a look with the others and then rose. "Well, that answers the can-they-hear-us-or-not question." She stood. "If I don't come back, you can split the things."

"You do not want us to come with you?" Rosario whispered, her lips barely moving.

"I have a feeling if we all showed up, they might not let any of us in. Alone, there's the chance I can learn something that can help us."

"Is it *us* now?" Dylan asked.

Rosario was the one who answered. "For now."

WITHIN SECONDS OF Ananke taking her seat at the conference table, the Administrator appeared on the video wall.

"Thank you for joining me," he said.

"Did I have a choice?" she said.

"We are not your enemies. No one dragged you here, nor would they have."

"Eh, excuse me. But isn't that exactly what you did? I don't remember walking in through the door."

"Our intent has only been to help you."

"You're saying you're my friend, then, is that it? I hate to ruin your day, but I have an ironclad rule about not making friends with people who use me."

"We haven't used you."

"Not yet, but you did say something about doing a job for you."

"I did, but I didn't say we'd force you to do that, either. We would like to hire you."

Ananke laughed. "Let me guess. And our payment is you having saved our lives."

"Again, incorrect. Saving your lives is not something we did for payment. As for the job, you will each be paid twice your normal rate. In advance. Anyone who chooses not to participate is free to leave."

"Into a world where you've already informed those looking for us where we'll be."

He looked caught off guard and even a bit hurt. "That would be cruel. We would never do that under any circumstances. If any of you chose not to participate, I would urge that person to remain here until his or her particular situation has been dealt with. And before you even ask, staying would not be mandatory. Our commitment to clearing all of your names will continue no matter what any of you decide."

"Sounds way too good to be true."

"I'm sure it does. But that doesn't change the fact that what I've told you is exactly what's going to happen. But I appreciate you are all cautious by nature. It's what makes you good at what you do. My words are just talk. Our actions are what will prove to you that we have not been lying."

Ananke leaned forward. "Who are you people?"

"Who we are doesn't matter."

"No, it does. A lot."

"Why? It has no bearing on the job we hope you will agree to do for us. And I know for a fact you have personally taken on many projects for which you knew little to nothing about your clients."

"That may be true, but none of those clients took me hostage first."

"You reviewed the information we left in your room. We did *not* take you hostage. We saved your life."

Like he'd said, there was no way for her to know if he was telling the truth or not. The only thing that was clear to her was that trouble awaited her if she attempted to return to her normal life anytime soon.

"Perhaps you should tell me about this job."

"WE NEED TO talk," Ananke said, standing in Liesel's doorway. "Can you come out and join us?"

When Ananke had returned, she found everyone exactly where she had left them. Rosario and Dylan had wanted to know what happened, but they all needed to be together for this.

"What is there to talk about?" Liesel said without looking over.

"Our future."

"I have no future."

"I get it. It's been a rough week for you." Ananke waved her hand back toward the main room. "It's been a rough week for all of us. But we have some choices to make. And you need to be a part of that discussion whether you want to be or not. So get off your ass and let's go."

Without waiting for a response, Ananke turned and walked over to her own room. As the Administrator promised, a file containing the photographs and other information pertaining to the job was waiting for her on her coffee table.

When she headed back out, Liesel had joined the others, though she was standing behind the bench, not sitting on it.

Ananke climbed in next to Rosario, set the file on the table, and then as succinctly as possible, laid out the choices the Administrator had presented.

"I will stay here," Liesel said. She turned toward her room.

"Wait," Ananke said. "You haven't heard everything."

"I have heard enough."

"No. You haven't."

For a moment Ananke thought Liesel would walk off anyway, but then the woman swiveled back around.

"Let me see if I have this right," Dylan said. "This job Mr. Administrator is talking about, he's going to pay us for it. Double our going rate. *And* he's going to clear our names so we can go home again."

"That's what he said."

Rosario frowned. "Sounds too—"

"Good to be true? Exactly what I told him."

"So you don't believe him?"

"I don't have enough information to determine what I believe."

Rosario considered this for a moment. "I am not staying here a minute longer than I have to. I will tell him I want to leave. If he does not let me go, then we will know he is lying."

"Or he lets you leave and shoots you in the back on your way out and we don't know one way or the other," Dylan said. "And, you know, you'd be dead."

"Better dead than a prisoner."

"That seems an awfully permanent solution."

Before Rosario could respond, Ananke said, "You might want to hear the details of the job before you go making any decisions."

"I do not care what the job is," Rosario said. "I do not work with kidnappers."

"Never?" Dylan asked. "Are you sure? I know my clients can get their hands pretty dirty sometimes."

"Kidnappers who kidnap *me*. How's that?" she asked, glaring at him.

"Well, that *is* a fine point, I'll give you that. But me? I can't deny I'm curious. Double fee sounds pretty good right now."

Ananke opened the file and removed a picture of a passenger van. "Two days ago, a vehicle just like this one left

118

a lodge near Yosemite National Park in California, carrying six students and three chaperones returning from an educational retreat. They never arrived home." She set another printout on the table. "This is a copy of a text sent to the families waiting at the pickup point for their kids."

The message read:

NO PRESS. NO POLICE.
NO FEDS. NOTHING.
SILENCE OR DEATH.
WE WILL CONTACT AGAIN.

"The messages were accompanied by these." She set six photographs next to the text message. In each was a different child, bound and gagged but easily recognizable. Four were female and two were male. "The only ones who know about this are the students' families and a few select others that now includes us."

"Jesus," Dylan said. "And the ransom?"

"It hasn't come yet."

"How much do six kids go for these days?"

"These three"—Ananke touched the appropriate pictures—"come from extremely wealthy families. We're talking Silicon Valley kind of money."

"What about the other three students?" Rosario asked.

"The retreat was part of a program to expose kids from different socioeconomic groups to one another," Ananke replied. "The other three are from working-class families."

Rosario looked troubled. "If the kidnappers need to send a message, these will be the kids sacrificed."

"Very likely."

"What is known about the kidnappers?" Liesel asked.

"Nothing. Our job would be to ID them, locate them, and bring the kids home alive." Ananke paused. "The question we each need to answer is whether to take the job or choose one of the other options."

The room fell silent.

"What's *your* answer?" Rosario finally asked.

Ananke had been contemplating that since she left the conference room.

The Administrator had presented her with enough information for her to believe the story about the missing kids was true, but there was more to this whole saving-Ananke-and-the-others-and-hiring-them thing than he was sharing.

Still, the kids were in real danger.

Her life in the last several years had been full of death. Since she couldn't return to it at the moment, it might be nice to do a little saving.

"I'm in," she said.

Rosario appeared surprised by the answer, and fell back into a dark silence.

"Hell, it beats hiding out for God knows how long staring at the walls," Dylan said. "I'm in, too."

"These children," Liesel said. "You are convinced they are in trouble?"

"As much as I can be. The thing is, if we find out we've been lied to, we can always walk away."

Liesel nodded to herself. "Yes, we can. Then I will help, too."

All eyes turned to Rosario. "All right," she said after a moment.

Ananke walked over to the wall near the room's main entrance and pressed the button she found there. "Assuming you weren't lying and haven't been listening in, we'll take the job."

"That's excellent news. Thank you all."

From the hallway they could hear the metal screech of another door opening.

"There is no time to waste."

TWENTY

UNDULATING FLOOR LIGHTS guided them into a locker room containing five stalls separated by privacy barriers. Four of the stalls were stocked with clothes hanging from pegs, footwear on shelves, and prepacked duffel bags on the floor. The fifth stall was empty.

The sizes and styles of the outfits made it obvious whose stall was whose.

In Ananke's were a pair of jeans, a white buttoned blouse, and a dark blue duster that went down to the top of her thighs. The duster had been modified with several handy interior pockets. She'd also been provided with a pair of stylish, reddish brown boots that slipped perfectly under the cuffs of her jeans.

After she was dressed, she unzipped her duffel. Inside she found two additional changes of clothes, a phone, a pair of compact yet powerful binoculars, comm gear, lock picks, a Heckler & Koch P30 9mm pistol with suppressor, extra ammo, and two thousand dollars in cash. The inclusion of the weapons bolstered the idea that the Administrator was telling the truth.

As she stepped out from her locker area, Dylan said, "You got a gun?" He was peeking around the barrier into the next stall where Liesel was holding her own P30. He turned back to his bag and began rifling through it. "Where's mine?"

"Tell me, Dylan, how often have you carried a pistol on a job?" Ananke asked.

"Well, I, uh, I-I…okay, never, but—"

"Looks like your job is driving," she said, nodding at the set of keys he tossed on the ground with the other stuff from his bag. "So same as it was on all those other jobs you didn't have a gun for."

He scowled at the keys, and then started shoving things back into his bag. "Fine. If I'm driving, then I decide when we stop and when we don't."

"Oh, look," Rosario said. "I have a gun, too."

WHEN THEY WERE ready, the Administrator's voice came over the speaker again.

"The phones you've been given have been preprogrammed with each other's numbers. There is also one to my office. I would prefer if Ananke serves as the main contact between us. As you have no doubt already assumed, she will act as team leader. Of course, if there is an emergency, you needn't go through her to get to me. Lastly, the fifth member of your team will be joining you at your destination."

"Fifth member?" Ananke said.

"A hunter."

Given the task they had before them, she thought adding a hunter wasn't a bad idea.

"Good luck," the Administrator said. "Find them, please. Get them home."

Lights led the team to a staircase that took them up to a metal door. Stepping outside, they discovered they weren't in a building but on a container ship. The vessel was moored against a dock of what appeared to be a busy port. Ananke knew the ship had to have been there since before they'd first woken or they would have felt the movements of the sea.

She studied their surroundings in hopes of getting a better idea of where they were. To their left and right was more port. Shoreside, beyond the port facilities, she could see hills dotted with homes. Given that the descending sun was behind them, hidden by the ship, the hills were to the east.

She looked up at the ship's superstructure behind them, and spotted walkways around several of the upper levels, but no way to reach them. She wondered if the Administrator was up there somewhere. Someone who worked for him definitely had to be on the ship. Either that or they'd been fed by ghosts.

"There's a gangway over here," Dylan called from the other end of the walkway.

They joined him and headed down to the pier.

"Holy crap, I hope that's our ride," he said, staring a dark blue Mustang parked next to a pier-side building with several other vehicles. He pulled out the keys and pressed the unlock button on the fob, but the responding flashing lights came from a passenger van two vehicles away. "Son of a mother...are you kidding me?"

Stepping onto the pier, Ananke looked back at the ship and noted the name *Karas Evonus* painted on the bow.

"California plates," Dylan said as they neared the van.

The cars parked around it also had California license plates. This wasn't particularly surprising, given that the kids had been kidnapped within the state.

As they climbed into the van, Dylan tossed an envelope that had been on the driver's seat to Ananke. "This must be for you, boss."

Inside she found false IDs for each of them and handed them out. There were also four printouts for room reservations at Hardwick Inn, located in Groveland, California, under their new assumed names. Groveland, Ananke knew from the map that had been in her file, was near Yosemite.

As they left the port, they learned the *Karas Evonus* was docked at the Port of Oakland, across the bay from San Francisco, leaving them a three-hour drive to the mountains where the kids were last seen.

Once Dylan got them onto the interstate headed east, Ananke began sifting through the contents of the file to commit the details to memory.

"I would like to look at those, too," Rosario said.

"And me, also," Liesel chimed in.

While the women studied, Dylan kept up a continuous monologue of jokes and stories that none of them paid attention to. Ananke had become so used to tuning him out that she was caught off guard when he tapped her on the shoulder and said, "What do you think?"

"About what?"

"About taking a toilet break, maybe getting something to eat. Am I just talking to myself here?"

"You don't want me to answer that."

They stopped at a gas station megaplex that boasted two fast-food places, a mini-market, and showers that could be rented by the minute. While the others used the facilities, Ananke went into the mini-market and purchased a burner phone and several SIM cards.

Outside, she found a deserted area near the Dumpsters and activated the cell.

"*Moshi-moshi*," Shinji said. "Nakamura Restaurant. Can you hold for a—"

"It's me," she said.

Not a sound for two whole seconds, then, "Would…you like to hear our s-s-specials?"

This was the first part of the code to be used in situations when Shinji felt it necessary to determine whether Ananke was speaking freely or in trouble. If the latter, there were several different responses she could make, each signaling him to do something different. For instance, if she said, "Yes, please," he would determine her location and arrange for her to be extracted ASAP. If the former, the response was more direct.

"Cut the crap," she said.

"Oh, thank God! Where the hell have you been? Are you all right? What happened? I thought you were either dead or Perkins got you."

"I'm fine and he didn't. I need to know what's going on out there."

"'I'm fine and he didn't'? That's all I get?"

"We can catch up later. Update now, please."

"Okay, okay. Well, um, word on the 'net is that you're supposed to be detained. But I guess that's not surprising, huh?"

"No, it's not. Have I received any messages?"

"Only one. Quinn. He said if you needed anything, let him know."

Given her current situation, most people would have distanced themselves from her. In fact, most had. Not Jonathan Quinn. She'd helped him out the previous summer, and he was not one to forget those he owed no matter what trouble they

BRETT BATTLES

might be in. His message was even more meaningful because the last she'd heard, he was dealing with a personal tragedy of some sort.

"Tell him I appreciate the offer and that I'm okay."

"Are you okay?"

"At the moment. Look, I need you to find out everything about a cargo ship called the *Karas Evonus*." She spelled it out for him.

"Okay. Do I need to know context?"

"Not right now. I'm also going to text you some names. Be very discreet."

"SOP." Standard operating procedure.

"Until I tell you otherwise, only text me back if I text you first, and do not call this number until I give you the go-ahead."

"Got it."

"Good." She hung up.

"HERE WE GO, Miss Handler." The woman behind the desk handed Ananke a key. "You are in room fifteen." She passed another to Rosario. "And Miss Rivera, yours is room fourteen. Now, let's see. Miss Cooper, for you, room seven." She handed a key to Liesel, then picked up another and gave it to Dylan. "And Mr. Drake, room five. Do you happen to know when your roommate will be here?"

"My roommate?"

"Yes…" She looked back at the screen of her ancient computer. "Mr. Brambles. His reservation was tied to yours."

"We're not sure of his schedule," Ananke said before Dylan could open his mouth. "If we hear from him, we'll let you know."

They picked up their bags and headed for the stairs.

As soon as they were out of earshot of the reception desk, Dylan said, "Roommate?"

"The hunter, I assume," Ananke said.

Dylan grimaced. "Why can't the hunter and I have our own rooms and two of you share?"

"If you would like, I am sure we can take a vote," Rosario said.

125

"But…you…" He stewed for a moment. "That's not fair."

Ananke patted him on the back. "Now you know what it's like to be a woman."

Though a few hours of sleep was what they really needed, Ananke wanted to get a look at the area where the van had disappeared. So they dropped their things in their rooms and were soon back on the road, heading farther east into the mountains.

Security footage had shown the kids' van leaving the Conifer Lodge, where the retreat had been held, at 8:42 a.m. on the day they vanished. The vehicle should have next appeared on cameras outside the Groveland fire station, but it never did, so whatever happened had occurred somewhere in between.

While Dylan drove, the women scanned both sides of the road. Except for gaps here and there where a house or other type of building had been constructed, the route was lined by trees. There were plenty of places where the van could have gone, but none was any better than the rest.

"An army could search through the area for a year and never find them," Dylan said as the Conifer Lodge came into view.

"Someone checked satellites, I assume," Rosario said.

"So I was told," Ananke replied.

"*Every* satellite?"

"That, I don't know."

"I am sure some were missed. When we get back, I'll look into it."

Ananke liked Rosario's confidence but didn't know how good the woman was. Even if she was the best hacker in the world, there would be only so much she could do on the laptop that had been in her duffel bag. "It'll go faster if you had help."

"I do not mean to offend you, but you would just get in my way."

"I wasn't talking about me," Ananke said. "I have a friend who won't get in your way. I'll put you in touch with him."

"A friend? Are we involving others now?"

"He works for me. Any job I'm on, he's on."

"I can do it myself. I don't need anyone."

Ananke's phone buzzed with a text.

"Give him a try," she said to Rosario as she pulled out her cell. "You might be surprised."

The message was from the Administrator.

Your hunter has arrived

"Good news, Dylan," Ananke announced. "Looks like your roommate's here."

IT WAS DARK by the time they returned to the Hardwick Inn.

As they entered the lobby, the woman behind the desk waved and said, "Mr. Drake, you just missed Mr. Brambles. I pointed him toward Mazy's Diner down the street not five minutes ago."

Ananke thanked the clerk, and she and the team headed back outside.

They found Mazy's Diner a few blocks down. A buzz of voices and clinking utensils and plates greeted them. Ananke stopped near a sign that read SEAT YOURSELF and scanned the room. All the booths and tables were occupied by couples and families. The only solo men she saw were seated at the counter and had the look of locals. Of course, the best hunters knew how to blend in.

She was in the process of assessing them one by one when a voice boomed across the dining room. "Kitty-kat!"

Until that moment, she had not been aware her blood could turn cold so fast. Eyes narrowing to slits, she turned toward the speaker. Standing outside the hallway to the bathrooms, smiling his million-dollar smile, was her misogynistic, narcissistic, supposed-to-still-be-in-prison ex-boyfriend.

Ricky Orbits.

A giant grin on his face, he began walking toward her. "Did you miss me, kitten?"

Trying to ignore the shiver of disgust running up her spine, Ananke whispered to the others, "Get something to eat," and then, with a flick of a finger, motioned for Orbits to follow her outside.

A slight breeze blew past the front of the restaurant as she stepped into the night and walked to the corner of the building. There she waited until Ricky appeared. Before he could say a word, she headed toward the back of the restaurant, stopping near a pile of pallets and empty pickle barrels.

A few seconds later, Mr. Wonderful arrived, still wearing his ear-to-ear smile. "Baby, ain't this great? I didn't think I'd get to see you for years. How about a little kiss?"

He threw his arms out and stepped toward her. But as soon as he was in range, she shoved him in the chest and sent him sprawling into the side of the building.

"Kitty-kat, what did I do to deserve that?"

"Seriously, Ricky? Seriously?" She grabbed his shirt and jammed him back against the wall. "Number one, I told you to *never* call me that again. Number two, you're supposed to be in prison!"

He snickered. "I know. Isn't it awesome?"

"How did you get out?" she said, teeth clenched.

"Apparently I'm in demand."

She bounced him off the wall. "Tell me how you got out!"

"All right. All right. Save the physical stuff for later, baby."

Her eyes flared, but before she could do anything else, he raised his hands in surrender.

"Just a joke, just a joke." He smiled again and leaned forward like he was about to impart top-secret information. "This woman shows up at Crestridge—you know, my home away from home—and says she can spring me if I'd do a job for her people. Like I'd pass up that opportunity, right?" He straightened back up, looking playfully suspicious. "You know this already, though, don't you? Miss Marsh is one of your friends, isn't she? Of course she is. Why else would I be here?"

"I would put you in solitary for the rest of your life before I would ever lift a finger to get you out."

He chuckled. "Now you're just being coy. Damn, woman, I knew you still loved me, but I didn't think it was this much."

He was dead wrong, though she'd come very close to

falling in love before she'd regained her senses that night she found him playing naked Twister with a couple of twentysomething Twister professionals. In a soft yet deadly tone, she said, "Jeopardize the mission again, and I'll have our client pull you off the team. Is that clear?"

"Hold on now."

She stared at him, an eyebrow raised.

"Fine," he said. "I'll be good." He cocked his head. "Aren't you going to answer that?"

"What?"

He nodded at the vibrating pocket of her duster. She jammed her hand inside and pulled out her phone. The caller ID read ADMINISTRATOR.

With a final shove to Ricky's chest, she walked away and pressed ACCEPT.

"Good evening, Ananke," the Administrator said. "Have you connected with Mr. Orbits yet?"

"You son of a bitch. What the hell is he doing here?"

"You need a hunter. My understanding is he's one of the best."

His understanding was correct, but she had no intention of confirming that. "And you just happened to have a get-out-of-jail-free card lying around you used to set him loose?"

"In a manner of speaking."

"I want him out of here."

"All right. Name me a hunter who can do a better job than Mr. Orbits and is available, and I'll get him," the Administrator said.

"Alan Kubik."

"Working in Kazakhstan, I believe."

"Noriko Motohashi."

"We've attempted to contact her but have had no replies."

"Russell Parker."

"Retired and not answering calls."

She dug for another name. "Donald Wilkinson."

"Also retired, I'm afraid."

Ananke stared at the ground, her mind scrambling. But the truth was, she'd just named four of the five top hunters in the world. Coming in at number three, Ricky rounded off that list.

"We can do this without a hunter," she said.

"If you had more time, perhaps. My job, however, is to provide you with the best tools I can. Mr. Orbits is an asset you can't afford to turn away."

As much as she hated to admit it, the Administrator was right.

Damn.

It.

"Fine. He can stay. But I can't guarantee I won't kill him at some point."

"Thank you. I'm sure he'll deserve it if that becomes necessary."

Ananke then caught him up on what little they'd been able to do so far. After she hung up, she turned back to Ricky.

"Is it official?" he asked. "Are we working together again?"

"So it would seem."

The Ricky grin returned as he lifted his arms. "Bring it in here, baby."

She turned and walked away.

TWENTY-ONE

A SINGLE SCREEN on the Administrator's wall flickered to life with the image of Committee member Monday.

"Orbits has joined the field team," the Administrator reported.

"And she accepted him?"

"She wasn't happy about it, but she understands the need."

"And the mission?"

"They've only been in the area for a couple hours, so nothing yet."

"What are they—"

"Apologies, sir," the Administrator said as the light for the emergency line on his phone began blinking. "May I put you on hold for one moment?"

When Monday nodded, the Administrator muted the video link and picked up his phone. The call lasted just over two minutes. When it was completed, he reactivated the video chat.

"That was one of the people I have with the families," he said. "A ransom demand has been received. Ten million per child."

"Interesting. And the deadline?"

"Seventy-two hours from"—he checked the time on his computer—"thirteen minutes ago. The ransom note came by an e-mail, and was sent only to the three families with the means to pay it. So far nothing has been received by the other three families."

"Thirty million dollars. That's quite a—"

"No, sir. Sixty. They want ten for each of the six children or none will be returned."

"Is that so?" Monday said. "Keep me informed."

"Of course."

TWENTY-TWO

Sierra Nevada Mountains, California

AS SHE WAS getting ready to go to bed, Ananke received the Administrator's message about the ransom demand and the deadline. She called the others and switched their rendezvous time from four a.m. to three a.m. She would have liked to move it up even earlier, but they had to get some rest. With under three days until time ran out for the hostages, who knew when they'd get the opportunity to rest again.

But sleep came in dribs and drabs, her mind still agitated by Ricky's presence. That he had such an effect on her was her own damn fault. She should have never become involved with him in the first place. All the warning signs had been there, on giant, horizon-filling billboards that she'd chosen to ignore. She'd been seduced due to her admiration of his skills and a bad-boy phase that was now, thanks to Ricky, behind her.

Could she work with him? Yes. They'd been on the same job the previous summer, the same one she'd helped Quinn on. Technically they'd been on conflicting sides, but she had avoided killing him then so she figured she could probably keep from sticking a knife in him now. It would have been nice, though, if the Administrator had informed her ahead of time that Ricky was the hunter. She'd almost lost her cool in front of the others, and she couldn't have that if she was running things.

Before her alarm rang at 2:30, she was up and on the phone with Shinji.

He gave her the rundown on what he'd found out about her team members, all of which confirmed what Ananke already knew or sensed about them. He then moved on to the *Karas Evonus*. "The registration is legit, but I can't find anything but a PO box address in Panama for the company who owns it, so it's got to be a cover for something. I can keep digging if you want."

"I do, but I'm going to need you to back-burner it for a while. I'm going to connect you with Rosario, and I want you to help her out. She might be a little resistant at first, so give her some of your charm."

"I have charm?"

"Fake it."

Ananke arrived at the van a minute before Rosario and Liesel got there. They shared nods but no one said anything. The peaceful silence changed the moment Ricky and Dylan walked out. The two men were in the middle of a one-sided conversation—Ricky talking, Dylan sleepily listening and nodding. As they neared, Ricky let out a loud belly laugh, as if he'd just said the funniest thing ever.

"Volume," Ananke whispered harshly.

"Sorry, sorry," Ricky said. "I was just telling Dylan here what RocketMan did on that—"

"Ricky, shut up."

"You got it. Sorry, kitten."

She glared at him.

"I mean, sorry, *boss*." He flashed a toothy smile.

She took a deep, centering breath and then looked at Rosario. "I want you to stay here and work on those satellite images and see whatever else you can dig up. I'll send you Shinji's number, the guy I was talking about. He knows you'll be calling him."

"Shinji?" Ricky bellowed. "Hey, I like that guy. Tell him—"

"Ricky," Ananke growled.

"—hi from me," he finished in a faux whisper.

Ananke pulled out her phone and texted Shinji's contact information to Rosario. "If you really can't work with him, let me know," she said as Rosario's phone buzzed.

Rosario looked skeptical but said nothing.

Ananke turned to Ricky. "You've been briefed?"

"About the kids? Yep."

"And can I assume you have a vehicle? Or did someone drop you off?"

"Nobody drops Ricky off." He pointed across the lot at a dark blue Chevy Silverado crew cab.

"They gave you a truck?" Dylan said. "Now that's just not fair."

Her gaze still on Ricky, Ananke said, "Go hunt. Any lead you find, you let me know right away."

He bowed deeply. "As you wish, milady."

He twirled around and headed toward the truck.

"Liesel and Dylan," Ananke said, "let's do some of our own hunting."

WITH THE TRAIL almost three days cold, Ananke decided to focus their initial efforts on buildings in the disappearance zone where the kids might have been taken. Even if they'd been kept someplace only temporarily, there might be clues to where they'd gone next. But at house after house they found nothing.

After they'd been at it for almost two hours, they pulled into the parking lot of an abandoned motel.

"Doesn't look like anyone's been here in ages," Dylan said as he parked.

It was the kind of place where guests stayed in individual cabins. It had undoubtedly been nice once but now was beyond repair. The central building where the front desk would have been lay in the middle of the complex next to the lot. Its windows had been knocked out years ago, and the roof sagged between rafters like a hammock.

As Ananke opened her door, she said to Dylan, "Kill the engine. It'll go faster if we're all looking around this time."

"Wait, wait, wait," he said with a smile and a shake of his head. "I'm the driver, remember? Not the gun-toting, haunted-house investigator. That's your job."

"And I'm the boss," Ananke said, smiling back. "Now get out."

As Ananke led Dylan and Liesel up to the main building,

the van beeped, signaling its locks had been engaged. She shot a look at Dylan.

"I don't know about you," he said, "but I'd like it if no one was waiting for us inside when we come back."

"Like who?"

"It doesn't matter who. Are you telling me this place doesn't give you the creeps?"

Ananke snorted and stepped across the threshold. A warped reception counter stretched across the room toward the back, but whatever else had been in there was gone. They searched the rest of the building but found nothing of interest.

When they exited, Dylan headed toward the van.

"Where do you think you're going?" Ananke said. "There's more."

"Not the cabins," he said, not hiding his dread.

"Yes, the cabins."

The first two cabins were as unhelpful as the main building. When Ananke reached the third, however, she paused outside the entrance. The layer of dust on the threshold was nowhere near as thick as she'd seen elsewhere. Shining her flashlight inside, she saw dozens of recent footprints and three large rectangular areas where there was also little dust. The spots were side by side and the right size and shape for sleeping bags.

As interesting as the discovery was, the recent occupants could have been anyone—hikers, campers, someone wanting to avoid paying for a hotel room. And though she knew the marks had been made in the last week, no one had done her the courtesy of writing the actual date in the dust.

"Ananke," Liesel called from outside. "Come look."

Ananke found Liesel along the side of the third cabin, pointing her flashlight at the ground. Smack dab in the center of the halo was a tire track.

"A street bike," Dylan said, looking over their shoulders. "You call tell from the tread pattern."

"There are two more." Liesel swung the beam and revealed the additional marks.

Dylan examined them for a moment. "Street bikes again,

different tire brands, though. The tracks are pretty wide, so I'd say the bikes are substantial. Maybe touring bikes, something like that."

"Is this it, or did you find others?" Ananke asked.

"No others," Liesel said.

Three sets of tracks. Three imprints of sleeping bags inside.

Without moving, Ananke followed the tracks with her light back to the area in front of the cabins, where they turned and disappeared from sight.

Still no way to know if they had anything to do with the missing kids.

They searched around cabin three a bit more, but discovered nothing else useful. While Liesel and Dylan checked the remaining cabins, Ananke called Rosario.

"Find anything?" she asked.

"It turns out that it was cloudy on the day of the kidnapping, so all visual spectrum satellite images are useless. There is, though, an NSA satellite in the vicinity that photographs in alternate spectrums. Unfortunately, it is not directly overhead, so the images we are interested in are at an angle. This means the mountains block a lot of the view, but there are parts of the road we can see. Shinji is going through it frame by frame now."

"So he's working out for you?"

"He is…useful so far."

Ananke grinned to herself. "I have something else for you to check out while you're looking at images." She told Rosario about the motorcycles. "Just want to rule out the possibility they had anything to do with this."

"We do not need the satellites for that. Security camera footage would be faster. Let me see what I can hack into. It should be easy enough to establish if the motorcycles were in the area or not."

ROSARIO HAD EXPECTED Shinji to be another wannabe hacker who could do a few tricks but was otherwise worthless. As a test, she'd tasked him with breaking into the NSA satellite database, figuring it would tie him up for hours. She then set about hacking into it herself.

She was still working on the secondary firewall when Shinji called back and told her he was in. Her response was at first disbelief, and then surprise after he provided her a pathway into the satellite's data.

Either he'd been lucky or he was better than she was. Considerably.

After she finished talking to Ananke, she initiated a new video chat with Shinji.

"Anything?" she asked.

"I found a clear view of the road about five miles west of the Conifer Lodge. The van never showed up. I even went an hour beyond when I should have seen it. Nothing."

"Show me the location."

She heard Shinji clicking a few keys before a map appeared on her screen, with a marker hovering over the spot he'd described.

"You are sure you did not miss the van?" she asked.

"You can look at the data yourself, if you want. But you're not going to find anything."

He was probably right, but she didn't know him well enough to take him at his word. "Send it to me."

"Oookay."

She could hear him typing for several seconds. A second after he stopped, a message box appeared on her screen, asking if she wanted to accept a file transfer.

"I converted it to a single movie," he said. "You can speed it up, slow it down. Whatever you want."

"Thank you." She initiated the download, then said, "We have something new to look into."

"What is it?"

She passed on Ananke's request. "We'll take fifteen minutes to find as many of the security cameras as we can. After that, we divide them between us and search footage in a twenty-four-hour window before and after the van left the lodge. If we do not see any motorcycles that fit the description, or we do but they leave the area before the van disappeared,

138

then we do not worry about them."

"That's still a lot of footage. I could automate the process. Set one of my computers to check all the cameras."

"You have an image recognition program that will do this?"

"I do."

"How fast?"

He paused. "Twenty minutes to get it running, then five minutes per camera processing."

"Accuracy?"

"About ninety percent."

That wasn't perfect, but a ten-percent error rate seemed a fair enough exchange for not wasting time they could spend on something else.

"Let's do it."

They found nine cameras in their target area, seven of which stored footage far enough back to be useful. While Shinji dealt with the footage, Rosario reviewed the satellite info he'd sent and confirmed the van had not driven past. She texted this information to Ananke and turned her attention to looking into the backgrounds of the missing kids and their chaperones.

The three rich kids all went to private schools and were stars in one way or another—debate, student government, and track. The lower-income kids went to public schools, where it would be generous to say extracurricular programs were limited. What they shared was their level of intelligence. All were part of gifted programs and had IQs above 140. This, apparently, had gained each of them membership in an organization called Point Five, a kind of nouveau Mensa club, which sponsored the retreat.

A soft *bong* signaled Shinji wanted to reconnect. She accepted the request, and then returned her attention to the article about Point Five.

"I found them," Shinji said.

Rosario blinked and looked at the chat box. "The motorcycles?"

"Uh-huh."

"In our time frame?"

"I have them on three different cameras in Groveland, driving toward the abandoned motel late on the afternoon before the kidnapping."

"Faces?"

He shook his head. "All wearing helmets."

"License numbers, then."

"The only camera with a decent angle didn't have the resolution to pick them out."

"Did you see when they left?"

"They didn't leave."

"They must have stayed longer than the search window. Expand the parameters and find—"

"Already expanded. Had my analyzer concentrate on footage from the camera with the best shot of the road, and ran through everything recorded up to just a few minutes ago. The motorcycles never went back west."

"You're sure it didn't miss them?"

"Positive. They either dumped the bikes somewhere and left in another vehicle, or they drove out a different way."

"How many other ways out are there?"

"Based on their last known location, four. But three are minor roads, partly dirt, partly paved, and lots of twists and turns. Difficult for anyone who doesn't know the area to navigate. Plus not great on those kinds of bikes. The only other way would be to drive through Yosemite and exit the east side to highway 395. I have my computer searching for cameras on that route right now."

"Okay. Let me know." As she reached to disconnect, she paused. "Shinji."

"Yeah?"

"Good work."

He nodded and the chat window shut off.

When he called back forty-five minutes later, his answer was unchanged.

The motorcycles had driven into the area the day before the kidnapping but had never driven out. It still wasn't proof the riders had anything do with the kids' disappearance, but it was troubling.

Rosario reached for her phone.

AS SOON AS she hung up, Ananke shared Rosario's news about the motorcycles with Liesel and Dylan.

"So more missing people?" Dylan asked.

"Or they were involved and left their bikes behind," Ananke said. "Or maybe hauled them out in a truck."

"Or they are still camping in the mountains," Liesel said.

"Or that, too."

Ananke stared out the front window of the van, across the parking lot at the Conifer Lodge. The sun had risen about thirty minutes before, but it was still too early to go noising around inside.

"Uh-oh," Dylan said.

Ananke glanced over and saw that he was staring at a sheriff's car heading their way.

"You don't think they're coming for us, do you?" he asked.

"Start the engine," Ananke said, her gaze glued to the approaching car.

Dylan turned the ignition. "We can't outrun him in this."

"You are a driver," Liesel said. "You will outdrive him."

"Right. I'll try to remember that." He grabbed the transmission, ready to drop it into Drive.

"Wait," Ananke said.

The sheriff's car had slowed. When it was still half the lot away, it swung in a wide U-turn and pulled to a stop at the curb. Two deputies climbed out and went inside the lodge.

Dylan shut the engine off. "Maybe they're just getting something to eat."

"Let's hope so. But we don't go in until they leave."

The wait wasn't long. Five minutes after the deputies entered the lodge, they came back out.

"Is that your friend?" Liesel asked.

Ananke groaned.

Walking between the deputies, hands cuffed behind his back, was Ricky Orbits.

TWENTY-THREE

Just After 3 a.m. Again

RICKY KNEW ANANKE was only playing it up for her crew.

No way she could still be mad at him. Their breakup had been at least three years ago, and had happened because of a simple misunderstanding. He hadn't actually liked either of the girls he was with when Ananke found him. Well, liked, sure— that redhead, whatever her name was, had been particularly talented. But not *liked*-liked. He'd just been blowing off some steam. What was wrong with that?

Of course, there'd also been that unfortunate run-in the previous summer that landed him in prison, but he should have been the one mad about that, not her.

No, she was just playing her cards tight to the vest, not wanting to show the others she had a favorite right off the bat. He had no doubt that as soon as they found some time to be alone, she'd be all over him. "Oh, Ricky, it's so good to see you." "Oh, Ricky, I've missed you so much." "Oh, Ricky, take me here."

Admittedly, those probably weren't the exact words she'd use, but something similar.

He allowed himself to muse about his once and future girlfriend for another few seconds before turning his attention to the job at hand. He had a vested interest in its success, after all.

"Just so we're clear, Mr. Orbits," Miss Marsh had said after filling him in on the job during their private flight to California. "Your continued freedom is contingent on the children being found alive."

"A few lost kids? No problem," might have been what he'd said, but what he'd been thinking was, he would never allow himself to be taken back to prison no matter the outcome of the mission.

Miss March turned out to be some kind of mind reader. "And in case you decide not to honor our deal…" She motioned to someone sitting at the back of the jet.

Up walked the bruiser who'd been with her at the prison, and his clone who'd been waiting for them on the plane. The former was carrying a leather pouch that he set on the table in front of Miss Marsh. He opened it so that it lay flat. Strapped to one side was an odd-looking gun, sort of Buck Rodgers meets vaccination gun. The man inserted a tube from the other half of the pouch into the barrel.

At the same time, his partner moved next to Ricky. "Take off your shirt."

Ricky snorted. "Huh. Right. I don't think so."

"Do it," Miss Marsh said, "or we'll return to Crestridge and put you back in your old cell."

"Hey, just joking. No problem. I'll take it off."

He removed the polo shirt she had given him before they left the prison, and flexed his toned arms, showing off his pecs. Prison had been useful in that respect.

"Not bad, huh?" he said to Miss Marsh. "Go ahead. You can touch—"

A small circle of cold metal pressed against his right side below his pectoral muscle, and *bam*! Something shot painfully under his skin.

"Hey!" he yelled, jerking away. "What the hell?"

He looked down at his torso and saw a red circle where the gun had shot him, surprisingly tiny for the amount of pain that had come with it.

The circle of cold was on him again, pressing below his shoulder blade.

Bam!

Twisting sideways, he tried to knock the guy's arm away, but his tormentor had already moved out of the way.

"Seriously! What the hell?"

The big man jabbed the gun into Ricky's bicep and pulled the trigger.

"Ow! I swear to God, if you do that again—"

"Pants off," the second man ordered.

"Are you kidding? Not a chance."

"Pants off."

"You can go ahead and turn this plane around, because they are staying on."

"Very well," Miss Marsh said. She rose and moved into the aisle. "I'll inform our pilot."

Ricky let her get almost to the cockpit door before he closed his eyes and said, "Wait."

She turned back, an eyebrow raised.

"Okay, okay," he said.

She didn't move.

He unbuckled his belt and dropped his pants to the floor.

"Thank you," she said, heading back to her seat.

"Underwear, too," the talking half of Tweedledee and Tweedledum said.

"Hold on. Where are you thinking of shooting me?"

"Underwear."

Again, he had but one choice.

Before he could pull them down, the man added, "Face the window."

Ricky turned begrudgingly and lowered his Fruit of the Looms.

"Bend over."

"I'm flattered and all, but not everyone who goes to prison is into this kind of thing."

"Bend over." This time the words were accompanied by a shove to Ricky's back.

Reluctantly, Ricky leaned toward the window. In rapid succession, he was shot twice in the butt, first in the right cheek and then the left.

"You can get dressed now," the talker said.

Once clothed again, Ricky sat—gingerly—back in his chair and glared at Miss Marsh. "What the hell was that all about?"

"Our insurance in case you decide to disappear. Consider yourself Lo-Jacked."

"Tracking bugs?" He figured it was something like that.

"As I said. Insurance."

"But why five, for God's sake?"

"You could deal with the pain of digging one out. Five, less likely. But even if you were inclined to try, you might have noticed some of them are really hard to reach. We'd find you long before you removed them."

As much as he wished otherwise, she was right. He had to see this thing through. Good thing he was the best hunter in the business. If he knew himself—and he did—he'd find the kids and have them home to mom and dad within twenty-four hours.

First, though, he needed to pick up the trail. He went to the spot all trails had in common—the starting point.

The Conifer Lodge was located not too far west of Yosemite National Park, in a shallow vale between tree-covered ridges on the north side of the highway. The lodge itself had seventy guest rooms, a popular restaurant on the ground floor, a gift shop, and an area for activities such as horseback riding and archery.

Ricky parked the Silverado in the lot among a group of SUVs, and then spent the next fifteen minutes watching the front of the lodge.

The security camera above the main door was easy to spot. From its position, he knew it wasn't the same one that had recorded the footage Miss Marsh had shown him of the van leaving the lodge. That camera had to be located down at the other end of the parking area. He didn't see any others, and if there was a guard who patrolled the facility, he sure didn't get around to the front very often, because Ricky hadn't seen him, either.

Ricky slipped out of his car and walked a wide arc around the archery range so that he could approach the lodge from behind. There were several outbuildings scattered across the back of the property. He used them to move within forty feet of the lodge's rear entrance without ever exposing himself. From there, he studied the building.

Stone steps led up to a partially covered deck and several sets of glass double doors to the main lodge. Ricky scanned the structure with his binoculars for more security cameras but saw none.

He sauntered over to the building and let himself in.

Turned out, the night clerk was the only person awake on the entire first floor. The kid, who couldn't have been more than twenty, sat behind the front desk watching a video on a computer, headphones on.

Ricky had asked Miss Marsh a lot of questions after he was chipped and she finished her brief. Among his inquiries had been one about the layout of the lodge.

He could tell she'd been impressed with that, but that was to be expected. Ricky was impressive. He didn't know how not to be.

She had floor plans sent to her while they were still in the air, and he'd been able to study them as the plane approached the airport outside Sacramento. So he'd likely find what he was looking for in one of the private offices on the other side of the door behind the front desk. Luckily there was a second way to get there that didn't involve having to ask the night clerk to get out of Ricky's way.

Getting to that back door, however, did mean he needed to cross the lobby.

After easing around the corner in a crouch, he crept over to one of the couches that faced a giant fireplace. The night clerk didn't even flinch.

Ricky slunk along the sofa as far as he could go and then paused. Now came the hard part. Between him and the hallway to the back door was thirty feet of floor that was in full view of the clerk. That was a whole lot more exposure than Ricky liked. The front desk was closer—under twenty feet. If he could get there, he could use it as a shield while he moved over to the hallway.

Or he could knock the kid out.

Kidding. Just kidding, he thought.

Eyes on the clerk, he took a breath and snuck across the stone floor to the safety of the counter. No movement or sound from the other side.

Ricky smiled. *Damn, I'm good.*

One second later, his shoe caught on a rough spot of stone, causing a squeak. He froze.

From the other side of the counter came the creak of a chair, followed by the tinny, muted sound of music. The clerk had removed his headphones.

Everything's fine. Go back to your stupid video. Nothing to see here.

Another chair creaked, longer this time.

Then a step.

Crap.

Ricky could feel the clerk standing no more than two feet away, the counter the only thing separating them. If the kid leaned forward far enough, he would see the top of Ricky's head.

Buddy, just sit down.

A tense silence.

Seriously, man. I said I was joking about knocking you out. Don't make me do it.

A floorboard groaned. Not a step, more the shifting of weight.

The sound of a door opening was totally unexpected. Even odder, it wasn't a regular door. The sound was more distinctive, like one for a—

Refrigerator?

A moment later it closed again, and then the hiss of an opening soda can filled the air. This was followed by the chair creaking again, and the disappearance of the tinny headphone music.

After giving it an extra twenty seconds to make sure the clerk had indeed retaken his seat, Ricky continued down the counter and entered the hall.

The door to the management section was locked, but it was one of those off-the-shelf, in-the-doorknob kind of keyholes and yielded to his picks in seconds.

A new hallway, smaller, with four office doors on the right and the door to the front desk area on the left.

Ricky made a quick survey of all the offices. The first two each had a couple of desks and a few filing cabinets crammed inside. The third and fourth offices had only one desk each. On the walls in the third were posters touting workers' safety and insurance benefits and employees' rights. The HR office, he guessed.

The fourth was clearly the lodge manager's. Along with a nicer desk and matching filing cabinets was a large, framed photograph of the lodge from at least fifty years earlier. Also hanging on a wall was a diploma revealing the manager's name as Scott Larson, and that he had a degree in hospitality management from Washington State University.

Ricky took a seat at the man's desk and fired up the computer.

As was all the rage, the screen was password protected. Ricky searched the desk area, and found a piece of paper with the man's login taped to the back of a family picture on Larson's credenza.

It took Ricky a little over a minute to find the registration information for the missing kids. They had used a total of six rooms: the three chaperones had their own rooms while the kids paired off.

Ricky brought up a list of other guests who'd stayed there at the same time. Since the summer season had yet to begin, there had been only thirty-seven others. Of those, twenty-eight remained at the lodge for at least an additional two days after the kids, while the other nine left the same day. The nine consisted of two families: one of four and one of three, who had both been at the lodge at least a week before the kids' arrival; and two solo male travelers who had checked in the day before the kids got there.

Ricky took a picture of the list.

Normally his next move would have been to call one of his contacts and have the person do background checks on the guests. But even if Miss Marsh hadn't explicitly warned him not to communicate with anyone from his old life, he had a feeling most of his contacts wouldn't have picked up the phone. He was supposed to be in prison for screwing up a job, after all.

148

No one would want anything to do with him.

That meant he'd have to hand the names over to Ananke. That bummed him out. Even if she was apparently in charge of their little gang, he would rather present her with fully researched information, or even better, with the kids themselves. How she'd love him for that.

C'est la vie.

He brought up the records for the kids again. According to the database, they and their chaperones checked out at 8:27 a.m. Getting into the security camera footage required an additional password.

Ricky typed in the manager's screen password and let out a quiet "ha!" as access to the security camera system was granted. It was amazing how many people didn't take the time to create different passwords, but he wasn't complaining. It sure made his job easier.

Whoever had set up the camera footage database needed a lesson in organization. The thing was a mess. Ricky figured it out, though, and tracked down the footage for the morning the kids had left. First, he verified that the clip Miss Marsh had shown him had indeed been recorded on the camera at the west end of the parking lot, at the time she had told him. Next, he switched to footage from the camera directly above the lodge entrance, and started watching at the 8:25 a.m. mark. The kids began trickling out by 8:28. They seemed bored, or maybe they were still tired—Ricky was willing to admit he wasn't exactly an expert when it came to anyone under twenty. By 8:33, all six kids and two of the chaperones were standing near the curb with their bags.

A white passenger van pulled up at 8:35, driven by the third chaperone. Luggage was loaded into the rear and everyone climbed in. The van departed at 8:41.

Ricky reached to stop the playback, but paused his finger above the space bar as a trio of motorcycles passed into frame, heading in the same direction the van had gone. It might have been a coincidence, but in a hunt, one could not afford to ignore anything.

He tried enlarging the image of the bikers, but the picture

became fuzzy pixels. He zoomed the image back out and noted what he could. Big bikes, with cargo bins straddling the rear wheels. The kind of bike you might want on a camping trip, and probably a common sight in places like Yosemite.

The bikers appeared to be all men, though they were hidden under leather jackets and sunglasses and helmets so he couldn't be sure. One had skin far too fair to be anything but Caucasian. The other two probably were also, but again it was impossible to tell from the crappy footage.

Ricky reverse it to when the kids were leaving the lodge and watched the whole thing again. As everyone was climbing into the van, Ricky paused the scene.

He scrubbed the video back a few seconds and played it again, and then repeated the process.

At the start of the section Ricky was reviewing, one of the chaperones, a middle-aged guy with bushy salt-and-pepper hair, had not joined the others inside the van. By all appearances, he was shutting the rear doors. That's how Ricky had interpreted it on previous viewings. But as the man went through the familiar motions this time, Ricky saw the guy glance over his shoulder in the direction the motorcycles would come from a few moments later. Not only that, the man appeared to nod in their direction, like he was acknowledging them.

Or telling them he was ready.

Miss Marsh had shown Ricky photos of all those who were missing. Though he hadn't been allowed to take the documents with him, she had let him use his phone to photograph each image. He shuffled through the images now, and stopped on the one that matched the man in the video.

"Hello, Mr. Andrew Carter," he whispered as he looked back at the computer screen. "What's your story?"

A door opened in the hallway outside the office.

Ricky shut the computer down and ducked below the desk.

What the hell is someone doing here already?

He checked his phone, sure it couldn't be much past four a.m., but it was almost five. He'd spent more time looking through the computer than he'd realized. This being a hotel, five in the morning was not particular early. He just hoped it wasn't the manager. Putting lousy-password-protecting Scott in a quick sleeper hold would severely compromise the team's low-profile mandate.

He could hear footsteps moving down the hall and then a door opening. This was followed almost immediately by the sound of voices. Ricky guessed whoever had just arrived was talking to the night clerk.

Was this the replacement clerk? If so, Ricky should be able to get out of there without anyone being the wiser, as soon as things settled down again.

But the new person did not stay in the reception area for long. The footsteps headed Ricky's way for a moment before stopping. Ricky heard another door open and the person step inside. He crept over to the wall the manager's office shared with the HR room and placed his ear against it.

The musical tone of a computer turning on confirmed the person had entered the neighboring office. Knowing this might be his best opportunity to get out of there unseen, Ricky snuck into the hallway, peeked into the HR office, and then scampered past when he saw that the woman sitting at the desk had her back to him. Moments later, he was once more in the public area.

He spent the next thirty minutes correlating the locations of the kids' and chaperones' rooms with those of other guests on his list. Interestingly, the room for one of the solo travelers was right next door to the one Andrew Carter had used. The hotel had been half empty at the time so it couldn't have been a coincidence.

God, if Ricky could just make one phone call and have someone look into the names, he knew he'd break this thing wide open before Ananke and the others had even had breakfast.

His stomach growled.

Breakfast. Now there's an idea.

It turned out the lodge restaurant didn't start serving until six a.m. Which meant Ricky had to wait. Which made him cranky. Which meant when the restaurant did open, the Denver omelet he ordered didn't arrive at his table until 6:17.

One look at it was all he needed to send it back. When the waiter returned with it six minutes later, the thing on the plate looked no better than it had before.

Clearly, the cook was unfamiliar with how to create a good Denver omelet. Ricky, if he did say so himself, was an expert.

"Maybe there's something else on the menu you might enjoy more," the waitress suggested after Ricky communicated his dissatisfaction.

"There's nothing I would enjoy more than a Denver omelet. It is what I've been thinking about for the last hour. It is what I came in here to eat. It is what I want." He picked up the corner of the plate and let it drop back on the table with a bang. "This, however, is *not* a Denver omelet."

The woman smiled uncomfortably. "I'm sorry, but I don't know what else I can do."

"I think the best thing would be for me to talk to your cook."

"Oh, I, um, don't think that's a good idea. The chef is very busy right—"

"Chef?" Ricky snickered. "Ma'am, the person in your kitchen is not a chef. He's a cook, and not a very good one." Ricky rose. "Trust me, he'll appreciate my feedback."

"Wait! You can't go in there!"

But Ricky wasn't listening to her anymore. He pushed through the swinging door into the kitchen and stopped a few feet inside. "Who's the one pretending to be in charge in here?"

It took two dishwashers, three prep cooks, a security guard—apparently they had one during the day—and the largest of the waitresses to pull Ricky from the man who claimed to be a chef and restrain Ricky until the sheriff's deputies arrived.

Ricky, of course, loudly proclaimed his innocence as he was ushered to the deputies' car in handcuffs, saying he'd only been trying to help someone who obviously didn't know what he was doing. The deputies, for their part, smiled and nodded and told him to watch his head as they helped him into the backseat.

TWENTY-FOUR

AFTER FOLLOWING THE deputies' car all the way back to a small sheriff's substation in Groveland, Ananke, Dylan, and Liesel watched the deputies transfer Ricky inside. Ananke didn't think there was a moment during the whole parade when Ricky's lips weren't moving.

"Do we go in and get him out?" Dylan asked.

"They're not going to just hand him over. So unless you'd like to get into a firefight over that asshole, then, no, we don't go in."

As tempted as Ananke was to let Ricky stay locked up, if the sheriff's department figured out he'd been staying at the Hardwick Inn, they'd quickly learn he hadn't been there alone. That would be a major problem. Like it or not, she had to do something.

"Progress?" the Administrator asked once she had him on the line.

"We have a situation."

"Is that so?"

She filled him in.

"And you don't know the reason he was arrested?" he asked when she finished.

"I can think of several hundred, but I don't know specifically."

He said nothing for a moment, then, "I would like you to return to the hotel until you hear from me again."

"We're not going to get a lot done sitting in our rooms."

"Until I have a better idea of what's going on, it would be prudent if you stay out of sight. I promise you'll be hearing from me very soon."

UPON RETURNING TO the Hardwick Inn, Ananke took fifteen minutes to freshen up before meeting up with the others in Rosario's room.

"Anything new?" she asked Rosario.

"One of our chaperones may be involved with the kidnappers."

"Oh, really? Do tell."

"The chaperones were all supposed to have come from local Point Five chapters—two from Palo Alto, and one from Daly City. Same chapters the kids are from. Marta Sorenson, the Daly City rep, needed to be replaced at the last minute."

"Why?" Ananke asked.

"Single vehicle car accident. Two days before the trip."

"Drinking?"

"No alcohol or drugs in her system. The police report says several witnesses saw her car suddenly speed up and clip the side of a semi-truck then flip over. She is still unconscious, so they have not been able to question her."

"Suicide attempt?"

"Possible, but she had no apparent money troubles. Also, she is recently married, and everything I have found indicates they had no problems. Her medical records also contain no mentions of mental health issues. My guess is no."

"You got into her medical records?"

"Shinji did."

Ananke grinned. "I told you he'd be a help."

"So far, he is…acceptable."

"Which one's the last-minute replacement?"

"Him. Andrew Carter. He was presented as a Point Five member from San Francisco able to fill in. A check of the San Francisco membership roll did turn up his name, but it appears that someone hacked their system and added Mr. Carter within the last week. Shinji checked the associated home address and employment information, but they were also false."

Ananke thought for a moment. "Shinji has a facial recognition system that can check a whole crapload of databases. Have him run the picture of Carter we—"

"Already in progress."

"Oh…um, great. I'm guessing no hits."

"Nothing yet."

Ananke's mission phone began ringing. It was the Administrator.

"Yes?" she answered.

"You are free to continue your investigation."

"Ricky?"

"Taken care of."

"In what way?"

The Administrator, as he often did, hung up without answering.

"What happened?" Dylan asked as Ananke lowered the phone.

"No idea. He just said it's taken care of."

"Don't you assassins say something like that when you kill someone?"

If only we were so lucky, Ananke thought. "We need to get back out there. Five minutes to freshen up then meet back at the van?"

"Works for me," Dylan said.

Liesel nodded.

Ananke walked to the door and opened it. As she stepped into the hallway—

"Morning, kitten!" Ricky stood in front of the door to her room, his hand in mid-knock. "I was wondering where you were."

She jammed her finger against her lips and motioned for him to come to her. As soon as he was in range, she grabbed him by the front of his shirt, pulled him into Rosario's room, and pushed him onto the bed.

"Whoa, baby. What was that for?"

"How about we start with you getting arrested?"

Ricky grinned sheepishly. "So you heard about that, huh? Big guy tell on me?"

"We're the ones who told him, you idiot! Right after we watched you get marched out of the Conifer Lodge and into that patrol car and taken to jail."

156

"I was wondering how he found out so fast. That makes a lot more sense now."

"What the hell happened?" she asked.

"There's a conspiracy in this country to keep people from knowing how to make a proper Denver omelet."

She closed her eyes in dread. "You didn't."

"Of course I did. Someone had to tell that cook what to do."

"You were arrested over food?" Rosario said. She considered that for a moment before adding, "I hate to say this, but I can actually appreciate that."

"Don't encourage him." Ananke said.

"Sorry," Rosario said, but gave Ricky a nod.

Ricky acknowledged her with a point of his finger, and then said, "So what are you all doing here? You can't get anything done this way."

If there was ever a moment when Ananke wished she could breathe fire, this was it. She settled instead for drilling holes in Ricky's forehead with her gaze. It wasn't nearly as satisfying.

"You're cute when you're angry, baby." He glanced at Dylan. "I'm right, aren't I?"

Dylan, looking uncomfortable, didn't respond.

"You know what?" Ananke said. "I don't care why you were arrested. We need to get back out there, and see if we can locate those motorcycles. I have a feeling they might—"

"Motorcycles?" Ricky asked.

She brought him up to speed on what he'd missed while he was locked away.

He grinned. "I've seen your motorcycles."

Ananke stared at him. "Today? Where?"

"Not live. A recording." Ricky told them about his visit to the manager's office at the Conifer Lodge and what he'd seen on the security footage.

Rosario showed him the clip of the bikers Shinji had found.

"Yep. Same guys," Ricky said.

"You're sure?"

"Sure I'm sure."

"That's actually helpful," Ananke said.

"If you liked that, you're going to love this," he said.

"What?"

"That chaperone you were talking about? Carter. He signaled the motorcycles before the van left."

"You saw this?" Liesel asked.

"I sure did."

Ananke couldn't help but sound impressed when she asked, "You find out anything else while you were digging around?"

"As a matter of fact…"

Ricky showed them the photo of the list of other guests who'd been staying at the lodge over the same days the kids had been there, and tapped the name of the guy who'd been in the room next door to Carter's.

"You were right," Dylan said to Ananke. "He is a pretty damn good hunter."

Looking flattered and surprised, Ricky said, "Did you really say that about me, kitten?"

Ananke looked at Rosario. "Have Shinji check the names out."

With a nod, Rosario motioned for Ricky to give her his phone.

"We know there's no sign of the van leaving the area," Ananke said to everyone. "Same with the motorcycles, but they would have been easier to smuggle out in a camper or truck. If we can find one of them, it could help us figure out who these people are. Maybe even point us to where they've taken the kids."

She had Rosario bring up a map of the area.

"We'll need all our eyes on this, so that means you, too," Ananke told her. "Shinji can handle research for now."

Rosario nodded.

"We'll split into two groups. My group will check places along these two roads." Ananke pointed at two routes leading south from the highway. "Ricky, you'll check this one." She pointed at the only road leading north.

"Whatever you want me to do, kitten…Oh, sorry."

Jaw tensing, she said, "Dylan, you'll be my driver." She looked at Rosario and Liesel. "I hate to do this, but one of you is going to have to go with *him*." She nodded at Ricky.

The women shared a look, then Liesel shrugged. "I will do it. He is…entertaining."

"I *am* entertaining, aren't I?" Ricky said.

Ananke rolled her eyes and said to Liesel, "If he becomes a problem, feel free to dump him at the side of the road. Or kill him. Your choice."

TWENTY-FIVE

The Bunker

THE HATCH OPENED, spilling ultra-bright light into the dark and dank space. Hands immediately went to eyes as those inside were blinded by the illumination.

Two thuds on the floor, and then the hatch closed again, plunging the occupants once more into pitch-black. A few muffled whimpers broke out, but no wailing like there'd been during the first few hours.

A shuffling of feet, followed by the sound of plastic ripping.

"Water," Erica Wright, one of the chaperones, said. "Everyone, come to my voice."

The children and Chris Jones, the other remaining chaperone, started toward her.

"Slowly," she said. "There's plenty for everyone."

"Ow," Nicholas shouted. "Hey, there's something else here."

Cardboard ripped.

"Feels like candy bars."

"Let me check that," Jones said.

Sounds of movement and a wrapper tearing.

"Granola bars," Jones announced.

"One each for now," Wright said. "If there are extras we'll divide them up later. Mr. Jones, make sure."

"I know, I know," Jones said.

Not for the first time, Wright wondered how long it would be before Jones snapped. The man had been going downhill since they were forced into this room. But with Carter gone and likely dead, both Wright and Jones needed to stay strong for the kids.

There was no other choice.

TWENTY-SIX

Just West of Yosemite National Park

ANANKE SCANNED THE house through her binoculars. Though it was not deserted, it looked as if no one had been around for a while.

A vacation home, likely. One with a very large, three-car garage in the back that had caught Ananke's interest.

She swung the glasses across the rest of the property. A dull forest green Honda Element sat to the side of the circular driveway. Based on the dust and pine needles covering it, the vehicle hadn't moved in a while, probably months.

She lowered her binoculars and whispered to Rosario, "We'll circle around and meet behind the garage."

They headed off in opposite directions, Ananke alternating her gaze between the path before her and the property. Still no signs of recent activity. If not for the garage, she and Rosario would be back in the van, headed to the next destination. But it was the biggest they'd seen so far, and could easily hide a van and several motorcycles.

She turned on her mic. "Anything?"

"Nothing so far," Rosario said.

"Dylan?"

He was still in the van, keeping an eye out in case someone came up the access road. "Nice and quiet, boss."

Ananke continued around the property until she was in the woods behind the garage. A few moments later, Rosario joined her.

She'd been hoping the building had a window along the back, but other than several vents near the roofline, the wall facing them was unbroken.

She motioned for Rosario to stay where she was, and then Ananke headed toward the garage. As she stepped out of the trees, her toe caught on a twig, causing her to glance down. Only it was not a twig, but a monofilament tripwire strung low through the brush. Before she could free her toe, one end of the line snapped.

"Down!" she yelled.

THE BUILDING WAS more storage shed than garage, but Ricky figured a van might fit as long as there wasn't anything else inside, so he picked the lock and pulled the rusty-hinged door open.

"Nope," he said to Liesel, standing off to the side. "I'm thinking this van isn't worth the time it's taking."

This was the sixth place they'd checked without finding anything.

"It might contain fingerprints or something that could identify the kidnappers. If we know who they are, it will be easier to find them."

"*Might* contain," he said as they started walking back toward the car. "There's your key word. But who'd be stupid enough to leave a van full of evidence?"

"But what if they did?"

He glanced at her. "You're like a piranha, aren't you? You grab on to something and don't let go."

She walked on as if she hadn't heard him.

After the comment she'd made when she agreed to go with him, he thought they would get along just fine, but man, did she turn out to be a tough nut to crack. She wore an all-business, tough-as-nails attitude like a second skin. Pretty, too, though he doubted she realized it, or, if she did, cared.

"Anybody ever tell you you've got nice eyes?" he said without thinking.

She turned on him, those same beautiful eyes narrowing to slits. "You are not my type."

"Hey, I wasn't flirting. I was just, you know, stating a fact, and was curious if anyone else ever told you."

For a moment, he was sure she was going to hit him, but after a long pause, what she did was whisper, "They smile."

"I'm sorry?"

"Someone once told me my eyes smile. A long time ago."

"He was right. That's it exactly. He an old boyfriend?"

Another pause, then, "An almost boyfriend."

That kind of comment called for further prodding. But when he opened his mouth to do that, a loud rumble rolled over the trees.

ANANKE FLEW INTO the woods on the concussive wave of the explosion.

For a moment, she lay on the forest floor stunned, with her ears ringing and no idea what had happened. Then she remembered the trip wire, and—

"Rosario!" Though she knew she had yelled, she couldn't hear herself. She struggled to her feet and turned in a circle. "Rosario!"

A wall of flames filled the space where the garage had been, while burning debris that had been blasted into the air was raining down in a fountain of fire.

"Rosario!"

Something touched her arm. She whirled around to find Rosario standing there, blood dripping from a cut on her forehead.

Rosario's lips moved, but all Ananke could hear was the buzzing echo of the explosion. She pointed at her ears and shook her head, then motioned back toward the van.

They ran through the trees, dodging pieces of the garage still falling from the sky, and spots of fire that had already caught on the ground.

When they emerged onto the driveway, Dylan was out of the van, looking toward the blaze. He ran to them, his mouth moving a mile a second.

Ananke waved him off. "No! Get the van started!"

He skidded to a stop and reversed course.

Ananke and Rosario reached the van as the engine roared to life, a noise—Ananke was relieved to find—she could actually hear. She let Rosario in first and flopped into the bench seat beside her.

"Get us out of here," she yelled at Dylan as she slid the side door shut.

He jammed the accelerator to the floor.

Looking out the back window, Ananke could see flames licking into the air from the tops of several trees. The house, too, was starting to burn.

She pulled her phone out of her pocket. The screen was shattered but she pushed the activate button anyway. Nothing happened. She grabbed the disposable cell she'd bought to contact Shinji. Thankfully, it had survived her airborne flight through the woods.

She punched in 911 but could barely hear the ring. When she thought she heard the operator's voice, she said, "There's been an explosion!" She gave the location as best she could, and added, "The fire's spreading into the trees! Hurry!"

She hung up, removed the phone's battery and SIM card, snapping the latter in two, and tossed the pieces out the window. Littering was not something she did lightly, but it was a small crime compared to the forest fire she'd inadvertently started, and reducing the chance of being caught due to a traceable SIM card seemed prudent.

"Take us back to the hotel," she said. "We have to get out of here before they start evacuating everyone."

"Evacuating?" Dylan said, his voice muffled but now understandable. "Do you really think they'll do that?"

"There aren't a lot of ways in and out of the area. Unless they get that fire under control quickly, the authorities won't want anyone around. And when they start forcing people out, the roads are going to jam up."

"But what about the kids? What if they're in the area?"

"They're not."

"How do you know that?"

"Because if they were, then they were killed the day they were taken. Whoever set that trap knew what the explosion would do, so they wouldn't be keeping their prized bargaining chips anywhere near it. Can you make this thing go any faster?"

Dylan punched the accelerator.

"What about Liesel and Ricky?" Rosario said.

"Right," Ananke said. "I'm out of phones. Can you call them?"

"AN EARTHQUAKE?" LIESEL asked.

They had stopped thirty feet shy of the Silverado and were looking in the direction from where the sound had come.

"You don't hear an earthquake without feeling it, too," he said. "I didn't feel anything. Did you?"

Liesel shook her head.

"I don't like this. Come on."

They jumped into the truck and Ricky started the engine. Instead of dropping it into gear right away, he called Ananke. The line rang several times before transferring to a mailbox that "has not been activated at this time." He called again. Same result.

"Do you know anyone's number besides Ananke's?" he asked.

"I have everyone's number."

"Why the hell didn't I get everyone's number?"

"Maybe so you wouldn't bother us?"

"Funny. Can you just try someone else, please?"

Liesel made a call but after several seconds said, "Rosario's not answering."

"We should go back to the hotel." Ricky shifted the truck into Drive.

"I agree."

They were almost back to Groveland when Liesel's phone rang.

"It's Rosario," she said.

Ricky tried to get the gist of the conversation, but for the most part Liesel only listened.

When she hung up, she said, "They are going to the hotel also."

"So they heard the explosion, too?"

"Ananke set it off."

He slammed on the brakes and turned to her. "Is she all

166

right?"

"She is okay. They are all okay. Now can we keep going, please?"

TWENTY-SEVEN

WORD OF THE fire had apparently not reached the people in Groveland yet. The town was operating as normal—campers filling their tanks with gas, café patrons eating an early lunch, and tourists walking in and out of the stores.

The fire station also seemed quiet.

Had it not gotten word? Ananke wondered.

What if the phone had been damaged after all, and the operator hadn't been able to hear her? Or maybe her disposable phone had sent her to a 911 call center not in the area. She was pretty sure there were safeguards against that, but she wasn't positive.

"Rosario, I need your—"

Lights on the fire station's front wall began flashing and the doors rolled open. Inside, more lights on the trucks spun beams of red while sirens blared.

"Never mind," she said.

Ananke hated fire, hated its unpredictability, and most of all the idea of dying in one. She would rather be tortured to death than barbecued alive.

As they pulled into the hotel parking lot, Ananke spotted Ricky and Liesel waiting by Ricky's truck. There were other people outside, too, guests and several employees of the hotel, all looking east.

"Didn't your parents tell you not to play with matches?" Ricky asked as Ananke climbed out of the van.

She barely heard him, as her attention was on the dark column of smoke rising above the forest.

"We've got to get out of here before the traffic backs up," she said. "Everyone grab your things and let's go. You have two minutes."

They sprinted into the building and were back at the vehicles before the deadline. When they pulled out of the lot, other guests, seeing that Ananke and her companions were fleeing, began running toward their own rooms.

"Go, go, go," Ananke told Dylan as he turned onto the highway.

They'd made it a few miles west of Groveland when Rosario's phone rang.

She answered it and glanced at Ananke. "She is." Another pause. "Okay. Sure." Rosario held the phone out. "It's the Administrator."

Ananke put the cell to her ear. "Yes?"

"Your phone is off."

"Permanently, I'm afraid."

"What happened?"

"I landed on it a little too hard after I was thrown into the trees by an explosion."

"Explosion? The fire?"

"Oh, you know about that, do you?"

"Details, please."

She updated him on her fun-filled morning.

"You couldn't have avoided the trip wire?" he said when she finished.

"Are you kidding me with that question? Look, if you want to play could-have/should-have you can hire someone else."

"My apologies. I'm sure you did all you could."

"Gee, thanks."

"Your explosion has changed the situation, however."

"I'd say. The forest is on fire."

"Yes, that, too. What I meant is, the kidnappers have made contact again."

Ananke paused. "Why?"

"They have moved the deadline up to eight a.m. tomorrow."

"Eight a.m.? *Tomorrow*? That's only twenty hours."

"A little under."

"How did they deliver the message? Text again?"

"E-mails, but to the same three families."

"When was it sent?"

"Four minutes after you triggered the bomb."

"Four minutes? That can't be a coincidence."

"No, it can't."

"Can you forward the e-mails to Rosario?"

"Already done."

Ananke finished the call and told the others about the change in deadline. Rosario connected her laptop to her phone and used the cell signal to log on to her e-mail.

"Got them," she said. She clicked a couple of times, spent several moments reading, and then handed the computer to Ananke.

The recipient's information was at the top, followed by the sender's e-mail address—not a name, only a string of seemingly random numbers and letters from one of those free e-mail services.

> SUBJECT: Your Daughter
>
> Hannah and her friends will die tomorrow at 8 a.m. The only way to prevent this is to transfer $20,000,000 split evenly into the following five accounts:

Below this was a list of account numbers, bank names, and routing numbers, all located outside the States in territories with lax customer identification laws.

> If the money is not received by 7:59 a.m., then you will be sent a follow-up e-mail with directions on where to find your daughter's body.

They compared the other two most recent e-mails to the first one. Three words had been changed in each to reflect the name and gender of the child.

"I'll send these to Shinji," Rosario said. "He can try to trace the send, and also look into the bank accounts while we're on the move."

As Ananke settled back in her seat, she spotted two fire trucks about a mile away, lights spinning. When they drew near, Dylan pulled to the side, waited until they passed, then sped up again.

"Where are we?" she asked.

"Just beyond someplace called the Moccasin Reservoir."

"I don't want to go too far until we decide where to go next. I think we'll be okay now, traffic-wise, so stop at the first good place you see."

He nodded.

The first good place turned out to be the parking lot of a mini-mart in a town called Chinese Camp. Ricky pulled his truck in beside them.

While everyone else went inside to grab something to drink and use the toilet, Ananke stayed in the van and studied the Google map of the area. By the time the others returned and piled into the van, the westbound traffic on the highway had begun to increase.

"We shouldn't stay here too much longer," Ricky said. "That traffic's going to be bumper to bumper before we know it."

"You see that?" Ananke pointed at a fork in the highway a few hundred feet to the northwest. "One way takes us back into the mountains, and the other toward Modesto. I don't know which way we need to go yet."

"Have you forgotten about your little kaboom, baby? It seems to me that back into the mountains is the last place we should head."

Ananke held up a finger an inch from his nose.

"This is the last time I tell you. I am *not* your baby. I am *not* your kitty-kat. I am *not* your kitten. My name is Ananke and I am your boss. The next time you say anything even remotely condescending, to me or to anyone else on the team— hell, to anyone else, period—I will have you tied up and inform the Administrator that you've decided to go back to prison. Have I made myself clear?"

"I'm a kindhearted man. You're taking this all the wrong way, baby."

"So be it," she said, pulling out her phone.

"Wait, wait. What did I do?"

"You said *baby*."

"Did I?"

She started dialing.

"Hold on," he said. "You don't need to do that. I get it. No more sweet stuff. It's a stab to my soul, but I'll do it."

She glared at him for a moment longer before putting her phone back in her pocket.

ALL FIVE OF Shinji's computer stations were working overtime. He'd even had to co-opt some processing power from the computer science department at Cal State Los Angeles, not that the school was aware of the intrusion, of course.

Two of his machines were dedicated to track down as much information as possible about the five bank account numbers the kidnappers were using. Two others were processing camera footage from all sides of Yosemite. The last he was using to analyze the metadata attached to the ransom e-mails.

Since they were all sent through an Internet e-mail service, the IP address associated with the sender was one owned by the service, not the actual computer the sender had used. For most people, that would've been as far as they could track things, but not for Shinji.

E-mail services such as the one in this case logged the computer IP address of the sender for their records, even though they didn't include it in the metadata. Most people didn't know that. They only knew an e-mail sent from such a place would appear anonymous. That's why those services were so popular for illegal activities.

Hacking into the e-mail system required exactly two minutes and seventeen seconds. Since Shinji knew the exact moments the e-mails had gone out, he was able to locate them in a flash.

"Good," he muttered.

The sending IP addresses were identical for all three e-mails. Not particularly surprising, but definitely reassuring. He

172

entered the number into an IP locator website and was presented with the follow results:

Country: United States
Region: Nevada
City: Tonopah

With this came latitude and longitude coordinates. He input these into Google Maps and hit RETURN. The satellite image zoomed in on the town of Tonopah, stopping directly on top of a building labeled STAR TRAVELER MOTEL.

While he thought it possible the kids were being held at a motel, he didn't think it highly likely. Still, it wasn't a dead end.

Shinji absently grabbed his can of Diet Mountain Dew, and had it halfway to his mouth before he realized it was empty. He tossed it into the nearly full recycle bin, snatched another from the mini-fridge under his desk, popped it open, and took a gulp.

He then set loose his considerable talents on the motel's computer system. As soon as he was through the firewall, he verified that the IP address belonged to one of the computers in the business center, and then hunted down the security system. As he had hoped, there was a camera inside the center, no doubt to deter anyone from stealing the equipment. He located the footage from around the time the ransom e-mails had been sent and let it play.

Sure enough, a man was sitting at the appropriate computer at the correct time. His features were hidden by the UNLV hoodie pulled over his head. That would have been disappointing if not for the fact that when he rose, he turned directly toward the camera for a solid three seconds, allowing Shinji to capture a clean image of his face.

Shinji used other motel cameras to track the man's movement through the building and into the parking lot, where he climbed into a white Nissan Altima and drove off. The car was too far away from the camera to get a full look at the license plate, but Shinji could make out three of the characters.

Those and the make and model of the car should be enough to find a match.

The discovery was too good to simply e-mail Rosario, so he reached for his phone. As he did, one of his computers dinged. He rolled his chair over and saw he'd received three hits on the Yosemite video footage. He brought up the clips and watched them.

When he finished the last, he grabbed his phone again. Boy, did he need to call the others now.

TWENTY-EIGHT

The Bunker

TESSA HERRERA STOOD in the center of the prison, directly below the hatch. She was scared, but not as scared as she'd been that first day when the armed motorcyclists had forced the van down a dirt road, and then made Tessa and the others transfer into the back of a waiting RV.

Her fear had hit its peak when, after they'd been driving for over an hour, the RV pulled to the side of the road and one of their chaperones, Mr. Carter, had been dragged outside. Everyone heard their captors shouting at him, enraged because he hadn't stopped asking questions since being taken hostage. Mr. Carter pleaded for them to not hurt him, and said he was sorry and that he'd shut up. For a few seconds there was silence, and Tessa thought maybe they were bringing him back in. The bang that rang out next was so loud, they all jumped.

"Oh, God," Conner had whispered.

Not having grown up in the best of neighborhoods, Tessa knew a gunshot when she heard one.

Moments later they were driving again, only without Mr. Carter in the vehicle.

When the RV next stopped, the students and their two remaining chaperones were blindfolded and led to a ladder they were told to climb down. When they were finally given permission to remove the covering from their eyes, they had just enough time to see they were in some kind of long room with curved walls, before the hatch above was shut and the space was plunged into complete darkness.

There they had been ever since.

Tessa had seen enough movies and TV shows to know the kidnappers were interested in a ransom. Why else would they have taken her and the others and stored them away?

They wouldn't be looking for money for her, of course. Her mom was a bookkeeper for the owner of a small dry-cleaning chain, and wouldn't have anywhere close to the kind of money the kidnappers would want. And her dad? Well, her mom always said nice things about him, but Tessa had never met him. The same lack of family fortune went for Renata and Mark.

No, the kidnappers were most likely only interested in getting money out of Grace's and Hannah's and Nicholas's families. They were the rich ones. Crazy rich, if Nicholas's bragging was true, and she was pretty sure it was.

She, Renata, and Mark happened to be in the wrong place at the wrong time and had no real value to the kidnappers. That troubled Tessa.

That was why she was standing under the hatch. It was the only spot she'd found where she could hear anything from above. Her hope was to overhear some of the kidnappers' plan and use the knowledge to somehow escape. She knew it was a long shot, but her only other choice was to sit around and wait for whatever was going to happen.

So far she hadn't learned much. Her biggest discovery had come a few hours earlier when she heard two of the captors called by name—Peterson and Nyland.

In the time since, she had heard nothing, but now she was picking up voices again, male like all the other times. They were too far from the hatch for her to pick up anything except their tone at first, but as they moved closer, words started coming through: *slow* and *driver* and *can't* and *time*.

Tessa tilted her head so that her right ear was pointed directly at the hatch.

"…later or could…"

"I don't…but if we…"

"We need…down. Right now."

Tessa straightened up, as she thought the hatch was about to open.

More talking. Even closer now.

"I'll just…it's over."

"You and me both."

"How long…to…do you think?"

"Cool it, asshole. You'll…like the rest…"

"Sorry. Guess I'm a little…"

Tessa's eyes grew wide.

That voice. The last one. The man who'd apologized.

Mr. Carter.

He wasn't dead. In fact, he seemed to be talking with the kidnappers like he was…

…one of them.

As this thought hit her, other things began flashing through her mind.

Mr. Carter replacing Mrs. Sorenson right before they left.

Mr. Carter's nervousness on the trip up to the mountains, though he'd played it off as excitement about the retreat.

Mr. Carter needing to go back to his room and "call home" more than anyone else did.

Mr. Carter vetoing the idea of an unplanned final hike before they headed home that morning, insisting the schedule must be adhered to, that it would be an inconvenience to the families expecting them home at a certain time.

Mr. Carter being pulled out of the RV and "shot" out of sight of Tessa and the others.

Tessa knew she couldn't tell everyone what she'd learned. Mr. Jones would likely go ballistic, and the other kids…well, you didn't tell kids that kind of thing, right?

Maybe if she got the chance, she could whisper it to Mrs. Wright. But she'd have to make sure no one else was around—not an easy task in the pitch-black of their cell.

She turned her ear to the hatch again, but the voices were gone.

ANDREW CARTER, REAL name Jeffrey Simmons though no one called him that anymore, said, "Sorry. Guess I'm a little on edge," and set the carton of bottled water on the ground next to the bag of apples Nyland had just put down. In an hour or so, they'd drop them through the hatch into the old doomsday shelter for the hostages' lunch.

"We're all on edge," Nyland said. "But nobody else is whining like you. Grab a beer. Calm the hell down."

He walked out of the dilapidated workshop that had been built over the shelter.

Carter paused near the center of the room and looked down at the hatch. Three of the kids down there were worth a lot of money. But one of the others was worth something, too. What and how much and why—he had no idea. He just knew what McGowan had told them.

"No matter what, nothing is to happen to the Herrera girl," McGowan had said after they brought the hostages to this godforsaken place, where they would stay until the ransom was paid. "And the job is not complete until we deliver her to the client. Alive."

While this may have been meant to instill vigilance in everyone, Carter saw the information for what it really was—a way to safeguard his fee in the event things went bad.

He smiled at the hatch, and then went out to grab one of those beers.

TWENTY-NINE

Chinese Camp, California

"IT'S SHINJI," ROSARIO said.

She turned her computer toward the others and accepted his video request.

The moment Shinji's tired-looking face appeared, Ricky leaned forward and waved. "Shinji! Buddy! How you doing?"

"Oh, hey, Ricky," Shinji said cautiously. "I'm okay, thanks." There was a pause before he added, "How are you?"

"Couldn't be better, my friend! Me. Ananke. Working together. It's a hell of a lot better than prison, I'll tell you that."

"I wouldn't know."

Ananke nudged Ricky away from the screen. "What's up?"

"Oh, do I have some stuff for you," Shinji said, his enthusiasm returning.

He first told them about where the e-mails had been sent from, and who had sent them. As he talked, he triggered a map to appear on Rosario's screen, showing the location of Tonopah. In two separate windows appeared images of the e-mail sender and his vehicle.

"There is nothing else around this place," Rosario said, zooming out on the map so they could see the town was miles and miles from anywhere. "If we are operating under the assumption that the new deadline was triggered by the explosion—"

"Which we are," Ananke said.

"—and was sent four minutes after it went off—"

"And it was."

"—and that the kidnappers could not know exactly when that would happen—"

"I don't see how they could have."

"—then the sender had to have been waiting in Tonopah for a day or two at least, correct? I mean, if he were in a big city, he could be out and about and still find someplace relatively quickly to e-mail the deadline change. In this place, though, if he is not in town, he is out of luck. So—"

"So the children are either nearby or the sender went there on purpose to wait until it was time to send a note," Liesel jumped in.

"Exactly."

Ananke nodded. The analysis was dead on. "We need to get there. Fast."

"Don't you want to hear what else I have for you?" Shinji said.

Everyone looked back at the chat box.

"What?" Ananke asked.

A video popped up and began to play. On the right side of the frame was a wooded area, and on the left the start of a meadow. Horizontally bisecting the image in the lower third was a two-lane road.

"This is from a north-facing security camera attached to a park-service building on Tioga Road, which is the eastern portion of Highway 120."

Highway 120 was the road that ran through Groveland, but on the west side it was known as Big Oak Flat Road.

"Here it comes," Shinji said.

Three cars passed through the frame eastbound, and another two west.

"There."

A large RV, the size of a touring bus, entered from the left. It had a trailer attached to the back, the contents of which were covered by a gray tarp. As the vehicle went by, Ananke saw that the back end of the tarp was flapping in the wind. As it lunged upward, she caught the glimpse of two upright tires.

"Motorcycle tires?" she asked.

"Definitely," Dylan said.

She frowned. "I'm sure dozens of people haul motorcycles down that road every day."

"Possibly. But then there's this."

Another clip played. A new location, same RV, but this time as it passed center frame, an updraft caught the flapping end of the tarp and kept it raised for a few seconds. This provided a much clearer view of the back of the bikes, and also revealed a third bike perched between them a bit farther forward in the trailer.

Again, in and of itself, the clip was not proof that the RV had carried away the kids.

"I assume you have something more," she said.

"Analysis confirms that the two visible tires are the same makes and models as those that made two of the tracks at the campsite you found. Also, that last clip gave my computer enough information to ID the bikes with a ninety-two percent certainty that they are also the makes and models of two of the bikes on the clip Ricky discovered. And don't forget, it's headed east, toward Nevada. Toward Tonopah."

Though still not conclusive, the connections could not be ignored.

Ananke sat back. "It looks like we know where we're going next."

SINCE DRIVING WOULD waste too much time, Shinji arranged for a Learjet to meet them at a private airfield outside East Oakdale, and soon they were on their way to Nevada.

As they flew over the Sierra Nevada Mountains, Ananke looked to the south for smoke but didn't spot anything. Had firefighters caught the fire in time? Or was she not looking in the right place?

You alerted the authorities. There's nothing more you can do, Ananke told herself. *Any fire is not your fault.*

Maybe, but it sure felt like it.

After they passed over the mountains and entered Nevada, the terrain rushing by below them became miles and miles of dry lake beds surrounded by barren rocky hills. When the pilot announced they were beginning their final approach, one thing was obvious. If there was such a place as the middle of nowhere, Tonopah was its capital.

The community's duel runway airport was east of town. As they neared the ground, the pilot warned that their landing might be a little rough.

And, boy, was he right.

The jet bounced all over the place as soon as it touched down. The reason became evident when they deplaned. The tarmac was in dire need of refinishing.

A gray Ford Explorer and a dark blue Dodge Ram pickup that Shinji had also arranged were waiting for them.

"Pickup's mine!" Ricky declared.

As long as Ananke didn't have to ride with him, that was fine by her.

Before leaving the airport, she touched base with Shinji to see if he'd come up with anything new.

"I have the RV turning toward Nevada on Highway 6, but after that, nothing. If they kept heading east, they would have had to change vehicles somewhere between the border and I-95. And if they didn't go that far, they're likely within fifty miles or so of Tonopah."

"What about our e-mailer?" Ananke asked.

"As of ten minutes ago, his car was parked in the lot belonging to the Goodwin Hotel and Casino."

"Is that a fact?"

THIRTY

A VIDEO CHAT request from Committee member Tuesday popped onto the Administrator's screen.

The Administrator accepted the call. "Mr. Tuesday, if you could give me just a moment, I can give you my full attention."

Tuesday did not look pleased. "Make it fast."

The Administrator put him on hold, and then, as he had been instructed to do if Tuesday requested any further one-on-one conversations, he covertly patched in Monday.

After activating Tuesday's line again, the Administrator said, "I apologize for the delay. How may I assist you?"

"I want an update on the kidnapping."

"We have an update for the full committee scheduled for this evening. Did you not receive your notification?"

"I am not about to wait that long! I brought this project to the Committee. Progress reports need to be available to me whenever I ask for them."

"Sir, that's not how the Committee works."

"This is a special case, and you know it. Additional oversight seems prudent."

The Administrator's gaze strayed to the monitor just left of the one Tuesday occupied, a change in focus that the Committee member would not register as anything but a pause. In the second monitor, Monday nodded.

"A valid point, Mr. Tuesday. Additional oversight would not be unreasonable." The Administrator made a show of opening a folder on his desk that had nothing to do with the field team's mission. It was a prop to put the other man at ease. "The field team has traced a lead to…" He paused, as if searching for the information. "Tonopah, Nevada."

"Is that where the kids are? Have they found them?"

"The team is en route, but they are not sure if that's where the children were taken or not."

"Then why are they going there?"

"It's where the computer that sent the ransom notes is located."

A startled pause. "Really? What about the person who sent them? Do they know who it is?"

"They're working on that." It wasn't exactly a lie. They didn't yet know the name of the man in the UNLV hoodie.

Tuesday grimaced. "What if it's a dead end? There's only, what? Seventeen hours left? Maybe we should just pay the ransom."

"That is also not how the Committee works."

"I don't mean us. I mean the families. We should tell them to pay."

"I'm sure you are aware that paying a ransom is no guarantee the hostages will be returned alive."

"And if the field team doesn't get to them before the deadline, the kids will be dead for sure. At least this way there's a chance."

"I'm confused, sir," the Administrator said. "If you think paying the ransom is the way to go, why did you bring this to the Committee in the first place?"

"I-I-I…" Tuesday sighed. "My apologies. Children in harm's way is something that always gets to me. I don't actually think paying the ransom is the right thing. I'm just…worried."

"We all are. I suggest that if we get down to the last hour or two before the deadline and the team has not yet been successful, then we can recommend paying."

"That sounds more than reasonable."

"Is there anything else I can help you with?"

Tuesday shook his head. "Just keep me updated on any changes."

184

"Of course."

Tuesday reached forward and his image winked off.

The Administrator verified that the connection had truly been severed before he transferred his boss's feed to the center screen.

"He clearly has no clue you've discovered his connection to the kidnapping," Monday said.

"You've read my report, then."

"I have. And I'm not happy about it. This should have been uncovered during the vetting process."

"It should have, and I take full responsibility. If you desire I tender my resignation, I—"

"If I wanted you to resign, I wouldn't dance around it. What I want is for you to be extra vigilant in your search to find us two new Committee members."

"Yes, sir," the Administrator said. "Would you like me to deliver the news to Tuesday now?"

Monday took a moment before saying, "No. After the mission is resolved. He is in no frame of mind to listen at the moment anyway."

THIRTY-ONE

THEY PARKED AT opposite ends of the Goodwin Hotel's parking lot to allow more flexibility if they ended up having to get out of there in a hurry.

To prevent drawing undue attention, Rosario, Liesel, and Ricky entered the hotel separately—Liesel and Ricky with instructions to search the lobby and restaurant area, while Rosario attempted a bit of techno magic at the reception desk. Ananke and Dylan would take the casino, but first they did a walk-by of the white Altima the target had been using.

A few crumpled food bags sat on the passenger seat, but otherwise the interior was empty.

Dylan nonchalantly tried the handle, but it was locked. "I could get it open in a snap, if you're inclined."

Ananke shook her head. The longer they loitered around the car, the greater chance the target would walk out and see them. There was, however, one thing she did want to do before they left the vehicle.

She retrieved her switchblade and tried to plunge it into the Altima's rear tire. Her angle was a bit off, so the blade caught on one of the steel belts and she wasn't sure how much damage she'd done. She considered puncturing it again, but before she could do so, several people exited the hotel and walked in their general direction. The one cut would have to do.

She and Dylan crossed to the casino entrance and went inside. Goodwin was no Caesar's Palace. The whole gaming operation took up no more space than a suite at the Wynn Hotel on the Vegas Strip. Even with the casino's smaller size, there were plenty of empty seats in front of slot machines and the three blackjack tables.

Ananke motioned for Dylan to check left while she went right. As she walked past the beckoning machines, she scanned the gamblers. Ninety percent were women, and of the ten percent of men, all were older than the guy the team was looking for. When she reached the blackjack tables, she looked back toward Dylan. He shook his head.

She gave the place another scan before rejoining him and heading into the hotel portion of the complex.

Rosario was at the front desk, talking to one of the clerks, while Liesel stood near the restaurant entryway at the other end of the lobby. Ricky was nowhere in sight.

Ananke nodded at Dylan to check the public hall that ran past the reception desk toward the back of the building. She then turned on her mic and whispered, "Liesel, anything?"

"He is not in the restaurant."

"Where's Ricky?"

"Said he was going to check upstairs."

"I never said anything about going upstairs."

"He said he had a…hunch, I believe is the word he used."

Ananke shut her eyes for a second to temper her frustration. Yes, Ricky knew how to hunt, but at the moment they were supposed to be working as a group. They needed to coordinate their efforts to avoid getting in one another's way.

"Ricky, come in."

A barely audible whisper came over the radio. "Can't talk."

"What's going on? Where are you?"

He said something else, but this time she couldn't make it out.

"Ricky?"

Nothing.

She tried again but he didn't answer. Swearing under her breath, she looked back at Liesel. "Did he specifically say where this hunch was taking him?"

"He did not."

While Ananke could waste time looking for him, it would be smarter to stick to the plan. So when Rosario stepped away from the reception desk and headed toward the elevators, Ananke did the same.

"You and Dylan keep watch here in the lobby," Ananke told Liesel as she crossed the lobby, arriving at the elevators a moment before the doors opened.

Conscious of the camera in the ceiling, Ananke and Rosario acted like they didn't know each other as they entered the car. Ananke then angled her head down to hide her face from the lens and whispered, "Did it work?"

Rosario flashed the screen of her phone. On it was the list of guests she'd secretly downloaded while she was talking to the check-in clerk. She studied the screen and highlighted several names.

The elevator dinged as they arrived on four, the highest floor.

Ananke exited first and looked around. Closed doors, used room-service dishes on the floor, a typical hotel floor. The only noise was a hum coming from an ice machine just off the elevator lobby—a lobby, she noted, that did not have a security camera.

"Did you find out the guy's room number?" she asked as Rosario joined her.

"There are eleven men staying alone. Give me five minutes, I could do some background checks and narrow things down."

"We don't have time for that. I have a better idea."

USING ANANKE'S METHOD, it only took them less than six minutes to check the fourth-floor rooms occupied by single male guests. There had been no answers at two, so they'd let themselves in and made sure no one was hiding inside. The other three were opened by men happily surprised to see two beautiful women at their door. None was the target, however, so Ananke and Rosario, acting as tipsy teases, apologized for getting the wrong room and stumbled off down the hallway.

When they reached the third floor, they heard a dull thud

from down the corridor. They shared a look and headed toward it. More thuds led them to a room halfway down the hall.

Rosario glanced at the room number and then at her phone. "It's on my list."

Ananke put her ear against the door. She heard a thump and the expulsion of a breath, and then, "Just calm down, asshole."

Ricky.

She picked the lock and shoved the door open.

At the other end of the short entrance hall, in the space between the bed and the dresser, Ricky lay on top of the e-mailer. The struggle that had been going on stopped as both men looked to see who'd come in.

"Hey, boss," Ricky said with a smile. "I found him!"

Rosario shut the door as Ananke strode into the room.

"What the hell do you think you're doing?" she asked.

"Capturing the bad guy? Isn't that why we're here?"

The e-mailer shoved at Ricky's chest, clearly realizing his bad situation had turned worse.

"Hey," Ricky barked. "Cool it. You ain't going—"

Somehow the e-mailer's leg slipped free, allowing him to swing his knee hard into Ricky's groin. As air exploded out of Ricky's mouth, the guy flipped him toward Ananke and scrambled to his feet. In a flash, he opened the sliding glass door at the back of the room and disappeared onto the balcony.

Ricky, eyes bulging, writhed on the floor at Ananke's feet, hindering her ability to get by him. Once she did, she sprinted to the door and outside.

The small patio was barely wide enough for the table and two chairs that occupied it, so the guy should have been right there, but he wasn't.

She looked over the railing. To both her relief and disappointment, no broken body lay on the sidewalk below.

She heard a pant and leaned a little farther out. "You little weasel," she said.

The target was hanging from a railing that ran underneath the patio.

Before she could figure out a way to haul him back up, he

swung once and dropped onto the balcony of the floor below.

"Are you kidding me?"

She clicked on her comm. "Liesel! Dylan! We found the target but he's trying to get away. Watch all exits and don't let him get out."

"There are only two of us down here," Dylan said. "How are we supposed to watch—"

"Just do it!"

Rosario, who had been backing her up in the doorway, moved to the side as Ananke ran back into the room.

"He jumped?" Rosario asked.

"To the floor below."

As they headed toward the door, Ananke glared at the still prone and cringing Ricky. "I swear to God, if we lose him…" She was out the door by then so she didn't finish.

Certain he hadn't stayed on the second floor for long, Ananke and Rosario skipped the elevator and flew down the stairs to ground level. Dylan was standing in the elevator lobby as they exited.

"He didn't come through here?" Ananke asked.

"Do you think I'd still be standing here if he had? What the hell happened?"

"Ricky happened," she growled.

Slowing their pace to not draw too much attention, the two women walked into the main lobby. Liesel was now across the room, where she could watch both the restaurant and casino exits.

"No sign of him?" Ananke asked.

Liesel shook her head.

Ananke and Rosario hurried outside through the main exit, and then headed along the path that ran beside the hotel, picking up speed until they were running. They whipped down the short side of the building and around the corner to the back, where the balcony the target had escaped from was located. There was no sign of him, not on any of the balconies or on the hotel grounds.

"His car!" Ananke said.

They raced down the back of the hotel, circled the building

190

into the parking lot, and rushed over to the guy's car. It was empty.

Ananke looked past the lot toward the heart of Tonopah, wondering if he'd run into town and was already blocks away. There was a way to find out.

She activated her comm. "Ricky, please tell me you're not still lying on the floor."

"I'm in the elevator," he replied, a strain in his voice.

"Good. When you reach the first floor, pull the fire alarm."

GAMBLERS AND GUESTS and hotel workers streamed into the casino's parking lot from every possible door. Ananke, Liesel, Rosario, and Dylan were spread out along the sidewalk that fronted the building so they could keep a watch on all exits. The still recovering Ricky was tasked with standing guard at their target's car.

Ananke was surprised at how many people had been inside. While she tried to get a look at each face, she knew the e-mailer could have snuck out in the middle of one of the many surges.

It wasn't long before fire engines and sheriff's cars started arriving, some having to honk at the gathering crowd to get through.

With the exiting crowd thinning to a trickle, Ananke swung around and searched the mob gathered in the lot. As far as she could tell, the e-mailer wasn't among them. She was just turning back when she noticed a car pulling out of a parking spot.

A white car.

She took three steps toward it before her view cleared enough for her to see it was a white Altima. Another step and the driver was visible.

She didn't see Ricky anywhere.

"Liesel!" Pointing, Ananke ran toward the car.

The e-mailer saw her coming and honked his horn get the people standing in his way to move. Some jumped at the sound, while others gave him the stink eye before moving to the side.

Ananke angled through a row of parked cars, sliding along

the rear fender of a Mercedes before reaching the aisle the e-mailer was driving down. She turned after him and sprinted down the asphalt in hopes of catching him before he reached the road. As she chased the vehicle, she noticed it was leaning downward at the back corner—where she'd stabbed the tire. As she'd feared, the cut wasn't as crippling as she'd wished. But it *was* having an effect.

The last of the crowd moved out of the Altima's way, giving the e-mailer a straight shot to the street. Ananke closed the gap to within two car lengths before the distance increased. She didn't stop until she reached the road, where it became clear she'd never catch up.

As she bent over to catch her breath, another vehicle raced up beside her and skidded to a halt.

"Get in!" Liesel yelled as she pushed open the rear crew cab of Ricky's truck.

Ananke started to pull herself in, but saw Ricky was behind the wheel. "I'll drive."

"Just get in," Ricky shouted, grimacing. "I got this."

The moment her butt hit the seat, Ricky slammed down the accelerator, the passenger door swinging shut without Ananke having to do a thing.

"What happened?" she asked, having a hard time keeping her anger in check. "You were supposed to keep him from getting to his car."

"He got behind me."

"He got *behind* you?"

"I swear, I was watching, but…I thought he would come from the hotel. He must have worked his way around the block to get to the car, and knocked me down when he saw me."

"You could have warned us he was getting away."

Rubbing the back of his head, he said, "By the time I…recovered, could think of it, I already heard you yelling." He must have taken her non-response as a silent rebuke, because he then added, "I know, I should have still heard him. I…I screwed up."

"Just drive," she said.

If it weren't for the need to respond to Goodwin's fire

192

alarm, Ananke was sure the sheriff's department would have been all over Ricky's truck as they sped through town after the Altima, but they made it all the way into the desert countryside unmolested.

Ahead, Ananke saw the Altima's back corner was getting closer and closer to the road.

"Slow down," she said.

Ricky scoffed. "Are you crazy? We've almost got him."

"Back away! Now!"

More a reaction to her tone than anything else, Ricky slowed the truck.

Less than ten seconds later, the rim of the sagging tire cut through the tread and sent a fountain of sparks into the air. A beat after this, the tire was shredded into a million pieces that spewed all over the road.

The car fishtailed wildly, twice going nearly perpendicular to the highway. The e-mailer tried to regain control, but each time he swung the car too far back the other way. The back end drifted off the road, allowing the empty rim to dig into the dirt shoulder.

At one moment, there was a cloud of dust, and at the next, the Altima was flying through the air.

The car flipped more than once before it landed on the passenger side. The tumbling didn't end there, as the car continued rolling over and over through the dirt and scrub. When it finally came to rest, the vehicle was back on its wheels.

Ananke jumped out of the truck before Ricky had fully stopped on the side of the road where the Altima was. As she raced across the desert, she could hear Liesel's footsteps not far behind her.

Not an inch of the Altima had escaped damage. One of the rear doors had flown off, while the trunk had been pounded down to half its original size. And though advances in safety technology had prevented the passenger cabin from collapsing, the metal skin that surrounded it had taken a serious beating.

The e-mailer was slumped in the driver's seat, his head resting on top of the displaced steering wheel, the now deflated airbag lying mostly in his lap. If he hadn't been wearing his seat belt, he would have probably been ejected through his missing window somewhere along the way.

Ananke tried to wrench his door open but it wouldn't move. She reached inside and touched his neck.

For a few seconds she thought she felt a pulse, but either it had been the last beats of his heart or wishful thinking on her part, because soon there was nothing.

Her head slumped forward. They had needed this asshole alive to tell them where the kids were.

"Dead?" Liesel asked.

"Yeah."

The two women searched the car, coming up with a small duffel bag full of clothes, a rental agreement for the car, and, with a glimmer of hope, the dead man's still-working smartphone.

Perhaps the e-mailer's untimely demise wasn't a total loss after all.

THIRTY-TWO

The Middle of Nowhere, Nevada

BY THE TIME Ananke and Liesel returned to the truck, Dylan and Rosario had arrived in the Explorer.

Ananke was relieved to see no other vehicles had stopped. Traffic on the two-lane highway was light. No one else had been close enough to witness the Altima's dramatic tumble across the dirt. At some point, though, someone would spot the mangled car sitting in the middle of the desert or the marks on the highway the bare wheel had made.

They needed to move on before that happened.

Dylan checked the map. "There's a rest stop a few miles to the west. Will that do?"

"Perfect," Ananke said.

On the drive, Ananke gave Rosario the dead man's phone and the rental agreement, and then made a more thorough check of the duffel bag, but as she'd guessed, it held only clothes.

"Ananke?" Rosario said suddenly.

Ananke looked over.

Rosario had been in the process of plugging the phone into her laptop, but had stopped and turned the cell's screen toward Ananke. Though the phone was neither ringing nor vibrating, a call was coming in, the caller ID reading V.

"Should I answer?" Rosario asked.

It was tempting, but Ananke shook her head. "We can't risk it."

If the person on the other end was also involved in the kidnapping—which seemed highly likely—it would be better for him or her to leave a message.

They watched the screen pulse one more time, and then V was replaced by MISSED CALL. Ten seconds later, VOICE MAIL appeared.

"Can you retrieve it?" Ananke asked.

"I should be able to."

Rosario got back to work hacking into the phone.

As they neared the rest stop, another call came in. V, and then MISSED CALL, and then VOICE MAIL.

Less than thirty seconds after that, a text message appeared on the screen.

V
Where the hell are you?

Ananke watched over Rosario's shoulder as the woman worked her magic, neither of them noticing that Dylan had parked and shut off the engine. It wasn't until Liesel opened the side door and climbed in that Ananke looked up.

"Where's Ricky?"

"Toilet," Liesel replied. "I think he wants to make sure his equipment is still working."

That earned a chuckle from the others.

"I'm in," Rosario said.

The lock screen of the dead man's smartphone had given way to rows of apps.

"Voice mails first," Ananke said.

Rosario navigated to the list. There were five messages, three already listened to. She played the first of the two new messages.

"Danny, call me back." The voice was male, raspy, with an aged but not too old quality.

Rosario touched the Play arrow for the newest message.

"Danny, goddammit. What's going on? Have you heard back yet? Call me as soon as you get this."

"Sounds like someone's getting anxious," Dylan said.

"You want to hear the others?" Rosario asked.

Ananke nodded.

Rosario played them in order of receipt.

Previous day, 9:10 a.m., same voice as before: "I know you're sleeping. Get your ass out of bed and call me."

Previous day, 5:43 p.m., same voice: "I swear to God, if you're playing blackjack, I'll…shit…don't lose too much. All clear here."

That morning, 7:37 a.m., same voice: "Still all clear. Hope you didn't get too drunk last night, asshole." A laugh at the end before the click.

It wasn't hard for Ananke to connect the dots. The dead man—Danny, apparently—was waiting for the go-ahead to send the ransom notes. He must have answered the call that had sent him into action. Or—

"Check his texts," she said.

Rosario opened the message app. V was the only conversation listed.

"Here's one from seconds after the explosion," Rosario said. She showed the screen to Ananke.

Barn's been found. Time to press SEND.

Danny responded immediately with:

On it

Four minutes later, he sent:

Messages away

V texted back:

Hourly check-ins from now on.
And the moment you get a response,
I want to know.

Every hour after that until seventy-five minutes ago, Danny sent:

Nothing yet

The most interesting text had been sent right about the time Ananke and the others were boarding the jet in California.

Head down. Trouble might be coming your way.

"How did they know we were coming here?" Liesel asked.

"That's an excellent question," Ananke said, the skin at the back of her neck simmering in anger.

"Aren't we the only ones who knew?" Dylan said. "Us and your man, Shinji. How much do you trust him?"

"With your life."

Looking a bit uncomfortable, Dylan said, "Had to ask, that's all. Didn't mean anything by it."

"There was someone else," Rosario said.

"Yes, there was," Ananke said. "Your phone, please."

When Rosario handed it over, Ananke climbed out of the Explorer and walked over to a deserted corner of the rest area, where she called the Administrator.

Before he could get out his first word, she said, "Is this all just one big setup?"

"I'm sorry?"

"This 'mission' you've given us, is it just some excuse to have us killed on a job?"

"What? That's rid—"

"Bring all of us recently excommunicated agents together, make us feel good about ourselves by giving us work, and then have us walk into an exploding barn, or perhaps track down someone who knows we're coming?"

"Of course not. Why would you say that?"

"Why? Because it turns out your ransom note sender was warned that we were on our way. The only person not on my team who knew our plans was you. Which—and excuse me if my logic is a bit hard to follow—means that either one of my team or you, Mr. Administrator, told him. The thing is, I know *we* didn't do it."

The line was quiet for several seconds before the Administrator said, "And you know he was aware you were coming how?"

"How doesn't matter. We know. I can't speak for the others, but I'm pretty sure you'll be getting more calls like this. I quit. I'd rather my previous employer send someone to slit my throat in the middle of the night than continue playing whatever game this is. At least that way, I'd have a good idea as to what was coming."

In a calm, measured voice, the Administrator said, "What about the missing children?"

"What missing children? Like I said, this is a setup."

"Only it's not. The kids are out there somewhere, and you are their only chance. I assure you, the mission is not a setup. And I am not the one who leaked your plans."

"If you didn't, someone working with you did."

"On that we agree."

Ananke blinked, not expecting his response.

"Whether you quit or not," he continued, "the leak will be identified and plugged. But I would very much appreciate it if you would remain on the job. I think the children are in more danger now than ever."

Ananke didn't want to believe him. She'd worked in the business for years, and knew clients lied all the time. But as much as she hated to admit it, her senses were telling her he was sincere.

Crap.

"Your mole might know where the children are," she said. "It could save a hell of a lot of time."

"So you're staying?"

Hoping she wouldn't hate herself later, she said, "For now."

"Thank you. If I am able to identify the leak in time, I'll pass on whatever I learn, but you should operate like you're not getting anything from me. In fact, unless something vital comes up, it might be better if we don't communicate again until the mission is complete, one way or the other."

If this really was a trap, that was also not the response she would have expected.

"That works for me."

THIRTY-THREE

THE LEAK COULD have come from only one source.

Tuesday.

The Administrator had told the man the field team was on its way to Tonopah.

And yet, Tuesday being the leak didn't make sense.

He wasn't involved with the kidnappers. He was, for all intents and purposes, a victim. His only goal would be seeing the kidnapping resolved with no harm coming to anyone.

No, Tuesday did not pass on the information. But he was, perhaps unwittingly, the source.

The Administrator's boss suspected someone was trying to sabotage the Committee.

What better way to do it than to tap into Tuesday's conversations?

The Administrator called his personal tech specialist. "I need a bug check. Covert. The potential victim cannot be aware of what you're doing. Whatever you find out, you will report only to me. Under no circumstances do you remove any bugs unless I give you the okay."

THIRTY-FOUR

Rest Stop
The Middle of Nowhere, Nevada

ANANKE HEADED BACK to the Explorer, still not sure she'd made the right decision to stay with the job.

"Hey, can I talk to you?"

She looked over her shoulder and saw Ricky walking, still gingerly, toward her from the restroom.

She almost kept going but he'd catch up to her eventually, so she turned and gave him an annoyed, "What?"

"Relax," he said, nearing. "I'm your friend, remember? And it ain't my fault he went all Evel Knievel. *He's* the one who decided to speed down the highway on a flat tire."

"Maybe. But he would have never been in that car if you hadn't let him get away."

"Okay, look. I may have made a mistake."

She stared at him, expressionless. "You *may* have made a mistake."

"And if I did, I just wanted to say, I'm…sorry." The word seemed to stick on his tongue before he could get it out.

He gave her his best puppy-dog eyes but she said nothing.

He groaned. "Come on. I'm laying it out here. Aren't you going to forgive me?"

"You haven't admitted to anything so you haven't really apologized, have you?"

"Well, I kinda did."

"Kinda?"

"Kitten, if we're going to—"

Her eyes narrowed, stopping him.

"What did I say? Oh, crap. Sorry." He looked genuinely surprised that last word had come out of his mouth. "What I was trying to say was, if we're going to be working together, then—"

She raised a finger in front of his face. "One time. That's all. When this is over, we go our separate ways. Understand?"

He screwed up his mouth, his brow scrunching together. "Uh, I think perhaps you're the one who doesn't understand. Didn't they—"

The driver's door of the Explorer opened and Dylan stuck his head out. "Rosario's got something."

Ananke hurried over and climbed inside, happy to be away from whatever bullshit Ricky was attempting to sell her. He followed a few paces behind.

"I think we found them," Rosario said.

"*Might* have found them," Shinji's voice chirped from the computer, his image in a small video box in the lower right corner, over a satellite map that filled the rest of the screen.

"Where?" Ananke asked.

"Somewhere in here." Rosario pointed at a red circle, about the size of a half dollar, overlying the center of the map. It covered a good portion of a desert valley about seventy miles to the north of their current position.

"That looks like a whole lot of nothing," Dylan said. At the map's current wide magnification level, there didn't appear to be any roads running through the circle, and the nearest highways were at least a dozen miles away.

"Took the words right out of my mouth, buddy," Ricky chimed in.

"How do you know this is the place?" Ananke asked.

"Cell-tower records," Rosario said. "Shinji used them to create a history of where the dead man's phone went."

"And this is where he went?"

"After starting in Yosemite and then heading east at the same time and route as the RV."

Ananke grinned, any lingering doubt that the kids had been in the RV gone.

"The phone traveled all the way to this point." Rosario

touched the map just below the highway that cut across the north end of the circled valley. "And then it disappeared."

"Disappeared?" Ricky said.

"Anywhere north or south of the highway and you'd lose cell signal."

"So he drove off into the desert?"

"Yes." She tapped the map. "If he had gone north, towers would have picked the phone up again when he reached this point. And if it had gone south"—she drew an imaginary border between the bottom of the circle and the highway on the south end—"it would have pinged towers along here. In fact, that's—"

"Unless he turned off his phone and pulled out the chip," Ricky said. "So in reality he could have stayed on the highway."

Rosario forced a smile. "He could have, yes. But he didn't. As I was about to say, the southern towers *did* pick him up the next morning at around eight right here." Again, she touched the screen near the southern highway.

"The guy could have still gone somewhere else," Ricky argued. "Say he turned off his phone once he was away from the towers, headed in another direction for the night, came back in time to drive all the way south, and then turned it on again and make it seem like he was in there the whole time."

Rosario magnified the map, brought the desert valley closer. "The only roads through that entire area are these." She pointed out four and adjusted the map to center on one of them. "This is the one that goes the farthest south. It's dirt, one lane, and looks in terrible shape. It also ends about thirty miles short of where the phone reappeared. So he'd have to make his own way from that point, which would take him hours. He wouldn't have had time to go anywhere else and get back."

"*Or*," Ricky said, "he drives all the way around on the nicely paved state roads, hops off in the south, drives into the desert until he's out of tower range, turns his phone back on and *voila*. He looks like he's been driving across the valley, but in reality the whole trip only took him two, maybe three hours tops."

As much as Ananke wished she could tell him he was an idiot, his alternate scenario—though a stretch—was possible.

"One more piece of information," Rosario said. "We also tracked the number for this V person who called the dead man. His phone disappeared at the same place and time, only his has not reappeared."

Ricky shrugged. "He could have disabled his phone, too."

"This is why I said *might*," Shinji said. "But it's the best lead we have."

"And least convoluted," Ananke said. "I think we should concentrate our effort within the circle, unless anyone has a better idea."

She looked around to make sure the others agreed. Even Ricky nodded.

"So you agree now?"

"I never said I didn't. I was just pointing out that there were alternate explanations. You're not looking for a group of yes men, are you?"

She shook her head. "I…appreciate your input."

Grinning, he said, "Thanks, boss."

Ananke looked at the computer again. "That circle covers a lot of ground. We need to narrow things down. I doubt they'd go far from one of the dirt roads. Can you see if anything jumps out?"

For the next few minutes, Rosario traced each road through the target area. When she finished, she'd found three places of interest.

Two were homesteads, a couple of miles apart. Each looked long abandoned, the houses and other buildings in various states of decay. Some of the structures, however, did appear intact enough to be used by the kidnappers.

The third location was an old mining facility halfway up the hillside on the east, about five miles from the closest homestead. Two decrepit buildings flanked a partially collapsed scaffolding over the shaft opening. There was also what looked like a flattened area large enough to park several vehicles.

It would make a lot of sense for the kidnappers to use one

of the locations as their base, instead of setting up camp in the wilderness. Still, Ananke knew, she and the others couldn't completely ignore the latter possibility.

She had Rosario move the map until the highway at the north end of the valley was visible.

"Zoom in there," Ananke said, pointing.

A moment later, a turnout on the north side of the highway sat center screen. Leading from it into the desert was a dirt road that ended after a quarter mile.

She tapped the dead end. "Correct me if I'm wrong, but that looks like a ridge."

Rosario studied the map for a second. "I believe so."

"From there, we should be able to see the whole valley."

"A good portion of it anyway."

Ananke leaned back, a plan coming together in her mind. When she was ready, she said, "Okay, here's what we're going to do. Rosario and Dylan, you'll take the Explorer back to Tonopah and pick up a few things we're going to need. As soon as you're done shopping, the rest of us will meet you here." Ananke pointed at the ridge again.

"So that means you're going to be riding with Leecie and me?" Ricky said, looking far too happy.

"No. It means you'll be riding with me." Ananke held out her hand. "Keys."

"Hold on there. I drive the truck."

"Keys."

"It needs a man's touch. We both know it."

Liesel whacked her elbow into Ricky's ribs. As air rushed out of his mouth, she said, "Give Ananke the keys."

The keys exchanged hands.

"And my name is Liesel, not Leecie. You will not forget this."

In a strained voice, Ricky said, "No. I guess I won't."

THIRTY-FIVE

The Bunker

CARTER WAS BEGINNING to worry.

McGowan had yet to reach Danny. This was especially troubling given that McGowan had passed on a tip from their employer that someone might have found out where Danny was.

Did his silence mean they'd captured him? Because if they got him talking, they'd find out about the camp soon enough and would be coming for Carter and the others next.

McGowan, however, was more angry than worried. "The asshole probably left town as soon as I warned him and is halfway to Vegas already."

Carter looked out at the motionless and soul-sucking desert from the shade of the RV's awning. God, he'd be glad to get out of there. He hated brown. He never wanted to see brown again unless it was on a beach.

Perhaps McGowan was right. Perhaps Danny had made a run for it. Perhaps everything else was still fine.

Perhaps.

But Carter would be a fool to bank on that. Nope, from this point forward, he needed to look out for number one.

As nonchalantly as possible, he pushed out of his chair and walked toward the RV entrance.

"If you're going inside, grab me another beer, would you?" Nyland asked.

"Sure," Carter said.

"And a bag of those spicy Doritos."

Carter nodded.

Five minutes later—after stuffing into a pillowcase a few bottles of water, some food, and other items he thought he might need, and stashing everything in a cabinet near the door—he brought Nyland his beer and chips.

"You not drinking?" Nyland asked.

"Maybe later."

"Your loss." Nyland raised his can. "Cheers."

Carter lifted an imaginary can of his own. "Cheers."

THIRTY-SIX

North of Nowhere

ANANKE LEANED AGAINST the truck and swept her binoculars across the valley. All but the very eastern edge was now in shadows. In another forty minutes, twilight would be in full bloom.

Even at maximum magnification, the ridge they were parked on was too far away for her to make out either of the homesteads. Ananke could, however, see the dark spot that was the scaffolding around the mine entrance. Too distant to tell if there were any cars or RVs near it, though.

Dominating the center of the darkening valley was a wide tan scar of a dry riverbed, created by eons of flash floods. Ananke checked the sky to make sure no rain clouds were gathering. Thankfully it was clear from horizon to horizon.

"Here they come," Liesel said from the other side of the truck.

Ananke lowered the binoculars and watched Dylan drive the Explorer up the dirt road to the ridge. As he parked, she, Liesel, and Ricky—who'd been lying across the truck's tailgate—walked over to meet Dylan and Rosario at the back of the SUV.

Dylan opened the hatch and pulled out a box. "We were only able to find four, so someone will have to go without. Even then, our choices weren't all that stellar, either." He pulled out four satellite phones.

"They are bigger than I wanted," Rosario said. "And not all the same brand, but they will do."

As long as a pint glass, the phones were also as thick as

paperback books—thankfully closer to *Misery* than *The Stand* on the Stephen King scale.

"I don't need one," Ricky said. "I work better alone."

"You'll be working alone, all right, but you get one," Ananke said. "And you'll answer every time I call."

He bowed his head dramatically. "Yes, ma'am."

"Rosario, you'll be with me," Ananke said. "So we can share."

Though they had comm gear, the signal quality would drop off considerably outside a couple of miles. Since the team would likely spread out farther than that, the satellite phones would fill in when the comms didn't work.

"Well, this is dumb," Ricky said as he finished mounting the phone's headset in one ear and the comm's in the other. "I look ridiculous."

"You do," Rosario said, her ears boasting their own wraparound look. "But it has nothing to do with the headsets."

Ananke, Dylan, and Liesel burst out in laughter. Ricky glared at them before he, too, joined in.

After the laugher died down, Rosario handed out the other items they'd picked up: flashlights, zip ties, and black clothing. By the time they were all geared up, the sun had set.

"Rosario and I will check out the farthest homestead. Ricky will drop us off on his way to the mine. You two," Ananke said to Dylan and Liesel, "have the closer place." She paused. "Before we go, disable all vehicle lights. Interior, brake, headlights, reverse. Don't miss anything. Once we're out there, no one should drive within a mile of any of these places. Park and walk the rest of the way. As close to the top and bottom of the hour as possible, check in with me." She paused. "Ricky, you'll be higher than any of us."

"I like the sound of that!" he said.

"Elevation-wise."

"Right. That's what I meant." He winked at the others.

"If you determine the mine is unoccupied," Ananke went on, "I want you to scan the valley and look for lights. If they're out there roughing it somewhere, they'll have something on."

"You're thinking like a hunter," Ricky said. "I like it."

"Anyone have questions?" Ananke looked around. "No? Good. Let's find those kids."

THE TWO VEHICLES entered the desert south of the highway in tandem, with Ananke leading the way in the truck.

As much as she wished they could race to their destinations, they had to be ultra-cautious. Navigating the two ruts in the sand that served as the dirt road was reason enough. Without the assistance of lights, it was all the more difficult. Even more important was keeping the sounds of their engines at a minimum to avoid alerting the kidnappers. At least they didn't have to contend with the moon, as it wouldn't be rising until the wee hours of the morning.

"We just passed out of cell range," Rosario announced.

Which meant they had entered the circle where the kids were being kept.

Hopefully.

They drove for another twenty minutes before they reached the fork in the road where the truck would part company with the Explorer.

Ananke triggered her comm. "Good luck."

"Thanks," Dylan said. "You, too."

The vehicles veered off in different directions, two black blobs moving through the gray-black night.

"A quarter mile," Rosario said, a minute later. She was monitoring their progress on her computer, which was hooked through her satellite phone.

Suddenly the front driver's side of the truck lurched downward. Ananke jerked the tire back onto the level surface and brought the vehicle to a stop.

"Nice driving there, boss," Ricky said.

She climbed out and took a good look at the road ahead, or, more accurately, the missing road. Apparently at some point in the not too distant past, a tributary of the now dry river had cut across the road, wiping away a fifty-foot section. The drop they experienced had been the truck dipping over the edge where the road had started to disappear.

Concerned that the sand might be soft enough to get stuck

in, she walked onto it. Though it was loose on top, it seemed to have a fairly solid base. She walked farther out to make sure that consistency remained the same. That's when she noticed the tire tracks.

After cupping a hand around the end of her flashlight, she turned it on and knelt down.

There were at least half a dozen imprints. A few were narrow enough to identify as belonging to motorcycles, while the others had been created by larger vehicles. From the design of the tread, she could tell none of the tires were made for off-roading. Street cars, then.

Perhaps even an RV.

She followed them across the wash to the other side where the road picked up again, before returning to the truck and telling Rosario and Ricky what she'd found.

"It's them," Ricky said.

"How can you know that?" Rosario asked.

"A hunter knows."

Ananke drove them across the tributary, sticking to the same path the other vehicles had used to avoid any sand traps.

"This is it," Rosario announced a few minutes later.

Ananke coasted to a stop and they all climbed out.

"If they're at the mine, don't do anything on your own."

"I won't," he said sincerely. This was the Ricky she liked, the focused Ricky, the cooperative Ricky.

"Stay safe."

"You, too, boss," he said, and then climbed into the driver's seat and drove off.

Ananke adjusted her backpack and looked over at Rosario. "Shall we?"

"LOOKS QUIET TO me," Dylan said. He handed the binoculars back to Liesel so she could take another look.

The abandoned homestead consisted of a house, a collapsed pile of wood that had probably been some kind of storage building, a separate stable, and a large area that had once been fenced in, where horses must have roamed. Neither of the still-standing buildings had a roof anymore, and only the stable had all its walls intact.

Liesel lowered the glasses. "No sign of anyone."

"Shall we make sure?" Dylan said.

She nodded. "Low and slow."

Crouching and with Liesel in the lead, they moved carefully through the scrub brush to the remains of the split-rail fence and took another look at the buildings. Still no movement.

When they reached the stables, Liesel motioned for Dylan to stay where he was, before she disappeared around the front of the building. He tried to listen for her footsteps, but she moved so quietly that he jumped when she suddenly walked up behind him and whispered, "Empty."

"How about scuffing the ground a little first, huh?"

She looked at him, not understanding.

"Never mind."

They moved on to the house.

The shorter wing of the L-shaped structure was in much better condition than the longer one. They crept to a window and peeked inside. Graffiti adorned the walls, and trash covered the floor. But there was nothing to indicate anyone had been there in a long time.

They moved around the front to the main, now doorless, entrance. Liesel gestured for Dylan to hold back while she went inside. As she neared the entrance, something caught Dylan's eye. It took a second before he realized it was a line, hovering in the doorway a few inches above the jamb, and Liesel was about to walk right into it.

"Stop!" he yelled as he launched himself through the air. He wrapped his arms around Liesel and knocked her down a second before her foot would have touched the line.

Though she lay still, her eyes darted back and forth. "Is someone coming?"

Dylan climbed off her, shaking his head. "You were about to kill both of us."

He walked back to the doorway, pulled out his flashlight, and shined it across the threshold. His eyes had not been playing tricks. It was a trip wire, ankle high.

Liesel pushed off the ground and moved in behind him.

Her eyes widened. "Thank you."

"You can buy me a pint later."

She retrieved her own flashlight and they both played their beam through the room. More debris and trash, but no other trip wires.

Liesel stepped inside, keeping her feet as far from the monofilament as possible.

Dylan swore under his breath and reluctantly followed.

Taking great care, they traced the monofilament along the wall into what must have once been a closet. There the line ran straight into a trigger box. A second monofilament line was also attached to the box. It ran out the other side of the closet, no doubt to another door. Attached to the other side of the box were four wires that ran, one each, into four bricks of C4.

Liesel stepped toward the explosives.

"Whoa, whoa, whoa," Dylan said. "Not sure we want to be messing with that."

She glanced back. "You have experience with explosives?"

"Damn right I do. I avoid them at every chance."

Moving much faster than he wished she would, she pulled the wires out of the bricks. With each yank, he flinched. When the last one came without a boom signaling the end of life, he let out a long breath.

After examining the trigger box, Liesel picked up an old nail and jammed it near where the trip wires were tied off. Next, she cut the three monofilaments, leaving a tail no more than a foot on each.

"Here," she said, and tossed the box at Dylan.

Caught off guard, he fumbled with the device and almost dropped it.

"Careful," she snapped.

"You might give me some warning next time."

"That nail should not come out."

He looked at the box. "What happens if it does?"

"Those cylinders on the other end of the wires—they are detonators." She mimed an explosion with her fingers. "It probably would not kill you, but would at least blow your hand off."

"Maybe you should carry it."

"You are the courier."

"Now you're just stereotyping."

RICKY DECIDED ANANKE'S instructions were more guidelines than hard and fast rules. She'd been erring heavily on the side of caution. She was good at that. But walk in the final *mile*? That was more overkill than he was willing to be subjected to.

A quarter mile would have been more reasonable, but he was willing to give in a little, so he stopped the truck a half mile away from the mine. He hurried across the desert and up the ridge that separated him from the mine site. When he neared the top, he dropped to all fours and crawled to the crest.

From this elevated position, he scanned the mine area through his binoculars, and confirmed what his senses were already telling him. This wasn't the place.

There were no RVs, no motorcycles, no cars, no trucks, no vehicles at all. And by the lack of tracks, nothing had been up here in months.

"Bummer," he mumbled.

He glanced out at the valley, wondering which of the other two groups had drawn the lucky straw, and almost instantly saw a muted glow.

He raised the binoculars. Reddish orange, and flickering.

A campfire.

It was about four or five miles away. Maybe a bit more. But definitely in the direction of the two homesteads.

Now whose spot is that? Ananke's and Rosario's, or Liesel's and Dylan's?

Ricky wasn't sure. He hadn't paid quite as close attention to the map as he probably should have. One of the pairs would be there, though, and the last thing they needed was for him to be walking around an abandoned mine while they needed help.

He pushed to his feet and scrambled back down the hill to his truck.

THIRTY-SEVEN

A LITTLE OVER halfway into their hike, Ananke and Rosario crossed the dirt driveway that connected the road they'd driven in on to the abandoned home.

Kneeling, Ananke swept the palm-controlled beam of her flashlight over the ground. More fresh tracks, like those on the river tributary—motorcycles and four-wheeled vehicles.

They continued on toward the homestead until a faint crackling ahead caused Ananke to whisper, "Down!"

She listened again. More crackling, tiny pops with no discernible rhythm, but distinct. A fire was burning somewhere ahead, maybe a hundred or hundred fifty yards away.

Staying close to the ground, they moved forward.

From the satellite image, they knew the property consisted of a main house, the remains of what had probably been a three- or four-vehicle carport, and an outbuilding of some type. The latter was not quite large enough to be a barn, more like a big storage shed or workshop. It was also the one least damaged by time. So it was the silhouette of this structure that Ananke looked for.

When she finally spotted it, something was strange about it. It seemed longer than it should have been, almost like it had grown a rectangular tail that pointed toward the ruins of the house. She looked at it through her binoculars, and then handed the glasses to Rosario.

"You were right," Ananke said. "They're here."

The extra shape was not part of the outbuilding. Even though it was mostly just a dark shadow, there was more than enough starlight to pick out wheels at the corners. It wasn't a building but a large vehicle, the same size and shape as the RV that had left Yosemite pulling a trailer full of motorbikes.

She swung the binoculars to the other side of the outbuilding, and for a moment thought there was another vehicle about twenty feet to the side of it. After staring at it for a few seconds, she realized it was a giant cylinder lying on its side. The properties' water tower, most likely, that had fallen over who knows how long ago.

She moved her gaze back to the vehicle. Nothing had changed. After clicking on her comm, she said, "If anyone can hear me, we've got eyes on the RV." She waited a moment, but there was no response. "Liesel? Dylan?" A pause. "Ricky?" Still nothing.

She started to pull out her sat phone, but Rosario touched her arm and pointed toward the outbuilding. At first Ananke couldn't figure out what she was supposed to be looking at, and then she saw someone halfway between the RV and where she and Rosario were, heading their way.

Ananke exchanged the sat phone for her switchblade and opened the knife, but the figure didn't come all the way to them. Whoever it was stopped about fifty feet away. A man, most likely, based on his shape, though that wasn't a given. What *was* clear was the barrel of a rifle sticking up over his shoulder.

They heard a zipper, and then a dull splash of a stream hitting the ground.

Definitely a man.

If they were closer, they might have been able to sneak behind him and take him down before he could raise an alarm, but at their current distance, the chance of him hearing them was too high.

When he finished, he zipped up and walked back toward the RV.

With Rosario following her, Ananke arced to the left, on a path that would take them into the desert on the other side of what was left of the house, and far from the RV and the man with a rifle.

When they stopped again, Ananke checked the breeze and confirmed it was blowing away from the house before she pulled out her sat phone.

Her first call was to Dylan.

"No one here," he said. "But Liesel does owe me her life." He told her about the C4.

"We need you to get over here quick. We found them."

She heard him pull the phone away and say, "Ananke and Rosario found them!" Then he was back. "We'll get there as fast as we can."

Next came Ricky.

"Almost there already," he said.

"What about the mine?"

"The place was deserted."

"No trip wire? No bomb?"

"Bomb?"

"Liesel and Dylan found a booby trap at their location."

"I guess there *might* have been one," he said.

"You didn't check?"

"I got a good enough look at the place. But then I saw the campfire, and I knew that's where I needed to be."

"Just hurry," she told him. "And don't do anything else stupid."

"What do you mean anything—"

She hung up.

Wanting to get a better look at the kidnappers' setup, she and Rosario circled around the water-tower end to the back of the property, sticking far enough in the desert that they wouldn't be noticed. From there, they could see the campfire Ananke had heard and Ricky had spotted. Its glow allowed them to get a better view of the RV and verify it was the one they were looking for. And if that wasn't enough to prove they were in the right spot, parked near the front of the RV were three touring motorcycles.

Ananke studied the setup through the binoculars. The RV abutted the far corner of the outbuilding, creating a wind and visual block for anyone approaching from the front of the property. The fire pit sat within the L the vehicle and building made. Though the light was too weak to cut through the darkness beyond the building's open garage-type door, it was enough for Ananke to pick out four men—two sitting near the fire, one leaning against the building wall, and the last lying on a lounge chair near the RV door, fast asleep.

She studied the area, wanting to commit as much as she could to memory—the placement of boxes, the bags of trash, the table next to the lounge with what looked like a radio on it, the portable barbecue off to the side.

As she did this, a sudden, pulsating beep sounded near the RV. The four men were instantly in motion, three of them rushing toward a container next to the vehicle. Just as they reached it, the camper's door flew open and two more men hurried out.

The guy who hadn't run toward the container was the one who'd been peeing. She could tell because the rifle she'd seen slung over his shoulder was now in his hands, the stock pressed against his shoulder.

She looked back at the others as they pulled more rifles out of the plastic box and handed them around.

One of the men stepped over to the small table and touched what she'd initially thought was a radio. The beeping stopped.

Ananke didn't know how or where or who had done it, but she knew one of her team had set off an alarm and taken away the advantage of surprise.

LIKE ON HIS approach to the mine, Ricky was not about to walk a mile in, especially now that they knew for sure the kidnappers were there. So when he found the rutted path that served as the mile-long driveway, he turned onto it and drove as far as he felt he could push it.

Unfortunately, without headlights, he didn't see the trip wire strung across the road a quarter mile back from where he finally stopped.

This line, instead of setting off a stash of C4, triggered a beacon that activated an alarm at the kidnappers' camp.

Ignorant of what he'd done, and happy as a lark at what he was sure would soon be another heroic Ricky moment, he cut across the desert toward the house.

THOUGH THEY DIDN'T know it, Liesel and Dylan left the SUV only about two dozen feet from where Ananke and Rosario had been dropped off.

They covered three quarters of a mile as fast as the terrain would allow, and then proceeded more cautiously from that point forward.

They were maybe a hundred yards from the big building when Liesel tapped Dylan's arm and pointed toward the west side of the property. He saw a shadow moving fast, *away* from the buildings.

"What is that?" he whispered. "Coyote?"

"I do not know. How big do coyotes get?"

"I don't know. Seemed kind of big, though. Should we check it out?"

They watched the shadow for a few more seconds, then Liesel shook her head. "If it was important, Ananke would have let us know."

They continued toward the buildings, the moving shadow quickly disappearing into the vast valley.

THIRTY-EIGHT

CARTER SLEPT IN fits and starts, his dreams an unending rollercoaster of disaster, all with him in the starring role.

When the beep of the perimeter alarm went off, it wove for a moment into his nightmare before his mind registered it was real. He shot up and looked around.

Whitmore and Nyland were already out of their beds, pulling on clothes.

"Get a move on it!" Nyland shouted at Carter.

Carter managed to say, "Right behind you," and then watched as the others rushed out of the camper.

The alarm could mean only one thing. It was over. Those who had gone after Danny were coming for them. Soon Carter would be either on his way to jail for the rest of his life or dead.

Only if you do nothing.

He blinked. Right. He'd prepared for this.

He scooted off the bed, shoved his feet into his shoes, and snatched his pistol off the counter. After attaching the suppressor, he grabbed his getaway bag from the cabinet near the exit and eased the RV door open.

As he'd hoped, the others were out of sight, headed off for the defense positions McGowan had assigned them in the event of trouble.

Carter crept down the steps and slipped along the side of the camper to the workshop. There he stopped and looked around.

He could see the feet of the person lying across the top of the RV. That would be Nyland, if Carter remembered McGowan's assignments correctly. Rocca would be around the front of the RV, low on the ground. The only other position he could remember was McGowan's. He'd be over near the collapsed house, giving them a wider view of whatever was coming.

Carter scanned the area but didn't see the others, so he crept inside the workshop to collect his insurance.

THIRTY-NINE

TESSA OPENED HER eyes and cocked her head.

What's that noise?

It was like a hum, but growing louder and softer like a siren.

She sat up.

Around her, she could hear the snores and breathing of the others. Someone else was awake, though. She could hear the person stirring.

"Hello?" she said.

"Who is that?"

"It's me, Mrs. Wright," Tessa said, recognizing the voice.

"Are you okay? You need something?"

Mrs. Wright had been the one who kept everyone calm and together. While Tessa had recognized that fact, she didn't think the others had.

"Do you hear that noise?" Tessa asked.

"You hear it, too?"

"Yeah, like a buzzer or something."

"I thought I was hearing things."

Tessa stood up and tried to figure out what the noise could be. A TV? Something on a radio?

"You should try to get some sleep," Mrs. Wright said.

"I will," Tessa said, but what she was thinking was, if she could get a little closer to the hatch, maybe she'd be able to figure out what was going on.

She rose onto her tippy toes and turned her ear upward. Just as she reached her full extension, the noise stopped.

She frowned, but remained there for another minute in case it started up again. Finally, she gave up and lay back down on the floor. But before she closed her eyes, she heard the familiar sound of metal scraping metal that always preceded the hatch opening.

Some of the others stirred, woken by the noise.

"What was that?" Renata asked.

"Quiet," Nicholas moaned.

"Is that the hatch?" Mr. Jones asked, the panic in his voice as strong as ever.

As if in answer to his question, the hatch moved upward.

It was dark on the other side, though not as dark as it was in their cell, so Tessa could make out the silhouette of the man looking down at them. There was something in his hand. At first she thought maybe it was more food he was going to drop down, but then he shifted and the shape of the item became clear.

A gun, one with a longer barrel than she'd ever seen on TV or in the movies.

"Tessa Herrera!" the man barked in a harsh whisper.

Tessa froze, her skin crawling.

From off to the side, she could hear someone moving toward the hatch, and then Mrs. Wright saying, "What do you want?"

"Are you deaf?" the man replied. "I said Tessa!"

The end of the rope ladder they'd used to climb down dropped into the cell, nearly hitting Tessa on the head.

"Send her up," the man ordered.

"Absolutely not," Mrs. Wright said. "You can't—"

The metallic slide of a pistol echoed down into the cell. "Send her up or I start shooting."

"What do you want with her?"

A pause. "She gets to go home."

"I don't believe you. She stays with us."

Thup.

The sound was powerful and yet muffled.

Mrs. Wright cried out in pain.

"Mrs. Wright?" Tessa said.

Using the chaperone's rapid stuttering breaths to guide her, Tessa stumbled over to Mrs. Wright.

"Are you okay?" she asked.

The woman's shirt was sticky.

"Tessa, get up here now," the kidnapper ordered. "Or do you want me to shoot someone else?"

"For God's sake, kid, get up the ladder!" Mr. Jones snapped.

Tessa didn't want to go, but if she stayed she'd be responsible for anyone else who was shot.

"I-I'm coming," she said, then added in a whisper to the others, "Someone help Mrs. Wright."

Climbing a rope ladder was difficult enough in normal circumstances. With her body shaking in fear, it seemed near impossible. When she finally neared the top, the kidnapper grabbed the back of her shirt, hauled her over the lip, and dumped Tessa on the ground.

"Don't move," the man ordered and then shut the hatch.

It was Mr. Carter.

Scared, confused, and furious at Mr. Carter's deception, Tessa said, "What do you want with me?"

"What I want is for you to do everything I say, starting with no talking unless I give you permission. If you disobey me even once, I'll shoot you. Nod if you understand."

Tessa nodded.

Mr. Carter grabbed Tessa's shoulder and twisted her around.

For the first time Tessa realized they were inside some kind of building. Before her was a large open doorway, and beyond it she could see a campfire but little else.

"Nice and quiet," Mr. Carter whispered as he shoved Tessa forward without letting go.

When they reached the opening, Mr. Carter yanked Tessa against his chest. "Don't forget I have this," he whispered, shoving his gun into her ribs.

He guided her outside and down to the corner of the building. The only light was the campfire to their left. Everywhere else was darkness. Too much for a city to be nearby.

Mr. Carter leaned around the corner to look down the side,

forcing Tessa to do the same. In the distance, she could see the shapes of mountains, not as tall as the Sierras but high enough to blot out some of the sky.

Mr. Carter's arm pressed against her tighter, causing Tessa to wince.

"Not a sound," he whispered so low she almost couldn't hear him.

At the other end of the building stood the shadow of a man. He had his back to them, and was looking around the far corner at something the same way they were looking around theirs at him.

Mr. Carter clamped a hand on Tessa's shoulder, and then they crept around the corner and down the building until they were only a few feet from the other man. The shadow remained unaware of their presence, until Mr. Carter moved up next to Tessa and tapped the man in the back with the long barrel of his gun.

The man whipped around.

Thup.

Tessa had assumed the man was another one of the kidnappers, and that Mr. Carter was being silent because of whatever trouble the other man was anticipating. So the flash of the gun and that weird muffled sound caught her completely off guard.

She sucked in a loud breath as the other man dropped to the ground, blood covering the front of his shirt.

Mr. Carter glared at her, and for a moment Tessa thought she was about to be next, but then he shoved her forward again toward the wild open expanse of dirt and low bushes.

"Move."

FORTY

FROM THEIR POSITION south of the camp, Ananke and Rosario watched the kidnappers spread out and noted where each went. Three of the men took up positions on or around the RV and the outbuilding, two others headed over to the water tower, while the last moved east to a pile of debris in front of the dilapidated house.

The way they'd deployed led Ananke to conclude the men were amateurs compared to the adversaries she'd run up against in her world. An operative like her would have sent at least two men into the desert to circle around and get behind the unknown intruder. Then again, she would have never allowed them to hang out in the same place to begin with.

If she had been running the operation, she would have had two dugout positions along the entrance road, an around-the-clock spotter on the roof of the RV, one guy watching the rear, and the last two at the camp.

She reminded herself the kidnappers *did* have access to C4 and knew how to use it, so rookie league or not, caution was still dictated.

She signaled for Rosario to follow her, but before they could move, a seventh man stepped out of the RV. He was carrying a bag of some kind and not moving nearly as fast as his colleagues. He crossed along the side of the vehicle and disappeared into the building.

Figuring he was part of the contingent staying close to the camp, Ananke decided to stay with her current plan and lead Rosario through the desert to the area behind the house.

There they split, Rosario circling around the east end of the ruins, and Ananke working her way along the more exposed west side, gun at the small of her back, knife in hand.

Every few steps she shot a glance back at the camp, but the men she could see were all focused on the desert to the north and weren't paying attention to anything on their flank. When she reached the front edge of the house, she stopped and softly clicked her tongue once into her comm. Almost instantly, she received a click back, indicating Rosario was also in position.

Ananke gave Rosario the signal to begin.

All was silent for several seconds, then, from off to the east came the dull thud of something hitting the sand. It wasn't loud enough for those back at the RV to hear, but what about the man in front of the house?

Ananke peeked around the corner.

As she'd hoped, her target's attention had been drawn eastward by the noise Rosario created.

Fast and quiet, Ananke skimmed along the front of the house, slipped in behind the man, and wrapped her arm around his neck before he even realized she was there. He tensed as she squeezed and tried to grab her, but his efforts were too late.

After he was unconscious, she laid him on the ground, removed his shirt, and tied it around his head to gag him. She then zip-tied his ankles and wrists together.

A quick body search came up with a cell phone, a wallet, and two hundred dollars in cash. She took it all, and his rifle, before retreating around the building to where Rosario was waiting.

"Who's next?" Rosario asked.

WHEN RICKY SAW a shadow move on top of the RV, he dropped to his belly.

It had to be a lookout, but one who wasn't that good at his job, since no bullets were flying in Ricky's directions.

He weaved a path through the sagebrush toward the large shed, staying as low as possible to hide his movements. He figured if he didn't hear from Ananke by the time he reached the building, he would sneak around the back of the structure and take the kidnappers by surprise. He wasn't worried about the details of how. As he was fond of saying, Ricky Orbits always finds a way.

A little more than halfway to his target destination, the ground in front of him suddenly dropped away. He halted just shy of the edge and peeked into the break. Another one of those damn flash-flood channels, he realized. This one much smaller than those he'd seen before but equally as deep, three feet across and about the same down.

As he lowered himself into the miniature canyon, he had one of his brainstorms. Though he could climb out the other side and continue on his previous path, he sensed he could take this tributary, as long as it stayed deep enough, almost all the way to the RV unseen. He could then sneak under the vehicle and come at the men from a direction none of them would be expecting.

Oh, he liked that idea. He liked it a whole lot.

Grinning ear to ear, he set off on his path to glory.

AS LIESEL AND Dylan neared the outbuilding, they spotted four of the kidnappers, one on the roof of the RV, another huddled against the vehicle's front bumper, and the other two crouched next to a collapsed structure on the side of the building opposite the camper.

Dylan thought it would be nice to know how many in total they were dealing with, but he kept it to himself since Liesel would probably slit his throat if he made any noise.

They went wide to the west so they wouldn't draw the attention of the men next to what now looked like an old water tank, but before they made it behind the outbuilding, Liesel raised a fist above her shoulder, telling Dylan to stop. She continued to the back corner on her own.

As Dylan watched her progress, he noticed a lump on the ground sticking out from the back of the building. Rocks? Some trash? Whatever it was, it seemed to be what had caught Liesel's attention. She lowered to a knee next to the shape and leaned over it. After a few seconds, she waved for Dylan to join her.

The shape turned out to be a man, his shirt dark with blood from a bullet wound to the chest.

"Dead?" Dylan whispered.

Liesel nodded.

They headed down the back of the building.

Ten feet before they reached the other end, Liesel suddenly stopped and shot a look into the wilderness off to their right. Dylan turned just in time to see the two human silhouettes rise from among the sagebrush. One was holding a rifle, and for half a second Dylan wondered why Liesel hadn't taken a shot at them. But when the two started walking toward them, he saw they were Ananke and Rosario.

Perhaps it was a good thing he didn't have a gun.

As soon as Ananke and Rosario joined them, Dylan started to whisper, "Boy, are we glad to see you," but the first word hadn't even fully crossed his lips when Liesel jammed her hand over his mouth and raised an annoyed eyebrow.

He knew it was unlikely anyone else would have heard, but the point was taken. He nodded that he understood and Liesel lowered her hand.

She pointed back toward the other end of the building, and mimed to the other two about finding the dead man.

Surprised, Ananke silently asked if Liesel or Dylan had killed him.

Liesel shook her head and shrugged.

After taking a moment to think, Ananke held up seven fingers, pointed toward the body, and lowered one. Next, she motioned in the other direction and lowered a second finger, leaving only five. She then crouched down and sketched out a plan in the dirt.

When everyone indicated they understood, she mouthed, "Good luck," and they moved out.

RICKY WOULD HAVE been happier if the walls of the narrow tributary bed went on a bit longer before tapering off.

The RV was *right there*. Sure, he could reach it in seconds, but that would mean crossing ten feet of open ground, where he'd be totally exposed to the lookout on the roof. If the guy was even barely competent, Ricky would be seen.

What Ricky needed was a distraction. What he had was

nothing. Not even a stupid rock he could throw at the side of the garage. Hell, there wasn't even a pebble. Just sand, sand, and more sand.

He considered radioing to get one of the others to make some noise for him, but he was too close. The moment he opened his mouth, he'd give himself away.

He swore silently. A perfectly good ambush opportunity wast—

Ricky froze.

The lookout's silhouette had risen a few inches.

Had the man seen him?

Oh, crap. That's just what I need!

Ricky put his palms on the sand to make his retreat, but paused.

The guy wasn't looking in Ricky's direction. He was looking over his shoulder, toward the far side of the RV.

After a few seconds, the lookout moved again, but instead of returning to his previous spot, he pulled back away from the edge and repositioned in a spot that took him out of Rickey's sight.

Well, wasn't that nice of him.

Grinning again, Ricky slipped out of the stream bed and crawled over to the RV.

ANANKE SLID AROUND the corner of the outbuilding and crept to the open doorway. No matter what she did, the moment any part of her body crossed into the opening, it would be seen by the guy who'd gone inside. Better to go all in. She shouldered the rifle in favor of her sound-suppressed pistol, and then, keeping low, rushed inside.

She swung the muzzle of her gun back and forth, looking for the target. But no one was there. What the hell? She'd seen the seventh guy enter the building, and had been sure he was still in there.

She swung around again, in case she'd missed a spot he might have been hiding in.

Nothing. He must have left when she and Rosario were over at the house.

That was disappointing. She'd been hoping to cross a third kidnapper off the list.

Even more disappointing was that the kids weren't inside, either. So the only other place they could be was inside the RV. Which meant there was probably at least an eighth kidnapper. They were like ants. Eliminate one and another appeared.

The kidnappers had been using the outbuilding for storage. Along one wall were a few boxes of bottled water and some sort of prepackaged food. There was also a generator, and two floodlights on stands sitting near a mound of concrete in the center of the room. Both were off. She wasn't sure what the men could be using them for, but until all threats were neutralized, there was no time to investigate.

She clicked her tongue and Rosario joined her inside.

Their remaining task was dealing with the two men at the RV—the one on top and the one crouched near the front. Liesel and Dylan had headed to a tipped-over water tank on the opposite side of the building, to handle the two men who'd hunkered down there.

Ananke took a good look at the RV from the darkness of the shed. The man on top was stretched out so that his heels were a few feet above the RV's side door. Taking care of him from behind would be child's play. First, though, she needed to deal with the guy around the front of the RV.

Ananke led the way past the campfire and along the RV, to just short of the front end. Easing forward, she leaned her head out only enough to see the man.

Good. He was crouched in front of the far headlight, looking out toward the driveway. The not-so-good part was the M16 semiautomatic he held.

Ananke pulled back and had a quick, silent confab with Rosario. Rosario moved to a position where she could aim her pistol at the man on the roof and take care of him if necessary.

Ananke gently laid the her rifle on the ground so that it wouldn't get in her way, gave Rosario a thumbs-up, and snuck around to the front of the RV.

The man was gone.

She swung her pistol in an arc and made sure he wasn't

anywhere in sight. The only other place he could have gone was around the corner of the vehicle to the driver's side. She lowered to her hands and knees so she could look under the vehicle and see where he was.

She saw him all right. Only he wasn't on the other side of the RV. He was lying, unconscious, directly below the front axle.

Beyond him, a pair of feet was wiggling under the carriage toward the back of the vehicle.

Ananke returned to the campfire side and looked under the RV again. The crawler had just reached the back bumper and was pulling himself from under the RV. There was plenty of starlight for her to see Ricky's face.

What the hell is he doing?

There was no way to call out to him without alerting those they hadn't taken care of yet.

She considered crawling after him, but as soon as he'd fully extracted himself, he stood up. A moment later, his feet disappeared upward.

Groaning, she hurried to the RV door. Out of the corner of her eye, she could see Rosario looking confused, but Ananke had no time to explain. Ricky was about to blow the whole operation.

She set her pistol on the ground, and then quietly opened the door and stepped onto the threshold. From there, she grabbed the roof and began pulling herself up.

When her gaze cleared the roofline, she checked the lookout first—he hadn't moved—and then the back of the vehicle.

There was a second when she thought her fears were unfounded, that Ricky was not about to slither over the top. But a moment later, that was exactly what he did.

Not waiting to see if the lookout spotted Ricky, Ananke grabbed the man's pant leg and leaned to the side as she yanked him off the roof. He tried to grab the edge as he passed over it, but missed.

Ricky looked at her in disbelief and whispered, "What did you—"

She shot up a finger. ""I'm trying very hard to find a reason not to put you on the ground with him. So don't say another word."

"But I—"

She glowered at him and he pulled an invisible zipper across his lips.

Ananke dropped to the ground, expecting to find the kidnapper lying there with the wind knocked out of him at most, with Rosario watching over him. But that wasn't the case. On his way down, he had apparently landed on one of the camping chairs. One of the aluminum legs had broken free and speared his chest. He was lying on his back with the chair leg sticking out of him like a flagpole, blood rushing from the wound.

BY ALL RIGHTS Dylan should have been dead.

He and Liesel had split up as they approached the water tank. He was supposed to go around the far side and let her know what he saw. In other words, get out of her way. That was fine by him.

Turned out he wasn't the only one heading in that direction. He totally didn't see the kidnapper until he was only a few feet behind the asshole. The guy wasn't supposed to be out there. He was supposed to be over at the water tank with his buddy.

Dylan's eyes widened.

Is the other guy around here, too?

He looked behind him, but the guy standing four feet in front of him was the only one there.

Still looking over his shoulder, Dylan took a tentative backward step, intending to disappear into the night, but he missed seeing the dried remains of the bush.

Crunch.

The kidnapper whirled around, his semiautomatic rifle swinging with him. Reflexively, Dylan charged and slammed into the guy's torso. As they flopped onto the desert floor, the rifle slipped from the guy's hands and bounced off the back of Dylan's head.

A gray tunnel started closing down Dylan's vision, but he forced it away.

The effort cost him any advantage he might have had, however, and when his vision cleared, he saw the muzzle of the semiautomatic pointing at his face. He rolled to his right, knowing that doing so probably wouldn't keep him alive for more than a second or two, but he couldn't just lie there and give up.

Thup.

His whole body tensed, as he was sure his skull was a microsecond away from being pierced by a bullet. When neither pain nor the appearance of pearly gates occurred, he had another thought.

That wasn't a rifle shot.

He peeled his eyelids back.

The guy and his rifle were gone.

What the—

Dylan twisted around at the sound of footsteps coming from the other direction.

"Are you hurt?" Liesel asked, the suppressor end of her pistol still pointed at the fallen kidnapper.

Dylan patted himself down, wincing a little as he touched the back of his head. No blood. "I'm okay."

"I think maybe we are even now."

"What?" Then he remembered the C4. "Oh, right. I think we are."

Liesel checked the downed kidnapper's pulse, but it was obvious to Dylan the guy had taken his last breath. She lowered his gun and helped Dylan to his feet.

"The other guy?" Dylan asked.

Instead of answering him directly, she clicked on her mic. "Water tank, clear. Two down."

"RV CLEAR," ANANKE said in response to Liesel. "Two down. That makes six. We're missing one. You two make a sweep of the west side. We'll do the east."

"Copy," Liesel replied.

Ananke looked at Ricky. "Go with Rosario, and don't give

her any trouble."

After giving her a what-me? look, he jogged off after Rosario.

As soon as they were gone, Ananke looked down at the dying kidnapper. Given what he'd been a part of, she wanted to feel zero sympathy for him, but, man, no one should ever have to die like this.

She crouched down beside him and nodded at the RV. "Any more of your friends inside?"

His lips parted, but whatever he planned to say was superseded by a violent, wet cough. Apparently the fall had done more than break some limbs.

She moved over to the RV entrance, listened for a few seconds to the silence inside, and opened the door. No other kidnappers, but no hostages, either. Was this camp just a ruse? Were the children not out here at all?

She squatted next to the kidnapper. "Where are the kids?"

Blood dribbling out one side of his mouth, he coughed again.

"Come on, answer me."

From the look in his eyes, she knew he had no intention of telling her anything.

"You're going to die. There's nothing anyone can do about that. Less painful or more, it's your choice." She pointed at the chair leg, her other fingers loose, making it look like she was going to grab it. "I'm really hoping you choose less."

His eyes widened, and then his gaze flashed past her, as if focusing on something else. She turned. The only thing behind her was the outbuilding. The glance could have been meaningless, but Ananke didn't think so.

"Thank you." She stood up.

Only two things were in the direction he'd looked—the near empty shed and the open desert. Perhaps there was another structure out there Rosario hadn't found on the map. But if so, why would the kidnappers set up camp here?

Her gaze drifted back to the shed. She hadn't seen anything that indicated the kids were in there, but she'd also not taken that close of a look.

She walked inside and scanned the space again. This time, she noticed something lying next to the two lights. A pile of…rope?

Yes, but not loose rope. It was tied together to form a ladder. One end was anchored to metal loops embedded at the edge of the concrete mound she'd noted before.

She swung the light across the mound.

How about that.

Not a mound. A concrete ring. And on top of it, a hatch.

Dropping to her knees, she undid the hasp and threw open the hatch. "Is anyone down there?" she called.

She shined her light inside and saw several bodies lying on the floor.

My God, are we too late?

"Hello?" The voice was adult, female, coming from the left.

Ananke leaned into the hole and pointed her light toward the sound. A woman stood in the middle of what looked like an old bomb shelter. Her hair was disheveled, her face smeared with dirt. Still, Ananke recognized her from the Administrator's photographs as Erica Wright, one of the missing chaperones. The woman was squinting, a hand shading her eyes.

Ananke could hear the others stirring now, and in her beam could see scared faces turning toward her.

"We're here to get you out," she said. "Hang on."

She stood up and touched her comm. "Status?"

"We have just finished the west," Liesel said. "No one else here."

"Rosario?"

No response for a few seconds, then, "We're all clear here, too."

Where had the seventh guy gone? If he was smart, he'd run for the highway once he knew the kidnapping had been blown. If not, well, there was a way to deal with that.

"Everyone back to the RV. I found the kids."

WHEN THE OTHERS returned, Ananke tasked Ricky and

Rosario with finding something to cover the now dead lookout, and had Liesel keep watch for the missing kidnapper.

With Dylan holding the flashlight, Ananke lowered the ladder through the hole. As soon as it was in place, everyone below started crowding around it.

"One at a time," she said.

Chris Jones, another chaperone, pushed everyone out of the way and grabbed the ladder.

"Children first," Ananke told him.

"I'm already here. I'm first," he said, climbing.

Not wanting to cause a scene, she let him continue.

"Thank God. Thank God," he said as he set his feet on the ground.

"If you could step to the side, please," Ananke said.

He didn't seem to hear her.

"Mr. Jones!"

He jerked. "What?"

"To the side, please."

"Oh, okay." He moved out of the way.

One by one, the children came up, Ananke mentally checking them off her list as they reached the top. After five of the children had reached the surface, Ananke poked her head into the hole again. Wright was the only one left, standing at the bottom of the ladder, one hand on the rope, the other strapped across her midsection.

"Where's Tessa Herrera?" Ananke asked.

"They took her," Wright said.

"Who took her?"

"The kidnappers. One of them called her up."

"By name?"

"Yes."

Why would someone take Tessa Herrera? She wasn't one of the kids from a wealthy family.

"How long ago?"

"Ten minutes. Maybe-maybe less."

For the first time Ananke realized something was wrong with the woman. "Can you come up?"

"I don't…think so." The woman tilted her hand away

from her belly for a moment. It was covered with blood.

Ananke scrambled down the ladder and then all but carried the woman up. "What happened?" she asked once they were out of the hole.

"He shot me when he took...when he took Tessa."

"Do you know which one it was?"

The woman hesitated. "I'm not sure."

"But you have an idea."

Wright frowned. "It's just...well, the voice sounded a little like our other chaperone. Andy Carter. But he-he was killed the day they took us."

Ananke turned to Dylan. "See what you can do for her, and keep everyone calm and in here."

"You got it."

She hurried outside and waved for the other three of her team to join her. "Were any of the people you took out Andrew Carter?"

Liesel shook her head.

Ricky frowned. "When would I have seen him?"

Rosario didn't need to respond because she'd been with Ananke.

"He's our seventh guy. He took one of the kids and I think he's making a run for it."

"When Dylan and I were on our way here," Liesel said, "we saw something moving into the desert. We weren't sure what it was."

"Where was this?" Ricky asked.

The moment Liesel pointed, Ricky started running in that direction.

"What are you doing?" Ananke asked.

He shouted, "I'm a hunter, remember?" but didn't stop running.

"Call the Administrator," Ananke said to Rosario. "Tell him we have the hostages and need him to arrange pickup. Also, we'll need someone to get rid of the bodies."

"Where are you going?" Rosario asked.

"To keep Ricky from doing something stupid again."

She sprinted after the hunter.

FORTY-ONE

CARTER KEPT TESSA hurrying through the desert for several minutes before he finally told her to stop.

He looked back the way they'd come, and the workshop that had hidden the old underground shelter seemed both a million miles away and still too close.

"Where are we going?" the girl asked.

He backhanded Tessa across the cheek. "I told you to shut up."

It was a good question, though. At the moment they were going nowhere but away, Carter's only goal to put as much space between himself and whoever was raiding the camp. But if they kept going in their current direction, all they'd find would be more desert, no matter which direction they went.

He looked back toward the workshop again. Everything *seemed* quiet. Maybe it had been a false alarm.

He took a deep breath and tried to figure out what to do. The alarm had been real. Someone was out there, likely the same person or people who'd gone after Danny. Carter couldn't go back. But he and Tessa would also never survive in the wilderness on foot. If he wanted a chance at cashing in on the kid, he would have to find a faster way out.

Perhaps it was his fear and panic that had kept him from thinking of the idea until now. It didn't matter, though. The important thing was, his mind had cleared enough for a solution to come to him.

If someone was indeed attacking the camp, they had approached quietly. So that had to mean they'd left their vehicle somewhere and walked the rest of the way in, right? It made sense to him.

The alarm had been set up to the north, on the long road leading to the house, so any vehicles would likely be in that direction.

"Come on, kid," he said, jerking Tessa's shirt.

TESSA STUMBLED BEHIND Mr. Carter for a few steps before catching her balance again.

Her cheek stung from where he'd hit it, but she was too focused on paying attention to his every movement for it to bother her. At some point he would make a mistake. And when he did, Tessa would make him pay for his betrayal.

CARTER LET OUT a quiet, triumphant laugh when he saw the pickup truck parked at the side of the road.

As soon as he was convinced no one had been left behind to guard the vehicle, he jogged over to it, pulling Tessa behind him.

The vehicle was dusty, but otherwise looked in fine shape. He tried the driver's door and laughed again when it opened.

"In," he said to the girl, pushing her toward the doorway.

"I don't know how to drive," she said.

"No one said anything about driving. Get in and climb over to the other seat."

Tessa did as she was told.

"Now kneel down in the footwell and face me."

"Where?" she asked, confused.

"The footwell!" He pointed at the area in front of the seat.

Once she was situated, he checked to see if the key was in the ignition. No such luck. But that was all right. He'd hotwired plenty of cars in his life.

He set his gun on the floor of the truck and shot Tessa a look. "Don't try anything."

She shook her head.

He set to work, snapping plastic out of his way and hunting for the appropriate wires. The problem was, it was too damn dark and he didn't have a flashlight. The truck's dome light didn't seem to be working. He had to guess four times before he finally found the right combination.

When the engine roared to life, he smiled and climbed inside. "Hold on, kid. This is going to be a little rough."

RICKY SKIDDED TO a stop in the open desert west of the outbuilding, giving Ananke the opportunity to catch up to him.

"They were here," he whispered.

He played his flashlight across the ground ahead of them, lighting up several fresh shoe prints—one set adult sized, one child's.

Ricky hunted for a moment and then said, "This way." He took off running again, this time heading north.

This was the purest form of hunting, Ananke thought. Old school, following physical tracks in the earth. And she sensed Ricky was really enjoying it. As much as she wanted to remind him they were chasing a kidnapped girl and there shouldn't be anything fun about that, she said nothing.

They must be heading to the highway, Ananke thought. Carter was probably hoping to hitch a ride from someone passing by. Or maybe, once he was in cell range, he was going to call someone who could pick up him and the girl.

Whatever the case, they needed to get there before he did, and the best way to do that would be by driving.

"Where's your truck?" she shouted. "We can take that."

"We're headed straight at it."

That did not make her happy. "Please tell me you have your keys."

"I've got them."

"And that you locked your doors."

"Why would I lock my doors out here? Besides, he could just break the window and get in."

"Yeah, but it would have slowed him down!"

Ricky increased his speed.

They reached the road to the house a minute later, and could see Carter and Tessa ahead. Then they heard the engine of Ricky's truck start up.

Ananke saw the gray outline of the vehicle make a U-turn and take off away from them. Ricky sprinted after it, but Ananke knew their only chance was to cut it off on the main dirt road.

"This way!" she shouted as she veered into the desert.

Glancing over her shoulder, she saw Ricky's flashlight bouncing after the truck for another few seconds, before he, too, turned toward the main road.

As she ran, she alternated between watching the ground in front of her and glancing at the moving shadow of the truck. Sooner than she'd hoped, it reached the end of the driveway and turned onto the main road.

No, no, no, no, no!

She dug as deep as she could and blasted through the brush.

The shadow was getting closer and closer. She could also see Ricky's light, and knew that unless he had a sudden burst of superhuman speed, the truck would be past him before he could get to it.

It was all on her.

She hurdled some sagebrush and checked the truck again. It would be close.

She took one more look at the terrain in front of her, memorizing the obstacles, and then focused on the truck.

Despite the unevenness of the road, Carter was pushing the truck faster than most drivers would. Would it have killed him to slow down just a little?

Sprinting with all her might, she raced onto the road just as the truck was passing by. She flung out her hands, grabbed the edge of the truck bed at the last second, and launched herself into the back.

CARTER JUMPED WHEN he heard a bang from somewhere in the back of the vehicle.

As he turned to glance through the rear window, the front end whacked into a bush and he had to refocus on the road.

He glanced at Tessa. "Look out the back. Tell me what you see."

The girl didn't move.

"Now!" he yelled.

She crawled into the other seat and looked out the rear

window.

"Well?" Carter asked.

"Nothing there."

ANANKE ROLLED HARD against the far wall of the bed, and had to quickly jam herself against it to keep from flying over the top.

She rose onto her knees and pulled her gun out from under her jacket. Keeping low so she wouldn't be seen in the truck's rearview mirror, she crawled toward the cab.

When she reached it, she looked up at the window and froze.

TESSA CLIMBED INTO the passenger seat and looked out the window.

She, too, had heard the noise, but thought they'd hit another hole in the road. She expected to see nothing in the back. Instead, she saw a woman holding a gun, looking up at her.

Was she one of the kidnappers Tessa had not seen or heard before?

The woman stared at her for a second, and then smiled and held a finger to her lips.

"Well?" Mr. Carter asked.

"Nothing there," Tessa replied, still looking at the woman.

"Then what the hell was that noise?"

"I don't know."

Mr. Carter glanced at her. "Back where you were."

Tessa waited until he looked away before she smiled at the woman and returned to the footwell.

ANANKE WASN'T SURE what the girl was going to do. But when Tessa spoke, her answer was short enough that Ananke could read her lips, and if that wasn't proof the girl hadn't given her away, Tessa's smile did the trick.

As soon as Tessa disappeared, Ananke hunkered down against the back of the cab to catch her breath. She knew from the drive in earlier that even at Carter's current pace, it would still be about ten minutes before they reached the highway. She could not allow that to happen.

There had been several points on the road between the highway and the truck's current location where Ricky had been forced to slow to a crawl to avoid damaging the vehicle. Carter would not be quite as concerned.

There was one point, however, where he would have no choice but to slow down. The narrow wash had a sharp downward turn to the left before an immediate hook to the right and a zigzag up the other side. Too fast and you run off the road, possibly tipping over to boot.

The wash had been about five minutes from the highway, which, given Carter's rush, put it about three minutes away.

Plenty of time to catch her breath.

CARTER DECIDED THEY were far enough from the others for him to risk turning the headlights on, but when he tried, nothing happened. A glance at the rearview mirror revealed no red glow of taillights, either. He tried turning the switch on and off several times, but no go. Apparently something was wrong with the electrical system.

His eyes were adjusted enough that the darkness wasn't much of a problem. The difficulty would come once they reached the highway. The last thing he needed was for the Nevada Highway Patrol to pull him over because of faulty wiring.

Nothing he could do about that, though. For now, he needed to concentrate on getting out of this godawful desolation.

Ahead the road dipped into another gully. At first, he thought it would be the same as the others they'd raced through, but when the front end tilted downward, he slammed on the brakes, cutting their speed to almost nothing.

This wash was not like the others.

He carefully negotiated a turn to the left that took him to the bottom, where the road sharply turned again to the right.

He heard the crunch a second before he realized something had punctured the front windshield. It happened again, and again.

Bullets, he realized.

He slammed the brakes all the way down as two more holes appeared in the window. The truck was still in the process of stopping when he started to duck behind the dash. Before he was all the way down, something from behind wrapped around his neck.

He twisted as much as he could to the side, and out of the corner of his eye saw an arm sticking into the cab through the rear window. He'd thought someone was shooting at him from ahead, when the shots had actually been fired from the truck's bed through the rear window. The five shots had weakened a circle of safety glass enough for the owner of the arm to shove it through.

He tried to pull off the arm as it squeezed his neck, but it had his head pinned tight against the headrest.

Gun.

His left hand shot down toward where he'd left his pistol. Though his fingers touched the very top of the weapon, he couldn't stretch his arm any farther.

He batted at the arm and tried to yell, "Let go of me, goddammit," but his voice came out not much louder than a hoarse whisper.

He heard a noise from the other side of the cab and glanced sideways toward it.

The passenger door was swinging open, and the girl—his ticket to financial independence—was climbing out.

No!

ANANKE'S ATTENTION WAS so focused on restraining Carter that she didn't know something else was happening until Carter yelled.

She looked over to see Tessa running across the desert.

"Tessa, wait!" she shouted. "I'm here to help!"

The girl kept going.

Couldn't just one thing go exactly as Ananke planned it?

She needed to incapacitate Carter, but while she could hold him in place, she couldn't get her arm around him enough to squeeze him into unconsciousness. More drastic measures were required.

She yanked her arm back outside, grabbed her gun, and shot him in the shoulder by the time he realized he was free.

Screaming, he flew into the steering wheel, and screamed again. But to his credit, he didn't give up. When he turned back toward Ananke, he held a pistol in his left hand.

She leapt over the side of the truck right before he pulled the trigger, and pressed the muzzle of her gun against the driver's side window.

"Drop it and open the door," she ordered.

She could see the question play out on his face—did he have enough time to bring his pistol around and get a shot off? The answer was no, of course. He just needed a little time to figure that out.

"I'm not going to ask again," she said.

He tossed the gun on the floor and raised his hands.

She took a step back. "Get out."

As he opened the door, he said, "You don't understand. I'm one of the hostages! We were just trying to get away, that's all."

"On the ground, Mr. Carter. Or would you rather I call you by your real name, Mr. Simmons?"

She could see the last of his hope collapse in his eyes.

He climbed out and knelt in the dirt.

"All the way down," she ordered.

"My shoulder," he said.

She shoved him in the back, and he dropped facedown beside the truck. She hog-tied him with the zip ties, grabbed his pistol from inside the cab, and chucked it as far as she could into the dark desert.

"The less you move, the less you'll hurt," she told him.

She took off after Tessa.

TESSA MOVED AS soon as she saw Mr. Carter was busy fighting off the woman.

Even when she heard the woman call after her, she kept going, wanting to get as far away from Mr. Carter as possible.

She didn't think about which way to go; she just went.

She was still running when she heard the woman say, "Tessa, stop," from only a few feet behind her.

She looked back and saw that the woman could have easily reached out and grabbed her, but she didn't.

"I'm not going to hurt you. I'm here to get you home."

Tessa kept going for a few more paces before halting. "You're really here to take me home?"

"I am."

"What about Mr. Carter? Did you kill him?"

"No. But he won't bother you anymore."

"He needs to go to jail."

"Don't worry. He'll be punished for his crimes."

"You promise?"

"I promise."

Tessa considered the woman for a moment, and then said, "Good."

The woman held out her hand. "I'm Ananke."

Tessa shook the woman's hand. "Tessa."

FORTY-TWO

TWO SUVS AND a panel van arrived at the homestead an hour before sunrise. The children and the two chaperones were loaded into the SUVs and whisked away to a waiting plane back in Tonopah.

Ananke and her team helped the two men who'd arrived in the van load the kidnappers, dead and alive, into the back of the vehicle. Among them was the still breathing Mr. Carter.

After the van departed, Ananke gathered her team around and called the Administrator on her sat phone.

"You're on speaker," she told him when he picked up the line.

"Everything wrapped up?" he asked.

"Yes."

"Excellent work, all of you," he said. "You will receive coordinates as soon as I hang up. Proceed there for extraction."

"Hold on," Ananke said. "The job's done. Where are you extracting us to?"

"Somewhere we can talk."

"In person?" Dylan asked.

"It would be best if you didn't delay."

He hung up.

"That wasn't very polite," Dylan said.

Ananke's phone beeped twice as her screen lit up with the Administrator's promised coordinates. She showed them to Rosario, who hooked her laptop into her own sat phone and input the coordinates into Google Maps.

The location was about twenty miles to the northeast, on a different dirt road off the highway. There was nothing there. Not even an abandoned building.

"Are we just going to go there?" Dylan asked. "It seems a little…out of the way."

"So what? You think they're planning on killing us?" Ricky asked him.

"The thought did cross my mind."

"Don't you think if they wanted us dead, they would have killed us here and tossed us into the back of the van with the other bodies?"

"Yeah, I guess."

Ricky snickered. "Leave the operational insights to the pros, Mr. Courier Man."

Dylan tensed. "Look, asshole, all I was saying is—"

"Relax, Dylan," Ananke said. "First rule of working with Ricky is, know when not to listen to Ricky. For instance, right now."

"Don't joke with him like that," Ricky said. "You'll deprive him of all the knowledge I can pass on to him."

"And that would be another example," Ananke said.

Dylan took a deep breath and nodded. "Lesson learned."

"There is still the question of whether we go or not," Liesel said.

"I think it's something we each need to decide for ourselves," Ananke said.

"What are you going to do?"

Ananke thought for a moment. "The faster we can get out of this desert, the happier I'm going to be. And honestly, I wouldn't mind a little in-person conversation with the Administrator."

"What if it's a trap?" Dylan said. "I mean, not to kill us, but to lock us up again?"

"If it bothers you enough, I can drop you off on the highway, and you can hitch a ride to wherever you want."

"I will go with you," Liesel said to Ananke.

"I want to know what is happening with clearing my name," Rosario said. "So I am with you also."

"Ah, hell," Dylan said. "Might as well join you. If they lock us back up, at least I'll know I'm not alone."

Ananke looked at Ricky.

"What?" he said as he rubbed a hand over his bicep. "Let's get moving."

LIESEL SPOTTED THE black dot in the southern sky first.

For over a minute, it seemed to be standing still, a pinprick in the blue sky. Soon enough, the illusion fell away, and the dot became a blob and then a cylinder and then a helicopter. The aircraft was a robust beast, large enough for a dozen passengers at least, and built for speed and distance.

As it landed, dust blew up all around it, momentarily hiding it from view. After the rotors wound down and the air began to clear, the side door opened and a man in a black suit stepped outside.

Gear over their shoulders, Ananke and her team left their vehicles behind and climbed aboard their ride. The moment the last of them was buckled in, the helicopter lifted into the air and headed west.

"CASSIDY HAS REPORTED in," Warren said. "He just heard from the Administrator. The children have been freed."

"What about the girl?" Avanti asked.

"Cassidy attempted to get more information, but was told a full report would be given to the Committee this evening. He did have the impression, though, that all the children were found."

"And the girl's father?" Avanti asked as he walked over to the window.

"Cassidy is convinced the man will be removed from the Committee, perhaps as early as tonight."

"But there is still a Committee."

"Yes, sir."

"Did the field team at least sustain some injuries?"

"I tried to reach McGowan multiple times, but no luck. I assume he's either dead or under their control by now. Cassidy should have more information after the meeting tonight." McGowan's demise had also been a likely outcome, and for that reason, neither he nor anyone working with him had known the true identity of their employers.

Avanti had hoped the mission would destroy the Committee, but that had never been likely. On the whole, though, the operation had accomplished much and provided him with a wealth of information about the field team and the day-to-day workings of the Committee.

Avanti stared out at the Pacific Ocean for several moments. "It will be interesting to see what they do next," he said as he turned back to the room. "In forty-eight hours, I want a dozen contingency plans on my desk to deal with whatever that might be. We must continue to be the thorn in their side."

THE FAMILIES OF the missing children were picked up from their homes and taken to a private hangar at San Francisco International Airport. Per the Administrator's instructions, all arrived at approximately the same time, and had to wait only a few minutes before the private jet rolled into the hangar and the hangar doors were closed.

The Administrator was there, of course, lurking in the shadows, unnoticed.

As he knew would be the case, Tuesday was also present. The man was the only member of the Committee to whom the Administrator had given the details of the children's return. Tuesday stood closer to the families than the Administrator did, but still far enough away to not interfere or be noticed.

As the children deplaned, they ran to the waiting embraces of their parents. Tears of joy and relief and exhaustion were shed by both sides.

Tessa Herrera was the fourth one to exit the craft.

Tuesday visibly tensed when she came into sight. This was the Administrator's cue. He moved silently into position six feet behind Tuesday. The Committee member watched the girl reunite with her mother in a deep embrace that seemed to go on forever.

Eventually, Tuesday turned to leave.

Startled, he said, "I…didn't expect to see you here."

"If I could have a moment of your time, sir."

"I'm running late already. I need to—"

"This won't take long." The Administrator gestured

toward an office where two of his own security stood, one on each side of the open doorway. "Committee business. I'm sure you understand."

"Of-of course."

The Administrator let Tuesday lead the way. Once they were in the room, he closed the door.

"It looks like everything turned out well," Tuesday said. "Given my involvement in this project, I thought it important to be here for the reunion. It really hammers home why we're doing what we're doing."

The Administrator smiled, and then pointed at a small stack of papers sitting next to a pen on the only desk in the room. "If you would please sign."

Tuesday's brow furrowed. "I'm sorry?"

"The document. If you could please sign, we both can be on our way."

Tuesday walked over to the desk and reached for the papers. "What is this?"

"It's your resignation from the Committee."

"My what?"

"Your resignation. And your acknowledgment that you understand the penalties if you ever mention the Committee again after we leave this room."

"I'm not signing this," Tuesday scoffed. "But I absolutely will be bringing it up in the meeting this evening."

"You will not be attending the meeting this evening."

"You have no power to keep me away. You work for the Committee on which I am a member. Not you. I demand we convene a meeting immediately."

"Your demand is noted and rejected."

"What the—"

"Sir, you have compromised the Committee in a way that could have very easily derailed our efforts."

"I have done no such thing."

"Tessa Herrera."

"What about her? She's...she's one of the children, right?"

"She's your child. With a woman who used to work in the

bookkeeping department of one of your companies. Conceived while your wife was on that trip to the Middle East which she never returned from. You were so ashamed you threatened her so that she'd never tell anyone, and arranged for her to be employed elsewhere. Worse yet, you have provided no financial assistance whatsoever."

A mass of emotions flickered across Tuesday's face. He muttered, "I don't know who told you that, but that's pure fiction."

"The document. Turn to the last page, please."

Tuesday reluctantly flipped to the chart.

"DNA comparison between you and Tessa," the Administrator said. "Congratulations, you have a daughter."

Tuesday stared at the sheet. "How did you…"

"How is unimportant. What's important is that you lied to us by telling us you had no connection to the kidnapping."

"And if I had?" Tuesday said with anger. "You wouldn't have sent the field team, and who knows what would have happened to her."

"If you care about her so much, why have you not helped her and her mother?"

"It's…complicated."

"She's your daughter. The only complications are the pathetic ones you invent." The Administrator paused. "Sign the paper so we can be done with this."

The man formerly known as Tuesday did as told.

"One more thing," the Administrator said. "If you do not do right by Tessa, the press will receive that chart. I'm sure they will be able to persuade you."

THE HELICOPTER FLEW through the Sierra Nevadas above a narrow river valley.

Though Ananke had no idea where they were relative to the explosion site outside Yosemite, she searched the forest for signs of smoke and fire. Like on their flight east, she found none.

Soon the mountains fell away, and they continued west over farms and towns and river plains.

Finally the tenor of the rotors changed, and the helicopter began to slow and descend.

Looking out the window, Dylan swore under his breath and said, "I knew it. They're going to lock us up again."

"No one's locking us up," Ananke said.

He looked over at her and gestured at the window. "They're taking us back to the boat. It's right there!"

"Technically, I believe that is a ship, not a boat," Liesel said, looking out another window.

"That's not my point."

Ananke lifted the side of her jacket and flashed him her gun. "No one's locking us up."

For the first time, Dylan seemed to realize the others also still had their weapons. "So we're all going to get killed in a bloody shootout? Is that the plan?"

"Buddy, you can't hate all the options," Ricky said.

"I never said I hated all the options. I'm just not fond of these two. I'm thinking more us walking away, the sun going down, a couple of pints in our future. That's an option I'll get behind."

The helicopter touched down in an open area near the end of the pier. Ananke glanced out the window. Standing well beyond the craft's rotor range were three men in dark suits. She had never seen the two big ones before, but the smaller man in the middle was the Administrator.

"Weapons drawn, or…?" Ricky asked.

She pulled out her pistol. "I guess it couldn't hurt to be ready."

Their escort didn't even raise an eyebrow at this, and simply opened the door and motioned for them to exit.

Ananke and Rosario went first, with Ricky and Liesel behind them and Dylan bringing up the rear.

They stopped a dozen feet in front of the Administrator and spread out into a line. Behind them, Ananke could hear the helicopter rotors speeding up again, and then the craft rising back into the air.

When the noise died down, the Administrator said, "I want to thank you again on a job well done. Now, if you will follow me."

"Follow you where?" Dylan asked.

The Administrator gestured toward the gangway to the *Karas Evonus.*

"No way. We're not letting you lock us up again."

"Mr. Brody, we have no intention of locking you up, now or ever. I made that clear before, and nothing has changed. Either come with me, or don't."

The Administrator walked away, taking his two companions with him.

"I don't know what you guys are waiting for," Ricky said, "but I don't see as I have much of a choice in this matter."

He followed the Administrator.

Ananke was pretty sure the others would do whatever she did. As tempting as walking away was, nothing that had happened in the last few days made her think the Administrator would lock them up again, least of all the fact she still had her gun. Besides, she still wanted answers.

She headed toward the ship and the others followed.

INSTEAD OF LEADING them back into the maze of hallways they'd been in previously, the Administrator unlocked a door along the ship's superstructure and took them up a set of stairs, into a room with large windows on three of the four sides.

The room was set up very similarly to the conference room down in the bowels of the ship—a large table with chairs around it. In this instance, six. In front of four of the chairs were file folders. The Administrator indicated where each was to sit, pointing Ricky to one of the chairs without a folder, and taking the other himself.

"In front of you is a report on the progress we've made concerning the problems that brought each of you to us."

"That's not exactly how I'd phrase how we got here," Ananke said.

"Please," he said. "Take a moment and look through them."

Before she opened her file, she asked, "What about the fire?"

"Fire?"

"From the explosion."

"Right. You'll be happy to know your call gave the firefighters an excellent head start. It is my understanding that a little over ten acres were burned, and no casualties."

The relief she felt was all consuming. Though she'd kept reminding herself it really wasn't her fault, she hadn't been able to shake the feeling that it was.

She opened the folder and looked inside.

Her no-good, backstabbing op leader Noah Perkins had been apprehended. By whom, the report didn't say, but there was a transcript of a taped interview—video file sent to her e-mail—in which Perkins laid out the setup of Ananke in great detail, implicating both himself and Marcus Denton. Denton's current whereabouts were unknown, as he'd disappeared within hours of Perkins's detention.

Her excommunication order was still in effect, but it was no longer being actively enforced. This was not exactly the redemption she needed, as most clients would be reluctant to hire her without definitive word that the Alonzo situation had all been a mistake. Still, it did mean she could go home without worrying too much about being shot in the back.

The report ended with, *Efforts are still underway to completely clear your name, but this may take up to a few months. Our recommendation is to take time off until the excommunication has been annulled.*

Looking up, she saw the others were just finishing up their files, too. She raised an eyebrow at Rosario.

"If this is all true, then I am okay," Rosario said. "I can work again."

"Me, too," Dylan said enthusiastically. He turned to the Administrator. "Thanks! This is better than I could have hoped." He looked back at the others. "He even put out word that I've just completed some high-stakes work and have his highest recommendation."

Ananke glanced at Liesel. "And you?"

"What does it matter? I still didn't save him."

"It matters." Ananke touched the woman's file. "May I?"

Liesel shrugged.

A scan of the report showed Liesel's problems with the Las Vegas police department had gone away, and that Mr. Wolf's company was now aware the only connection Liesel had to Katarina Stolzer was trying to stop the woman. Her job in the company's security department was waiting for her whenever she was ready to return. Whom she would protect now was not mentioned.

"As you see, we have upheld our promise," the Administrator said. "With the exception of Mr. Orbits, you are all free to return to your lives, though with any minor caveats that might have been in your individual report."

"Where is Ricky going?" Ananke asked, not wanting to care, but caring nonetheless.

"He will be staying here with us. That was our agreement with him."

"Fine by me," Ricky said. "This place looks a lot more fun than Crestridge."

"What's he going to be doing? Just hanging out here for the next ten years?" Ananke asked.

"Please. Nine and a half," Ricky said.

"That actually brings me to the other point I wanted to discuss," the Administrator said. "From time to time, my organization will have jobs that come up on which we'd like to use you as a team again. You worked very well together, and we feel you will do so again. The terms will always be payment up front and double your going rates. All we would ask in return is that when we call, you answer."

"What kind of work? More kidnappings?" Rosario asked.

He paused. "The type of work will not be like the assignments you get from others. We're not interested in government intelligence or corporate espionage. Our mission is to provide help where it's needed but would otherwise not be given."

"Who the hell are you guys?" Dylan asked.

"Who we are is not important. The jobs we would have you do are. The kidnappings, for example. There was nothing there for us to gain except saving those children."

"This all sounds very altruistic, but something's bothering me," Ananke said. "How is it you chose the five of us?" Before he could answer, she said, "Let me rephrase that. How did the five of us end up available to you all at the same time? Well, the four of us, I guess. Ricky wasn't doing much of anything."

"You're right about that," Ricky said.

"Simple," the Administrator said. "We were tracking you. You and several dozen others we thought would fill our needs, that is. You four happened to be the ones who became available around the time we needed you."

"Whoa, there," Dylan said. "Are you saying that if my clients had waited another week or two to move their C4, I'd be a dead man because you would have already chosen someone else?"

"Quite possibly, yes."

Dylan looked far from pleased with that answer.

Ananke was still bothered by the four of them being available at the same time, and via similar situations. But she didn't think she'd get a straight answer, so for the moment she kept her thoughts to herself.

"You said you would want us to answer when you called," Rosario said. "What if I am on another job?"

"Then you are unavailable to us for that particular mission."

"As easy as that?"

"As easy as that."

"There is much, I think, you are not telling us," Liesel said.

"You're correct. But I've told you all I am able until you choose to participate."

Ananke had heard enough and was itching to get out of there. "I assume we can have some time to think about it."

"Of course. In fact, we really don't need to know your answer until the next project comes up."

"And when do you think that will be?"

"No way to tell for sure. Could be as soon as a week, or as much as a month."

"Until then we're free to go home?"

"Of course. Transportation is waiting for you on the pier."

"WELL?" MONDAY ASKED. "Are they with us?"

The Administrator was still in the windowed room of the *Karas Evonus*, now talking to his boss via video chat on his phone. "They have asked for time to consider the offer."

"What's your sense? Will they take it?"

"Hard to tell. The courier will. He needs the work and the money. The women, though, I'm not so sure about."

"That's not the answer I was hoping for."

"Me, neither."

"You're ready if they refuse."

"The safeguards are in place, yes. And they will be taken care of…organically."

"Let's hope we don't have to start back at zero again."

"No, sir."

"What about Tuesday? How did that go?"

"Exactly as planned."

"Good. I'm glad to be rid of him, though I guess I should be thankful he did us the favor of exposing the fact that there's a traitor among the other five." Monday reached for his keyboard to terminate the call. "I'm counting on you to find out who it is."

"Yes, sir."

THEIR TRANSPORTATION WAS a rental Lexus sedan, with four airline tickets waiting inside that would fly each of them back to their home.

Dylan, behind the wheel again, drove them from the port, this time on a route that would take them across the bay to San Francisco International Airport.

Before they hit the Bay Bridge, Shinji called Rosario's phone, looking for Ananke.

"We've been freed," Ananke told him. "I should be home for dinner."

"That's great," he said.

"We were told that, for the most part, our problems have been cleared up. Can you check on your end?"

"Of course."

"Great. Thanks. Let us know as soon—"

"Ananke, I called for a reason."

She paused. "What's up?"

"Quinn tried to get ahold of you. He wants you to call him back right away." He gave her the cleaner's contact information and hung up.

She punched in the number.

"Yes?" Quinn answered on the first ring.

"It's Ananke."

He said in a deadly serious tone, "I need your help."

She sat up, shifting immediately back to operative mode. "When and where?"

"Now. In London."

"What's going on?"

"I'll fill you in when you get here. It's…personal."

She glanced at the others. "How much help do you need?"

"All I can get. Do you have some people you can trust?"

She glanced at the others. "As a matter of fact, I do."

60159873R00157